I0685348

The Sexification of Em

by Laura Kat

Copyright © 2014 by Laura Kat

1 Everydayness

Downstairs, hiding out in the laundry room, I take a scoop of laundry detergent and add it to the mass of clothing piled in the washer. I see my daughter's tiny T-shirt float to the top of the machine and I can't help but think: *How pointless is this?* I know that as I stand here, somewhere above my head on the main floor, my girls are spilling food all over themselves. Spilling is one thing they've mastered. At two and four years of age, they could teach a class in it. I once stood and watched helplessly as they squeezed fruit punch from a juice box on their cousin's first communion dress. With their talent for soiling, the laundry never ends.

The lid of my beat up industrial-sized washing machine bangs down. *This is not what I thought motherhood would be like. I didn't envision waking up before the sun everyday only to run around thanklessly completing the endless duties that make a household function: grocery shopping, cleaning everything from dishes to kids' bums, cooking and feeding, packing swim bags, backpacks or lunch-boxes, and getting ready for gymnastics, daycare, school, or grandma's house. You name it, I do it. I'm the reason my girls have clean clothes, brushed hair, nutritious food to eat, educational toys to play with, and a good bedtime routine.*

I shudder at the thought that I feel imprisoned somehow by all of my motherly obligations. *Life is so overwhelming sometimes. I never imagined the humdrum everydayness that would make up my existence. I guess I always thought having kids would be all fun and games. Like life would be all about reading bedtime stories, fixing boo-boos with kisses, first steps, and bubble baths.*

The fresh scent of the fabric softener wafts through the air as I stare at the basket of clean clothes on the floor. *If I don't fold it now, it'll only mean more work for me later.* A couple of minutes pass and I put the last pair of folded pants on top of the pile before I begrudgingly pick up the basket. Turning towards the door, I pause. I want to revel in the silence for a moment longer.

It's then that I hear the all too familiar cry of my two year old. It sounds as though she is being tortured. I know better. My keenly trained mommy ears know that those are just her overzealous crocodile tears. She's crying out for attention, to have her every whim satiated, or to stop the unrelenting teasing of her sister. Whatever the reason, I'm aware as I reach the landing on the stairs that I need to take a deep breath and muster up some patience.

Once upstairs, I glance down the hallway. In my older daughter's room there are naked Barbies and Lego sprawled out as far as the eye can see. I've only been downstairs a minute or two and already the toys have taken over.

Frustrated by the state of her room, I carry the laundry in the other direction, towards the increasingly distressed two year old in the living room. As I approach I step down hard on a princess crown that has been tossed carelessly about. It crumbles under my weight, the pain shoots straight to the stress-centre of my brain which is already being overwhelmed by the chores, the mess, and the screaming toddler. Turning the corner to see what all the commotion is about, I see my husband lackadaisically lounging on the couch. He's thoroughly engrossed in some stupid app on his iPhone and completely oblivious to the child now in full-fledged tantrum mode at his feet. I put the laundry down and pick up the screaming child in one motion. I glare at him as he glances up briefly from crushing digital candies.

This is the man I love...the man I have grown up with. Yet at this moment all I feel is contempt. In the back of my brain I am fully aware that I have everything I ever wanted, but right now I can't help but think: *This is not what I signed up for.*

2 The Fantasy

My name is Emilia and I am a woman just like you. Sure, we all have different lives, but in essence, we are the same. We want to be loved. We want to have time to do the things we feel are important, and to spend time with people that matter to us. We are all running through life striving to be the best: daughter, friend, girlfriend, lover, wife, mother... In the process we are being inundated with information about finding ourselves and being intrinsically happy. We are chasing the modern day fairytale.

Ever since I was a child I have been drawn to 'happy endings'. For me, it started with the Disney fairytales. How I loved watching Cinderella dancing across the ballroom floor. I mean, who could resist the notion that she was lifted out of her shitty existence to a life of ease and opulence? Watching Belle's love transform the Beast, and seeing Prince Philip fight Maleficent to rescue Aurora from her sleepy existence – I was hooked!

I moved on as I got older, to an eighties romantic comedy addiction. The characters in the movies were only slightly older than I was. I could strive to be the wallflower plucked from obscurity into a life of love and popularity. Even today, if Jake Ryan were waiting outside my house, I would be hard pressed not to run away with him. I lived vicariously through Molly Ringwald. I could totally see past the hideous pink taffeta dress she made for her prom. I so desperately want my life to resemble the tumultuous antics of all the John Hughes characters. I longed to attend the party that would result in the love of my life whisking me away. Where was my John Cusack?

This was also about the time I started spending my summers at the cottage with my elderly Grandparents. Sounds like an odd segue I realize, but my Grandmother had an extensive collection of trashy romance novels. Every night when my Grandparents would go to bed, I would pour through the pages, fixated on the slow progression of a young girl's journey toward love. Frankly, the trashier the better. Harlequins were my favourites. I spent my summers from age fourteen to sixteen in the mid-nineties, with only wenches, heaving bosoms, and mysterious rebels to keep me company. This was pre-internet, pre-cellphone, pre-anyway-to-keep-in-touch-with-my-friends-or-society-as-I-knew-it. So, the books themselves took on a life on their own. The characters felt like friends. I reveled in their highs and wallowed in their lows. I was compelled by the rags to riches and the good girl taming the bad boy plots. The inevitable 'happy-ever-after' was pivotal. I craved the magical connection that the books championed. The idea that the sparks of love could ignite at first touch captivated me. The notion of kismet felt real. I desperately wanted to be the kind of girl that a boy would find irresistible. I was dying to feel special and cherished like the heroines of my favourite novels.

By the time I was in my late teens I had moved onto Generation X movies and adult romantic comedies. I was transfixed by movies with frustrating sexual tension and seemingly impossible obstacles for the characters to overcome; where the grand romantic gesture reigned supreme. They were such a big part of my life that I still pull quotes from these movies in my everyday life. Not just the famous quotes either.

Movies made me feel romantic love long before I had ever experienced it firsthand. Whether they were the Disney movies I watched as a child in the eighties or the romantic comedies I devoured during my teen years in the nineties, they provided me with the imagery and soundtrack that encapsulated my vision of what love should be. They depicted what it might look like. They gave my heart a glimpse of how it would feel. They made me want to be in love.

I wanted the fantasy: to be kissed in the rain, to be compelled to hold hands because I simply couldn't bear to be without my man's touch, and of course to wake up cuddled in his arms. I longed for the head over heels, all-consuming kind of connection that seemed so tangible in the movies.

My mental image of what life was 'supposed' to look and feel like was formed slowly over time. I was supposed to fall in love with my best friend, to marry him, to start a family. We were supposed to joyfully raise our children, have sophisticated careers and grow old together. I associated unconditional love and existential purpose with this vision.

Movies and books weren't the only reason I continued to perpetuate my romantic notions. My home-life also contributed to this ideal. My parents were very happily married. Through the good and the bad they loved each other.

As a child, I remember seeing my mom and dad being goofy in the kitchen. My dad was trying to kiss my mom and she was making it a game of cat and mouse. It was sort of like a tickle fight but with kisses. There was something so joyous, so genuine about their absolute infatuation with one another. My parents were best friends and partners, no matter what life handed them. They had the kind of perfect synergy I aspired to attain.

When it was all said and done, I firmly believed in the fairytale. Pop-culture, romance novels and even my own family had promised me a 'happily ever after'. So now I'm sharing my pursuit with you...

Part One: Once Upon a Time...

3 Meaningless Rebound Relationship

"Hey Britta, how do you say, 'I want' in Spanish?" Sitting on the floor of Britta's bedroom, we are interrupted by a loud knock at the door. Britta jumps up so excited by the noise that I'm positive it must be one of the guys she knows from Briarview High. She runs to the door and sure enough, a guy I'd met only briefly once before is standing outside. He's wearing a new Briarview '96 letterman jacket. *He is totally Britta's type. Hot and cocky.* No pun intended.

"So your parents are gone?" he says.

Wow, news travels fast, I think to myself. I glance back at my textbook knowing that Britta's going to be consumed by her overt flirting for a while. I hope to memorize a few more verbs for the exam on Monday.

I have to do well on this exam. Doing well is kind of my thing. I guess I have high expectations for myself. I'm kind of a closeted geek. Maybe it's not so much the success, but the fear of failure that drives me. The idea of not being successful actually causes a tightening in my chest. I physically dread failure. So, I study. I work hard and I aspire to greatness in all things Emilia. Today's feat, conversational Spanish.

I hear Britta's giggle as she bounces towards me. Britta has long blond hair and gorgeous deep brown eyes that are captivating. She has a way of sucking all the attention out of a room. Her beautiful frame and her keen fashion sense make her seem relevant and cool at all times.

"Do you have any cash? The guys have I.D. and they're gonna pick us up some drinks for later."

Annoyed by the prospect of watching Britta fawn over this guy all night, I remind her that I have a date with the guy she fixed me up with. He goes to some crazy expensive all-boys prep school, *which I guess is kinda cool*. We're only going for coffee, but it means I won't be around tonight.

She looks at me pleading with her brown eyes. "You can bring him back here. I'll call Steph. Come on." I sigh loudly, so she knows I'm annoyed. I'm helpless against her. She's one of my closest friends and let's face it, I'd do anything for her.

Looking quickly around the room I realize I've left my bag in the car. "I've gotta run to the car," I say as she grins a self-satisfied grin. "You owe me big," I add on my way to the door.

I breeze past the guy at the door. He smiles and I nod a little. I don't want to be rude, but Britta has a lot of admirers and I simply don't feel the need to invest my time anymore.

As I approach my car, I'm distracted by the loud music and excessive movement in the car parked behind mine. Nirvana's "Entertainers" is blaring from the radio.

Great tune. I kind of sing it under my breath on my way to the car. As I get closer I see that the movement is coming from a guy in the driver's seat rapidly drumming on the steering wheel. I unlock my car and realize that I've been noticed. The guy behind the wheel has stopped drumming and he is looking at me. The glare from the windshield kind of obstructs my view. I smile, lean into the car and begin fishing through my centre console for my emergency gas money. I hide it there so I'll never be stranded. Under Britta's influence I've already spent it hastily on alcohol three times now.

As I back out of the car I immediately sense that I'm not alone. I turn and there is the steering-wheel-drummer himself. *Dave Grohl's got nothing on him*, and that is saying something.

"Hi," he says with a smirk at the edge of his lips.

I can't help but think that seconds earlier he must have been staring at my ass. "Hi," bursts out of my mouth, sounding somewhat startled.

"I'm Tom's friend, Evan."

Tom must have been the guy I breezed by at the door. My eyes meet Evan's and I freeze for a second. I want to breeze past him too...but there is something about his gaze that stops me. He has striking blue eyes. I am drawn in by the dark ring around the breathtakingly intense blue colour. I'm not sure what it is. Slowly, I become aware that I'm just gawking at him. I'm speechless. I try to shrug off this foreign feeling as I attempt to casually introduce myself.

"I'm Emilia." I finally spit out. Usually, I introduce myself as Em, but this time I feel nervous, giddy even.

I am level headed and self-assured. Well, as much as any eighteen-year-old can be. As I stand here in the driveway, however, I find myself blushing and I hear a nervous giggle escape from within. *This is totally not me.*

"Are you going somewhere?" he asks.

It dawns on me that I'm now standing beside the driver's side door with the keys in my hands. "I was just getting some money," I manage to say.

"Oh good," he smiles. I melt. A flush of warmth spreads throughout my body. Thoughts race through my head. *I wonder if he's simply making conversation or if he really wants me to stay.* I watch intently as he turns and approaches the door. I'm fixated as he motions for me to walk with him.

He is not like any of the guys I've been interested in before. He's edgier somehow. Not preppy or manicured. He looks like the kind of guy who could front a band. He has broad shoulders that are accented by his faded ACDC T-shirt. His jeans, complete with wallet chain, fall perfectly against his body. *That butt...*I can't help but follow.

Mesmerized, I find myself back in the house. Moments earlier, I was confident and annoyed. Now, all traces of these feelings have vanished. I'm driven by a new-found electricity in my body. I am keenly aware of every part of myself. My hands feel awkward. My mouth is dry. *What's wrong with me?* I've never felt this way before. It's weird. I'm all together too self-aware.

I have never been one to care about my clothes. Right now, I'm looking down at my ill-fitting shirt and old jeans and wishing I'd put more effort into my appearance. *Maybe I can borrow something of Britta's? Why am I so flustered?*

It's not like I haven't hung out with guys before. I even had a boyfriend for a couple of months. His name was Brad and we met in chemistry class. He was nice and very good at chemistry. Well, the school kind of chemistry anyway. We hit it off over a chem-lab and went out a couple times after that. I liked his preppy style and he got along really well with my friends. It took me a while to realize that I kinda liked him more as a friend than as a boyfriend. I stuck it out for a while longer after that, though, because I didn't know how to break up with him. He eventually 'let me down easy'. *Thank God!*

That was over a month ago now. Since then, Britta has been trying desperately to set me up with this prep school guy, or Fix-Up-Boy as I like to call him. She's been championing the benefits of 'meaningless rebound relationships'. I'm not sure why, maybe it's her persistent nature, but I've finally given in and agreed to go out with Fix-Up-Boy. I tell myself that it'll be a good distraction from school stress, but I kind of know that her 'meaningless rebound relationship' idea has weaseled its way into my brain. Oddly, I find myself considering what this would look like for me.

To Britta, 'meaningless rebound relationships' always involved sex and lots of it. For me, this is not exactly the case. I'm not planning on anything like that. My reality is that I've only ever gotten to third base and barely at that. I have never really wanted to go any further. Brad tried several times to persuade me, but something never felt right. I guess I was afraid I'd make a decision I'd regret. I've probably seen too many movies or read too many romance novels, but I kinda expect fireworks. I want chemistry to be more than a class I take. Maybe that's it? Maybe I just wasn't that hot for Brad or any of the guys I've made out with. Whatever the reason, one thing's for sure: I'm saving myself. For what, I have no idea, but I am.

Tom and Evan are taking drink orders and flirting with Britta. I feel invisible. I take the opportunity to look Evan over. He is tall….at least six feet. He has chestnut brown hair that is short but long enough on top to fist my hands through. *Oh my word, where did that thought come from?*

My eyes begin their decent down his body. His shirt accents the muscles of his shoulders and chest. My gaze continues to travel down slowly. His waist is trim and hips look powerful. *Hmmm...*my mind goes blank for a second as I contemplate the hint of an outline on his jeans.

"What would you like Emilia?" I hear the words. My heartbeat races and I gasp a little. He's said my name. It sounds so poetic, so melodic coming from his lips. I quickly bring my eyes up hoping my dirty mind hasn't been caught in the act.

Blushing, I start to answer and Britta blurts out "Emilia? Why so formal? She's just Em." I feel smaller somehow. "She's a lightweight. Get her a cooler or some wine." Just when I think it can't get any worse, she follows up with, "She's going out on a date for most of the night anyway." *I could kill her!*

Britta's used to getting all the attention. She does this thing sometimes where she makes me seem completely insignificant. It usually doesn't piss me off, because usually I don't give a shit about the guys she flirts with. Right now I give a shit! *Maybe Britta likes Evan? I thought she liked Tom, but maybe I'm wrong? What if she likes Evan? I can't compete with Britta, can I? What am I thinking? I don't even know this guy.*

I look at Evan. His strong chiseled jaw line frames his perfect lips so well. A piece of his brown hair falls in front of his eyes and he raises his hand to brush it away. As his fingers comb it back in place, his shirt hugs against him. His muscles flex under the faded fabric and I can feel the saliva collecting in my mouth. A sliver of skin between his pants and his shirt is visible for a fraction of a second and I think I can feel my brain imploding. His stunning eyes meet mine briefly and seem confused somehow. My mind starts racing to figure out whether his confusion is a good thing. *Maybe he doesn't want me to go out with Fix-Up-Boy? Maybe he likes me? Or, maybe he saw me check him out and thinks I'm some kind of weirdo?* Feeling way too uncomfortable in my own skin I stand up and say quietly, "I'd better get ready."

"I'll help," Britta exclaims almost bubbling over with excitement. She loves to play 'real-life Barbie' with me. I'm still pretty annoyed with her as we enter her small bedroom. I sit on her tiny twin bed and my annoyance quickly dissipates as Britta begins gushing. She gushes her every feeling, thought, and question about Tom. Girl talk at its finest. I take a much needed sigh of relief. *She's not into Evan.* I still hate how she's so self-serving sometimes, but at this moment, I'm just happy she doesn't have a thing for Evan.

I listen for what seems like an eternity as she takes my hair out of my ponytail and begins brushing and smoothing it. Usually it's quite curly, but earlier in the day Britta had experimented with her new straightening iron. My shoulder length hair is now half way down my back. It feels strange, like I'm pretending to be someone else. It doesn't look professionally done by any means, but I have to admit that by the time she's finished, I look stylish.

I glance down at my clothes. My shirt is okay but it's probably a size too big for me. My jeans are uber-comfy, but their style-appeal is lacking. *My hair transformation seems wasted on this ensemble.*

"Britta, maybe I could borrow something of yours to wear," her eyes light up.

"You must really like Chris!" she says as she hurries over to her small closet. Chris is Fix-Up-Boy. I've spoken to him a couple of times on the phone. He seems nice and I have been trying to find a distraction. As she rummages through her over-stuffed-wardrobe I admit to myself that I've found a more interesting distraction. In fact, the entire time we've been in the bedroom my thoughts have never left the striking blue eyes down the hall.

I look in the mirror and barely recognize my body. I'm wearing a tight, low-cut green shirt. My green eyes seem to come alive in this colour. Britta's jeans hug my curves and my hair flows down my back. My body is not model-like, but I'm not big either. My boobs are small but I've never really minded. My waist is small too. My butt however, is quite curvy. It's probably my best feature, especially in Britta's form-fitting jeans. I feel good as we exit the bedroom. *I hope Evan's still here. Maybe I should blow off Fix-Up-Boy and hang here?*

Tom and Evan are in the kitchen. Tom is on the phone talking to a friend, telling him Britta's address. It's starting to sound like Britta is in for quite a party. I follow Britta into the kitchen. Evan's leaning up against the counter. I notice him looking at me. I can't help but add a little strut to my walk as I approach. When I reach the doorway, I lean my shoulder against the door-jam. I'm still not sure what to do with my hands. *I hope like hell I look hot.*

Evan's gaze drifts steadily from my hips up to my breasts and finally rests on my eyes. He smiles a devious grin and I feel the strange rush of electricity flow through my body again. He must be aware that I can see him checking me out but he seems to relish the idea that we both know he's up to no good. Confidence oozes out of him as he holds his eyes on mine. I can't look away. I don't want to. I don't want to destroy the power that is radiating between us. My own confidence begins to rise as he licks his lips ever so slightly and I find myself tingling all over.

Tom hangs up the phone and says, "Whoa Em." My eyes dart away from Evan's as though I've been caught with my hand in the cookie jar. I notice Britta's obvious dislike of Tom's utterance. So I smile at Tom and say, "Britta has worked her magic."

Evan says almost in a whisper "No magic about it. She made a beautiful girl look...well, beautiful."

I wasn't even sure I was supposed to hear him, but, I did. My heart is pounding. I feel entirely too exposed. I have to get out of here. I panic. Fleeing, I quickly say, "I'm gonna be late." Glancing at the floor, I head to the door. Britta scurries after me.

"What was that?" She whispers as we reach the door.

"What do you mean?" I play dumb.

"You know exactly what I mean. I have never seen you...I don't know...like that with anyone," she states.

I want to stand here and analyze what she means. I know what I was feeling, but *what did that look like? How was I different?* I need to flee. I can't risk talking about this with her now, not with him in the other room. I'm overwhelmed by the fact that this guy's mere presence can have my mind and body racing. The shock of it forces me out the door.

Dismissing Britta's last comment with a huff, I say, "I'll see you later." The words leave my mouth and I am fully aware that *I'm definitely coming back here later.*

I jump in my black Pontiac Tempest and back down the driveway. The car belongs to my parents, but they've pretty well given it to me. It's nothing fancy. It has a pale, grey fabric interior. The letters on the automatic stick shift don't quite line up properly so it looks like I'm always driving in second. The power windows are temperamental. For me though, it means freedom. *I love my quirky little ride.*

I realize as I am pulling up to a stop sign, that I need to call my mom and check in. I need to remind her that I'm staying at Britta's tonight. She thinks I'm studying for my Spanish exam. *I probably should be.*

Right now however, my thoughts are consumed by the hot guy in Britta's kitchen. *Did I really hear him right? Did he call me beautiful?* A huge grin spreads across my face from the thought. I turn up the radio to try and escape the overwhelming feelings I'm having over this complete stranger.

Marvin Gaye's "Sexual Healing" is now pumping loudly out of the speakers. One speaker starts to rattle so I adjust the sound. Just another little quirk my car has. Rolling down the window, the warm humid air rushes in. My senses are in overdrive. I pull into the bakery parking lot. It is almost eight-o-clock and the sun is starting to lower in the sky behind the building as I enter.

Fix-Up-Boy is already sitting at a table. I see him nervously fidgeting with his napkin. He's attractive. He has spiky blond hair and greenish eyes. He has on a blue, three-button polo shirt and khakis. From our phone conversations, I know that he attends an all-boys private school downtown. I'm fairly sure that Britta has set me up solely for her own personal gain: increased access to hot wealthy boys. It's obvious as I approach the table that he is not her type. He's not at all confident or charismatic…two must-haves for Britta.

I should have known he would be sort of lame, otherwise Britta would have claimed him for herself. It's not like she means to be selfish about boys. She just is. I knew it when our friendship started three years ago and I've kind of accepted it. Having a boyfriend has never really concerned me, so it hasn't really been that much of an issue. Britta is what she is: fun. Her carefree nature used to stand in stark contrast to my studious and reserved persona. Over the course of our friendship though, she has managed to pull out a more easy-going kind of Emilia. Maybe that's why I let her manipulate me, because deep down I like being a little less inhibited.

Our friendship has slowly changed me in other ways too. I'm starting to take the whole boy-girl relationship thing more seriously. That's probably why it's still bugging me that she put me down in front of Evan and it is definitely why I'm so annoyed right now as I approach Britta's cast-off Fix-Up-Boy. Smiling politely, I suck up my annoyance and prepare to be nice to the poor sap. *It's not his fault Britta wants an in with his friends.*

Chris is reserved and soft spoken as he greets me. He's not unlike the other guys I've dated. He has charm-school manners that any mother would love. He even stands up as I get to the table and politely waits for me to sit down before he does. *What a gentleman. Maybe this won't be so bad?*

   We begin chatting about school. He's graduating this year. I still have one more year before graduation. We talk about his family. They want him to take a trip with them to Paris over the summer. He wants to go to New York. *New York's cool, but Paris – I've always wanted to go to Paris. I'd choose the Eiffel tower over Times Square any day. I prefer the romantic potential over the hustle and bustle for sure. Chris and I have less in common than I thought.*

   He's a sweet guy, I guess, but I feel no chemistry. Until recently I had no idea what that really meant. Now, however, my mind is wandering to Evan's broad shoulders. This is so unlike me. I never daydream about boys. I've seen girls in movies get goofy over boys they've just met. I've poured through a great deal of fiction that thoroughly and poetically describes a kind of undeniable attraction and longing. Until now I had always thought it was just that: fictitious. Sure, I hoped that connections like that existed, but now I'm beginning to believe they do. I mean, an hour ago I laid eyes on Evan for the first time and here I am wondering what his hands might feel like on my skin. I blush as Chris, fix-up boy, rambles on about the universities he's applied to.

   While he is talking I hear Britta's giggle come from behind a booth across the bakery. I see her. From my seat

I can see Britta, Tom, Steph, and Evan trying to be inconspicuous as they spy on us. I freeze. It is clear something's up when Tom gets up and heads towards us. *What is he doing?* Chris sees me looking at Tom just as he reaches our table. I'm about to introduce them when Tom starts speaking with a very thick Italian accent.

"Oh what a beautiful couple! Bellissima," Tom says, completely straight-faced.

Now I'm very confused. I can see Britta and Steph snickering away in the booth at the end of the row. I try to get a glimpse of Evan but the others are blocking my view. Chris is oblivious and he is politely thanking Tom.

Tom then pulls a camera from his pocket and says, "One picture, so beautiful."

At this point I'm sure that I'm on the receiving end of a dare. Chris leans into the centre of our booth and puts his arm awkwardly around my shoulder. I'm helpless. I smile as well. The flash blinds us momentarily and Tom leaves almost as quickly as he came. The rest of the booth empties out. As they make their way onto the sidewalk I faintly hear the eruption of laughter.

I'm seething with anger. *How could Britta and Steph do this to me? The others I don't know very well but they – they're my best friends. Or, at least I thought they were. Britta is certainly plummeting her way down my friendship chart today. As for Steph, she's going to have some explaining to do. I wonder how Britta spun this embarrassing episode so that Steph would go along with it. What makes it worse is that they did it in front of Evan. I can't imagine what he thinks about me after that.*

"That was strange," Chris says and I nod.

After twenty more minutes or so we decide to leave, ourselves. We make our way out. Chris asks if I can give him a lift home. When we approach the car I realize that asking Fix-Up-Boy back to the party is no longer an option. I know that I'm not really interested in him but a crazy thought occurs to me: *If he comes with me, I might be distracted from the magnetic pull that Evan seems to possess over me.* No, *who am I kidding, I welcome the magnetism.*

We pull up outside his house and Chris leans in for a kiss. I don't really want to feel his lips against mine but I guess I have no real choice. He's a 'nice guy' and I did have a 'nice' time. Almost instantly as our lips touch his hand is on my thigh, grabbing and inching up between my legs. I reach down to push his hand away as his tongue forces its way into my mouth. Pulling away and gasping for air I find myself almost shouting, "What are you doing?"

He gives me the sleaziest look and says, "What? Not in the car? That's cool...my folks are out."

Stunned I blurt out, "What's that supposed to mean?"

"I know you public school girls..." he hisses.

This isn't actually happening? He didn't just say that did he? You've gotta be kidding me? What the hell has Britta gotten me into?

My face winces with a look of disgust as his words register. "Get out now!" I shout forcefully.

"Come on, ease up," he coos.

"Out!" I assert as I shove my hands against his shoulder.

He slinks out of the car and as he is closing the door I yell, "Gentleman my ass!" feeling less than classy as the words leave my lips. I speed away as if he's chasing me, knowing full well he isn't. Adrenaline racing through my veins, I feel like I have totally been part of a bad after-school special. The weird thing is that I never saw it coming. He was so sweet until...he wasn't. *Jackass!*

I pull over a few streets away and try to muster a sense of calm. *Shit...first my friends are assholes, making me the brunt of their joke and then Fix-Up-Boy turns into Mister-Grab-Ass-Sleaze-Ball.* My mind is reeling. I'm not sure what to do. *Do I go to Britta's? Should I just go home?*

Shit, it occurs to me that I still haven't called my mom. It is almost ten thirty now and I haven't talked to her all day. *If I don't hurry she is going to call Britta* to ask where I am. Then any option of a party night will be out of the question. I quickly signal and get back on the road. I'm heading to Britta's.

4 My Type

I pull onto Britta's street and notice several parked cars that were not here when I left. I can see Steph's car. I'm angry at her but relieved that she's here at the same time. As I approach the door, the sweet smell of marijuana is wafting in the air. I enter Britta's place and head straight to the phone. My fingers aptly call home. I'm hoping that my mom hasn't called already or that she isn't already in bed.

"Hey, Mom."

"Hi, honey. I was just starting to get worried about you." A sense of relief washes over me. At least there isn't a search party on its way.

"I'm hanging out at Britta's. We're studying."

Some guy stumbles through the back door into the kitchen, giggling like a fool. He is obviously high. I panic. I don't want my mom to hear him. I cover the receiver and rush into Britta's room.

Her room is dark. I instantly realize I'm interrupting something. I hear moaning and groaning. *Shit.* I continue to hold the receiver and I duck back out into the hall.

"I gotta go Mom. We're about to start a movie." It sounds so reasonable as it comes out of my mouth.

"Night honey. Love you," she says.

"Love you too." Click.

Immediately guilt sets in. I really don't like lying to my mom. If she ever found out, I would be devastated. Not because she would punish me or anything. More because she would tell me, so sincerely, how disappointed she was in me. That would not be 'succeeding in all things Emilia'. That would eat me up inside.

The fact remains that Britta's parents never go away, and what's done is done. I try to ignore my conscience on my way back to the kitchen. I grab a drink out of the fridge. It's a wine cooler. I remember Britta saying, "Get her a cooler or some wine," and instinctively realize that this is meant for me. I hate wine coolers. I like vodka coolers and I like wine, but wine coolers are vile. I wish I hadn't been so distracted when Tom was taking drink orders. Twisting the top off, I hear a 'ppsstt' sound. I take a sip. *Fuck that tastes bad!* Today's been such a crazy day that I lift the funky wine cooler and start chugging it. The bubbles fizz-up as it flows down my throat. I'm disgusted, but I don't stop. Finishing the bottle, I place it on the counter and grab another.

Now I am ready to face Britta and Steph. I walk out in the backyard. It is dark outside. There is only one small light above the door. It casts a dim hazy light down and across the yard. There are about a dozen people there. *I am surprised, I expected more.*

Steph throws her arms around me. Steph is by far my closest friend. She's so smart and confident I can't help but be drawn to her. She has a unique style too. She doesn't buy into fashion trends. If she likes it, she wears it, as is evident by the retro pleather jacket she's wearing tonight. Her long brown hair is pin-straight. Tonight she has braided her long thick asymmetrical bangs and secured them to the side with a bobby pin.

"Hey, how was your date?" she giggles.

She thinks I'm going to be amused by the bakery antics. I'm about to tear a strip off her when I see Evan looking at me. He's sitting in a lawn chair with a group of guys. I can no longer think. I know I want to say something, but my mind is fumbling as I hear myself saying. "Good, no thanks to you." Not nearly as searing as I would've come up with if I wasn't so distracted.

"Where's Britta?" I ask.

"Guess?" she says as she rolls her eyes.

Oh...of course, I realize the origins of the moaning and groaning in Britta's bedroom. I'm kind of glad actually; *this way I don't have to face Tom. What would I say to the fake-Italian-photographer anyway?*

Steph starts telling me about her new job as a lifeguard. She's so excited. I pretend to listen to what she's saying but my mind and eyes keep wandering over to the patio. Now some girl is blocking my view. I want her to move out of the way. When she does I'm thoroughly disappointed.

She's moved. She's moved right onto Evan's lap. *What is she doing? Is she his girlfriend?* My heart sinks. I become keenly aware that I know absolutely nothing about him. I try to see if he's flirting or touching the petite busty blond on his lap. As I do, Steph probes, "Em, what's wrong with you? Are you even listening?"

"Of course I am," I lie and follow it up with, "lifeguarding sounds awesome." *Shit, I hope she is still talking about her job.*

Steph smiles and says, "Yeah, well...I better get going."

"No, don't leave now, I just got here." *She can't leave.* With Britta in the bedroom I'll be on my own.

"I have the early shift tomorrow," she hugs me and heads inside.

Not knowing what to do with myself I follow. Now I'm in the kitchen. I can see Steph closing the front door. She's gone. Here I am in Britta's house where I've been a million times before, only this time I feel totally out of place. All of Britta's Briarview friends are in the yard. Normally, I have no problem mingling with random strangers. Britta puts me in this situation often. This time though, I'm staring through the ugly lace curtains into the yard wondering what to do. *Maybe I should go. It's not too late. I could tell my mom that I changed my mind and decided to come home. Ugh. This is totally not me – lying to my mom, blowing off studying. What am I doing?* I take a big swig of my vile-tasting-liquid-courage, then another, until I have finished the bottle. Grabbing another from the fridge I head back into the yard.

The sound of a very poorly played guitar hits my ears instantly. Two seats over from Evan, a total stoner has just arrived and is trying to play and sing Oasis' "Wonderwall". It's awful but I guess everyone else is too drunk, high, or wrapped up in their own conversation to care. I approach the patio and as I do, the girl on Evan's lap giggles and leans back into him. *She must be his girlfriend I tell myself. Actually, this is good*, I reassure, or should I say lie to, myself. *Now I know he's not into me and I can forget about him.* I sit in the empty seat opposite Evan and his flirty girl. I'm right beside Wonderwall-Stoner.

He looks up over his guitar, stops playing and says, "What do you want to hear baby?"

Firstly, I hate being called baby. Secondly, now everyone is looking at me expectantly. I smile sweetly trying to buy myself some time and rack my brain for cool tunes. The first song that comes to me is... "Do you know 'She Talks to Angels' by the Black Crowes?"

"Great tune," Wonderwall-Stoner says as he quickly goes about bastardizing it with his poor pitch and bad tempo.

I sigh. The attention is no longer on me.

"I love that song," a husky voice across from me says.

Holy shit it's Evan! He likes my song and what's more, he is talking to me. The girl on his lap shifts forward and he motions for her to find another seat. To my surprise, she gets up and sits on another guy's lap. *Maybe she isn't his girlfriend!* I blush at the thought. I smile at Evan. He stands up and as he does he motions for me to follow him. I have never met anyone who 'motions' to get people to do things before. It is strange but for some reason the quiet commanding nature of the action is so hot. Without even thinking, I follow him down the driveway to the front of the house. As he walks in front of me I have an urge to touch the small of his back. *I want to wrap my arms or possibly my legs around him.* I blush again at the thought. *What is going on with me?*

We get to the front of the house. We're alone. I am nervous but somehow invigorated.

"I couldn't think with all that...well um...I guess we could call it music that Jeff was playing."

Jeff must be Wonderwall-Stoner. I giggle realizing I wasn't the only critic in the yard.

"I liked your song choice though," he adds.

"Thanks." I smile melting into his compliment as if I had something to do with the Black Crowes being awesome.

"How was your date?" he asks with the faintest gleam of jealousy in his eyes. I'm elated. *Maybe he's into me or maybe he will be 'into me', wink-wink, nudge-nudge.* I am embarrassed by my own thoughts. Perhaps this vile excuse for alcohol is really getting to me.

"It was okay until some creeps interrupted it. Then my date became Mister-Grab-Ass." I can't believe I had uttered those words. *So much for being charming and classy.*

He laughs but then takes a more serious tone. "Are you okay? He didn't hurt you or anything?"

"No, I didn't really like him anyway."

"No, why not?" he seems genuinely interested.

"Not my type I guess." I can't help but say this with a slightly seductive tone.

"What's your type?" he murmurs with a very seductive tone. *He's done this before.* The idea should bother me, but instead I just think: *He is definitely better at this than I am. I'm going to have to step up my game.*

I try to channel the sultry heroine, Kendra, from one of my steamiest romance novels. I take a step closer to him so that we can feel one another's body heat. There is a subtle increase in his breathing. *Oh my, I'm having an effect. Thank you, Kendra.*

"Tall, dark hair, blue-eyes, broad shoulders, mysterious, confident, and charming," I say.

Right when it is about to get interesting, some girl calls Evan's name from the backyard.

"Come on." He grabs my hand and opens the front door. His touch sends a bolt of lightning through my body. I can hear the girl's voice getting close to the front of the house as the door closes behind me.

We duck into the closest bedroom. It's dark. It is Britta's younger brother, Alex's room. He is away with Britta's parents. I feel weird being in here. Britta, Steph, and I try to avoid Alex and his pimply drooling friends as much as possible. I think he's like fourteen, and as far as I know fourteen-year-old boys' bedrooms are far from sexy and romantic. Yet here I am, holding this gorgeous guy's hand with only thoughts of sex and romance on my mind. We step over some clothes and books. He reaches over to the lamp beside the bed and turns it on. It casts a soft glow onto his handsome face. He sits down at the head of the very small twin bed and I sit in front of him at the foot of the bed. Our eyes are fixated on one another. I'm trying to contain my excitement and look cool and calm. Inside I'm doing back flips.

He breaks the silence. "She won't leave me alone."

"Who is she?" I ask.

"Sarah. We're just friends, but whenever she has a drink she can't keep her hands off me."

"Oh Miss-Grab-Ass," I quip. "Perhaps I should introduce her to my date," I joke nervously.

He laughs.

"I thought she was your girlfriend," I say hoping he will tell me that no such creature exists.

"God no!" he states emphatically and follows it with his seductive tone from before. "She's not my type."

"Oh?" I say coyly. "What is your type?"

He moves down the bed, places his hands at my ankles and begins circling his fingers over my jeans. His touch is amazing. It is light and gentle. Who knew that touching my ankles and calves could be so erotic? The slow rhythmic circles are shooting waves of pleasure throughout my body. *If he can do that simply by touching my ankle this is gonna be a very interesting night.*

"I like girls that are real."

What is that supposed to mean? Despite his gentle caressing I'm confused. I was expecting the same crap I said to him about his appearance and a few standard character traits. Instead I get 'real.' *What the hell is 'real'? Aren't all girls 'real'?* I need clarification.

"What do you mean 'real'?"

He leans in closer. Tucks my hair behind my ear and whispers softly. "You know girls who aren't afraid to be themselves. Smart. Strong. Sexy." His last word sends a warm shiver to my core. *He's good. He's very good at this seduction thing.*

I can't help it. My normally rational, level-headed self is completely enraptured. I'm putty in his hands. He slowly moves his hand back through my hair resting it at the nape my neck. He pulls me forward so my lips are against his. We are kissing softly at first but it doesn't take long...it builds passionately...feverishly. Our tongues are intertwined. His fingers are threaded in my hair. His other hand is on the small of back. My legs are somehow wrapped around his waist. My hands are traipsing up over his broad shoulders and down his back. I am ALIVE! Every part of my body is hungry for his touch.

He pulls away and his eyes meet mine. We're panting. "What?" I gasp. *Why is he stopping?* My insides are screaming for more.

"This is okay, right?" he whispers. I'm confused by the question. *Can't he see that I want him so badly? Why is he stopping?*

He reaches down to the hem of his shirt and pulls it over his head. *Ah...he is so sexy.* He's muscular but not in a meat-head way. He's toned and sleek. I immediately have an urge to lick him all over. I refrain...for now.

I touch his chest starting from his collarbone and slowly winding down towards the button on his jeans. I'm so turned on. I breathe in a deep ragged breath. Just before I get to his button, I stop. I reach for the hem of my shirt. I pull it over my head and hope to hell I looked sexy in the process. He is looking at me with soft eyes. He takes his finger and touches my bra strap on my shoulder. He drags it ever so slowly down the strap, along the edge of the cup of my bra towards the centre of my chest, and then back up. My nipples grow hard within the bra. He turns his head and slowly begins to kiss me slightly below my earlobe down towards my bra.

I grab a hold of the button on his jeans and he lets out a sigh. I feel so in control, so desired, so full of pure lust, as I begin to undo his zipper. My hand brushes down his fly as each tooth of the zipper springs open. I can feel how hard he is on the back of my hand. My hormones surge. I never thought my body could feel this...this...

Shit what is that? The door flings open. A rush of light flashes into Evan. It takes me an instant to realize that I'm being illuminated too. Tom, Britta, and Sarah burst through the door and their hysterical laugher invades the room.

"What the fuck?" Evan blurts out.

I grab for my shirt. I can't find it. Evan hands me his T-shirt and I quickly put it on. I look over at him and he is doing up the button on his jeans.

"Em!" Britta stops dead and looks shocked. She obviously didn't expect to find me here.

Sarah looks crushed. *Why does she look so crushed?* The thought is fleeting as Britta grabs my hand and rips me out of the room. She pulls me into her room like she's my mother and I'm in big trouble. While I'm being ripped away I glance back at Evan. He takes a step forward as if he is about to follow me. Our eyes meet. The look he gives me is sympathetic, apologetic even. But, the small smirk on his lips is more telling. It's flirtatious and offers a glimmer of a deeper infatuation.

"What are you doing?" She scolds.

"What? I like him," I say.

"He is not your type." *Apparently this is the line of the night.* I can't help but smirk, thinking about my earlier conversations.

"You think this is funny?" She continues to lecture me.

"What's your problem, Britta? And, what do you mean he's not my type*?" Like she knows my type. She's the one that set me up with Mister-Grab-Ass.*

"He's a player." Her words hurt but I refuse to believe her. *What does she know? Then again, what do I know? Until tonight I had never even heard of this guy. I haven't even had a real conversation with him and now I'm questioning my best friend. Well, maybe not best friend after today, but whatever. I need to know more.*

"How do you know?" I ask.

"He's always in a bedroom at a party," she says. *Which kind of explains why they burst into the bedroom as a joke.*

Maybe I'm the flavour of the night. I can't think. It was so good. I was being completely reckless and yet I felt in complete control.

"Maybe I just want to reap the benefits of a meaningless rebound relationship," I snap back using her own theory against her.

"Em, I really think you're in over your head here."

I hear her but...I've never felt anything like this. *I might be in over my head but I need to, NEED TO feel his touch on my body again.* I look Britta in the eye and say, "I just want to have a little fun. Don't worry. I'm fine." *What's it to her anyway? She does this kind of thing all the time.*

"Promise me you won't let things go too far. I don't want you to get hurt."

"Promise," I say but I'm not sure this is a promise I want to keep.

On the way back to Alex's bedroom I pass Sarah in the hall. She's just standing there. I realize she's probably been in the hall since we first left the room. *What's her deal?* She looks at me and I smile politely. She glares back at me. *She's not a fan*, I think to myself. Normally I hate when people are mad at me. I usually go out of my way to try to win over anyone that has a negative view of me. Right now though, I have a different agenda.

I turn to enter the boudoir, if you will, the set of my steamy indiscretion ready to channel Kendra once more.

Now all the lights are on in the room and it's a real shit hole of a room. There are clothes and comic books all over the floor. There is a huge poster of Jim Morrison and some smaller pictures of trashy girls in bikinis haphazardly stapled to the wall. To think, moments earlier I was giving this room more action than it has ever seen.

Evan's sitting with Tom on the bed. I can tell they've been having a heated conversation. As I approach they both stop talking. Tom meekly nods an apology. He gets up and leaves closing the door behind him.

"Sorry about my friends," Evan says as he takes my hands and sits me down on the bed. We are back in the same spot we were before the interruption. I smile. "Maybe it's a good thing they came in," he adds.

What? I am totally caught off guard. *I did not hear him complaining about what we were doing. In fact, I literally felt that he was enjoying himself.* I must have a confused look on my face because he starts to clarify his comment even before I can respond.

"It's...well...I think I might really like you." *Yeah you do!* A small cheering section erupts in my brain. "And well, I don't want to screw this up."

"What do you mean?" I say blushing and batting my lashes. *Who bats their lashes anyway?* I have never done it before, but as I sit now cross-legged on the bed I, for some reason, am unmistakably batting my lashes. *Crazy.*

"Well, I don't know what it is but, I think you're, well...real and I really like that about you. I'm afraid if I do my thing, we won't get to know each other."

His thing? He has a thing. Is he sitting here in front of me admitting that he is a player and in the same breath asking if we could be something? Maybe he's playing me right now? I'm wary now about getting too invested but, who am I kidding? Even if he is playing me, I'm hooked. *Batter-up.*

"Okay, let's get to know each other then," I say sweetly and then follow it up seductively with, "As long as you promise to do 'your thing' sometime."

"Oh, that I can guarantee."

We spend the rest of the night lying in the wet-dream-bedroom on Britta's brother's twin bed. I'm curled up at his side with my head on his chest. I slowly stroke his chest and he gently plays with my hair. It is all very P.G. *I want more. I think he does too.* For tonight, it's just fun asking questions and giggling at each reply. We talk about our friends, school, his graduation, and his plans for business school.

By morning we are both exhausted, as I ask one final question. "Tell me something that no one else knows about you." I expect some deep dark secret. His response is far more endearing than that.

"I'm afraid of sharks."

"Sharks?" I giggle. *We live in Canada. We don't even have shark-infested waters.* He seems embarrassed as I say, "That's not what I expected you to say."

"I'm not a complicated guy. Not many things scare me. Sharks don't intend to hurt people. Sometimes they just do."

I smile quietly to myself. Lying here on his chest, I think perhaps he is telling me a deep dark secret. *This confident, smart, sexy guy is afraid of unknowingly being hurt. Maybe we're not so different.* I close my eyes and drift off on his chest.

I wake up stiff and in pain. I can't feel my left arm at all. I sit up and see that Evan is still sleeping. I'm relieved because, to be quite honest, the vile coolers have made my mouth feel like something has curled up and died in it. I slowly stand up and creep out of the room into the bathroom. I look in the mirror and I'm not pleased with the reflection. I'm still wearing Evan's shirt and my hair has a large matte at the back. I smile at the thought that Evan's hands created that matte with his gentle touch. I pull his shirt up to my nose to smell his natural scent...*Mmmm.* Riffling through the top drawer under the sink, I find a comb and some toothpaste. It takes some work but I get my hair looking somewhat stylish again. The toothpaste is cold as it squirts onto my finger. It is not a great solution, but it will have to do. I finish freshening up and creep back into the bedroom.

Evan's looks so peaceful sleeping. Britta's green shirt is peeking out from under the bed. I quickly remove Evan's giving it one last whiff and pull on the green one. I know I have to get home so I can get ready for work, but I want to say goodbye.

Taking some clothes off of a desk chair that I didn't know existed until now, I wheel it over beside the bed. I begin by slowly circling my fingers on his ankle as he had done to me only a few hours before. I hope I'm affecting him in a similar way. He stirs. A sexy smile appears on his lips and I whisper, "Good morning." His peaceful look is quickly transformed into one of pure... *Yum.*

His eyes flutter slowly opening and he lifts his body up to rest on his elbows. I can see all the muscles in his chest and I'm salivating.

"Good morning," he says in a suggestive tone. "You look nice."

"You're not so bad yourself," I purr back. It sounds so cheesy coming from me, but what can I do? It's already out in the universe.

"I've gotta get going. My shift at the store starts at one and I still have to go home and take a shower." I work at a mid-range clothing store. I'm a lowly sales clerk, but it gives me gas money and I get a discount on clothes.

"Oh," he says, "I thought we could do breakfast or something." The way the 'or something' rolls off his tongue, it sounds incredibly tempting. But, the rational side of me is not as much of a push-over without the repulsive coolers following through my veins.

"Another time," I say and I'm proud of myself for resisting the urge to qualify my response with a 'maybe.'

He sits up quickly and in one motion grabs me in his arms and kisses me. His lips are soft and full. It is not the lustful tongue down my throat kiss from last night but it is igniting a fire within me. I open my mouth to intensify the kiss and he pulls back.

"You cheated!" He says.

Confused, no stunned by the comment, I give him a quizzical look.

"You brushed your teeth. It's not fair that you brushed and I didn't," he jokes.

Relieved and smiling I smugly reply, "That's one thing you should know about me. I never play fair." I'm not entirely sure what I even mean by that. Maybe the stupid coolers have caused temporary brain damage. This moment feels so moviesque that perhaps I'm simply pulling out film style banter? Who knows? *I better get out of here before I say something really stupid.* I stand up, give him a quick peck and leave.

I'm in my car ten blocks away before I realize that I never gave him my number. *Shit. What was I thinking? Britta will give it to him, right? We never even talked about hanging out again. He didn't even really ask. Why was I so sure of myself? He has given me no real reason to be. Shit. Shit. Shit. I really like him. I think he likes me too. I guess it's up to him now.*

At work I'm a mess. I can't stop thinking about him. It's really starting to bother me that Britta thinks he is a player. *She has no reason to lie to me about something like that – unless she likes him! No, she was all over Tom last night.*

If Evan really is a player then why was he the one that put a halt to our rapidly advancing make-out session? He's got an edgy charm that tells me he could have any girl he sets his sights on, but last night he chose to only snuggle and talk with me. Maybe I'm different. Maybe he feels the magnetism too. Or, shit, maybe he doesn't. What if he's not really that turned on by me? What if he didn't want to fool around with me anymore so he made up that shit about wanting to get to know me? I agonize over the prospect. *No, last night had to have meant something to him.*

Little memories pop up throughout the day: Evan's feather light touch as he absentmindedly traced his finger up and down my arm while he told me about his love for his childhood cottage, the feel of his breath against my neck as he listened to me talk about wanting to eventually be the kind of teacher that makes students feel special and important, the secure feeling I had when I woke up nuzzled in his arms. I can't contain my goofy smile.

That night I call Britta to ask if he's got my number. She says no and starts my interrogation.

"What happened with you guys?"

"Nothing really. We just snuggled and talked mostly."

"Seriously? Cause you were totally doing more than that when we came in."

"Yeah, thanks for that," I say sarcastically. "What the hell was that all about anyway?"

"Sarah was looking for Evan, and Tom thought it would be funny to crash in on his latest conquest."

"Conquest?"

"Yeah Em, conquest. I told you Evan's a total player. Every time I see him he has a different girl hanging off him."

"That doesn't mean he is sleeping with them," I defend.

"Well, his reputation would say otherwise."

"And, since when are you one to care about reputations?" It is a low blow. But, I'm super annoyed at her hypocrisy. Plus, she's kind of been a shitty friend lately. Britta's silent for a minute and I start to feel sort of bad for inadvertently calling her a slut. *Okay maybe not quite inadvertently, kind of intentionally. Okay now I really feel bad.* "Sorry Britta. You know I didn't really mean to..."

"I know what you meant. It's cool. What can I say?
Why should boys have all the fun, right?" She laughs but it
sounds slightly off. Like she's upset.

"What about Tom?" I ask trying to change the subject.

"What about him?"

"You like him right?"

"Yeah, but he doesn't do the girlfriend thing and let's
face it I'm not girlfriend material."

"I'd date you. If I was a dude," I quip.

"Shut up!" She snort laughs into the phone.

"But, since I'm not a dude...I've got a favour to ask."

"Let's have it."

"Okay. If Evan asks for my number can you give it to
him?"

"Are you sure, Em?"

"Yeah, I'm sure. I know what you think, but I like him.
It can't hurt to get to know him, right?"

"Don't say I didn't warn you," she says as she
concedes.

"Thanks Britta. You're the best."

"Yeah, yeah...Later, Em."

"Later."

I call Steph to give her the lowdown but Britta has
already gotten to her and she is now saying things like, "He
could totally have a STD you know." I hang up, firmly
believing that I'm on my own.

Perhaps studying will clear my head. I spend the rest of the night studying. Well, fantasizing and strategizing with my Spanish textbook open in front of me anyway. It's like my brain is on vacation. *I've gotta snap out of this.*

Three days go by and nothing. I've written two exams already and I start to think it isn't gonna happen with Evan. He hasn't even asked for my number yet.

That night when I get home from work there's a message from Britta. "Britta called. She wants you to call her back. Something about a number." I don't think my feet hit a stair on the way to my room in the basement. I swing open the door and grab my phone. I've had my own line ever since I started working. I can't risk Britta sharing her escapades freely on my parent's phone line. I call Britta and it's true. Tom called Britta today to get my number for Evan. Now it's just a matter of time. I wait. I wait. I hole up in my room all night so I don't miss the call. I hover over my sleek, black, corded handset phone willing it to ring but it's silent. At midnight I admit defeat and go to bed.

The next night I am talking to Steph on the phone while I give myself a pedicure. I feel bold today so I choose Robust Red nail polish. Steph is telling me about this guy at the pool, Nick, who is giving her a hard time. I'm sure he has a crush on her, but she is completely shooting down my theory.

Steph's my best friend ever. I'm way closer to Steph than I am with anyone, even Britta. We have been friends since the end of grade nine and I love her beyond words. She and I totally get one another. Steph is the one person that I know, regardless of time and space, I will always have in my corner. We love, respect, trust, and genuinely dig each other. When we're not together we are usually talking on the phone. She stays at my house a couple nights a week and I do the same at hers. We call each other's parents 'Mom' and 'Dad' for Pete's sake.

Steph is distraught over this dude at the pool and I'm trying to console her when I get a beep, it's another call. Thinking it must be Britta I quickly flash over.

"Hey," I say.

"Hi, can I speak with Emilia please?" an incredibly polite husky voice says.

Shit. This is definitely not Britta. Could it be? No. It's probably Mister-Grab-Ass-Sleaze-Ball calling to apologize, I tell myself.

"Speaking."

"Hi, it's Evan from Britta's place the other night," he states like I wouldn't remember or something.

"Hi," I say again. My mind is racing. *What should I say? Quick, think of something witty, cute, interesting, any of the above.*

"I hope it's not too late to call," he says.

"No, not at all, this is my own line. You can call it anytime." *That doesn't sound desperate at all. Pull it together, Em.* My heart is pounding and I realize I'm holding my breath. I stand up to walk around the room but the phone cord pulls tautly and I'm forced to sit back down on my bed. *Breathe Em, Breathe.*

"Cool," he murmurs quietly.

"So...I had a good time the other night...um morning, with you," I say, once again sounding too desperate. *I need a new, cooler approach.*

"Yeah, me too."

"It's too bad our friends burst in when they did." *Remind him of the hot parts, that's not a bad plan.*

"Oh yeah?" He sounds surprised. "It is too bad. What do you think might have happened if they didn't?"

Oh you bad boy. That is how you want to play this? A little 'what-are-you-wearing-sexy-time-conversation.' Can't say that I have done this before but I'll bite.

"Well, things were just getting good if I remember correctly."

"I don't know. Things were pretty good already, but I did like where they were headed," he replies.

"I seem to recall that we were wearing entirely too many clothes." *Oh my word! Did I say that?*

"I would have liked to take that lovely bra off you."

"I would have liked that too. I was enjoying taking off your pants."

"You were, were you?" he hisses.

"Very much so," I say as seductively as I can. *Am I really doing this? Is this really where our first phone conversation is going?*

"I think you could feel how much I was enjoying it."

"Very much so," I say again this time blushing.

He lets out a small gasp and I breathe in deeply. As I do the other line beeps. *Shit, it's probably Steph. I totally hung up on her.* There is a silence. *I don't want to get the other line*, but it keeps beeping.

"Is that your other line?" He asks.

I embarrassedly answer, "Yeah...let me get rid of them."

Click.

"Hey."

"Hey, you totally hung up on me."

"Sorry Steph. Can't talk. It's Evan on the other line. Wish me luck. I'll call you later."

Click.

"Sorry about that. It was my friend Steph. It seems like friends are always bursting in on us just when things are getting good," I joke.

He laughs. "Well, maybe we should get together sometime without friends then."

Holy shit. He's asking me out. He's really asking me out. Be cool. Deep breath. "Sounds like a good idea." My voice sounds oddly high pitched as I attempt to control my excitement. "What were you thinking?"

"Well, I work at The Coffee Bean until eleven every night this week. If you don't mind meeting me after that, we could go out or something."

"How's Friday?" I say.

"Sounds good. I can pick you up or you can meet me at work."

"I'll meet you there."

"Alright."

"Alright."

"Well...goodnight, Emilia."

My heart skips a beat. "Goodnight, Evan."

I hang up and dance around my room like I just scored a touchdown at the Super Bowl. Then I call Steph back to gush over my date, leaving out the sexy-talk portion of the conversation because I don't think Steph would approve.

"So your date is starting at eleven?" Steph asks.

"Yeah. I'm gonna have to tell my mom I'm staying with you that night. Is that cool?"

Steph's parents are hippies. They don't believe in curfews or invasion of privacy of any kind. So Steph can pretty much do whatever she wants, whenever she wants. I, as her best friend, reap the benefits of this when necessary. See, at my house, even though I'm eighteen, I need to follow some simple rules. I have a curfew of eleven on school nights, two-thirty on weekends. I have to check-in by calling my mom a couple times a day so she doesn't worry. As long as I follow the rules, I can continue to live rent-free and drive their car. Not really a bad deal.

"I don't know. I'm not sure about this guy. I was talking to a girl I lifeguard with; she goes to Briarview like Evan. She's only a freshman but she says her friend fooled around with him at a party and never heard from him again. Em, he..."

I cut her off. "Steph, I know that he's been around. Britta's practically tattooed *player* on his forehead. But, he's been really sweet so far. He said he wants to get to know me and that he doesn't want to just fool around. He was the one that put the brakes on the other night. Maybe, he wants to change? It's just a date anyway."

"Yeah, I guess," she says sounding worried.

"So I can stay at your place?"

"Okay, as long as you promise to stay here at some point that night," Steph says.

Because Steph has been given all the freedom in the world, she is honestly the most level-headed person I know. She has no need to rebel whatsoever, so she always makes responsible sound decisions. It totally works for her. Me on the other hand...

"Of course I'll come back to your place to sleep," I say as sincerely as I can only to follow it up with "unless the night goes really well." I Laugh knowing full-well there's some truth to this.

"You'd better be joking," she says.

"Only time will tell," I smirk. "Goodnight, Steph"

"Goodnight, slut" she jokes. But, point taken.

I drift off to bed with a smile plastered across my face. Friday can't come soon enough.

5 Bottle the Feeling

"Can you pass me the potatoes please?" Steph asks my dad.

We are eating dinner around my family's small, somewhat beat up, dining room table. We used to eat around this table every night when I was little. That was before my brother Jay went off to university.

Jay's five years older than me. As a kid I used to think Jay was the coolest guy on the planet. I followed him around like a little puppy dog, bouncing around eager for his attention. As we got older though, our age difference made him more distant. Other than having the odd crush on his friends when I was in Junior High, our lives were fairly separate. Dinners were the only times we hung out and now that he's away that's gone too. Without Jay, family dinners aren't quite the same. We still try to sit down together but it happens more sporadically now. When it does happen, I draw all of my parents' attention.

"So, what are you girls up to tonight?" my dad asks.

My dad's a great guy. He and my mom have been married for twenty something years. He's smart and strong. I've always felt safe and loved in his presence. He's not infallible by any means but I think he's a good man, and I think I'm lucky to have him.

"A bunch of us are going out with a group of guys from Briarview," I say. Stretching the truth a bit but, I know my dad prefers the idea of me out with a lot of people and not only one guy. I try to fool myself into believing that it's for him that I'm lying. Steph gives me a small kick under the table. She hates when I'm not honest with my folks.

"Oh, that sounds like fun," my mom says.

My mom is the sweetest most giving person I have ever met. Her small five foot frame somehow houses a humongous heart. Throughout her life she has always selflessly cared for anyone and everyone she meets. It's like she can see to the core of a person's needs and gently, and ever so empathetically, sooth them. It's why she and Steph get along so well together. My mom knows that Steph longs for a sense of belonging that her parents' freedom philosophy cannot provide. Steph wholeheartedly belongs to my family, thanks to my mom.

"Where are you headed?" My mom asks.

"Ah ...um..." I stammer.

"We're meeting up at The Coffee Bean. Then we'll probably go out to The Dessert Bar or something. We'll go back to my house to sleep," Steph rescues me.

"Oh I love that dessert place. They make the best brownies," my mom says as I take a sigh of relief.

I owe Steph. I'm not usually at a loss for words with my parents but I guess this time I really feel like I have something to hide.

The rest of the evening goes by painstakingly slowly. We head over to Steph's where she and Britta fuss over me for what feels like hours preparing me for the date. I am poked and prodded, blushed, and glossed. When they're finished with me I look stylish again. My hair is its natural curly this time, but they have done a good job taming the frizz. Make-up is on the natural side too. I'm just pleased that it looks like I have long lashes, something I'm normally lacking for sure. I'm wearing a plain blue tank top that is made from some fancy flowy material that I bought at work this week. I have on my nicest jeans. They make me feel like I'm not trying too hard.

Britta has reluctantly let me borrow her cool, black faux leather jacket. She and Steph keep throwing me repeated warnings, as if Evan is some sort of man-whore with a beeline aimed at popping my cherry, and a foot in the bedroom door of another conquest.

They don't see the Evan I see. They don't feel the connection I feel.

I take one last look at myself in the mirror. *Here goes nothing*.

Ten minutes later I'm in my car on the way to The Coffee Bean. I am so excited and nervous I can hardly contain myself. I keep reminding myself to breathe. Turning up the radio, I hope that it will distract me. Pearl Jam's "Betterman" is now blaring out of the speakers. I'm singing at the top of my lungs to drown out my thoughts. *Great tune.* Screaming it at the top of my lungs has really gone a long way to help calm my nerves. *I'll have to remember that trick in the future,* I tell myself.

I pull up outside The Coffee Bean. I'm a couple minutes early. I make the decision to go in and say hi anyway. As I approach the front door on the make-shift patio, a pathetic grouping of tables outside on the sidewalk, I see Sarah, the girl from Britta's party. She is sitting at a table with one other girl. I have to pass her to go inside. Not sure what to make of her presence I simply say, "Hey," with a polite smile.

"Oh you again. I should have known," she replies sounding less than thrilled to see me.

Not sure what she means by this, I continue to smile politely and keep walking. *She is probably just jealous* I think as I begin to open the door to go inside.

"Don't fool yourself into thinking you're the only one," she snaps at me as I'm entering.

I let the door close behind me and without giving her the satisfaction of a response. I walk straight ahead towards Evan who is cleaning the espresso machine. Inside I try to brush off the comment, but I know it is now in the back of my brain. *Am I one of many?* My brain starts to spiral into a vortex of self-preservation when Evan's soft voice hits me with, "Hello, pretty girl."

His eyes meet mine and all thoughts of other girls or running for the hills are a distant memory. I'm just here. It's just us. Everything else falls away.

I blush. "Hi. I'm a bit early. Sorry, I thought it would take me longer to get here."

"That's cool. We can start our date here if you don't mind me running around for a few minutes first. I have to close up."

I nod and he motions for me to sit down at a table close to him. He and another guy named Bruno begin cleaning up and closing out the till. I do this kind of thing at work all the time so I kind of know what's involved. After about five minutes, he and Bruno take the deposits for the night next door to the bank and leave me inside by myself. I watch through the window as Evan talks with Bruno and then comes back in by himself, locking the door behind him.

"Now what can I get you to drink?" he says as he turns out the majority of the lights and puts up the CLOSED sign.

"We're staying here?" I say surprised by the idea.

"If that's okay with you? Bruno is the owner's son and he said it was cool. So what would you like?"

This is so romantic and cool. We have this dimly lit coffee house all to ourselves.

"I don't know? Surprise me."

"Do you like coffee?" He asks.

"It's not my favourite but I drink it with lots of sugar and cream."

He laughs. "So you don't like coffee but you like sugar and cream then."

"I guess," I say.

"I know what I'm making you..." he trails off.

I sit and watch him expertly stream and froth, boil and whip. When he's done I have a work of art in front of me.

"It looks amazing."

"Tastes even better," he says as he grabs a spoon and sits down on the chair across from me. He slowly dips the spoon in the chocolate-dusted whip cream and brings it to my lips. I close my eyes as it reaches my tongue. *Mmmm...so good.*

"It's delicious," I purr.

He laughs quietly, "You've only had the cream and sugar so far."

I giggle, it's true. "Maybe I just prefer things simple, without all the bitterness," I joke back. I joke when I'm nervous.

"I will make a note of that."

"This is really nice," I say.

"Well, I wanted our first date to top your last coffee date."

"That isn't aiming very high," I laugh and then realize I may be insulting him so I follow it up with, "this is a hundred times better than my last coffee date."

We spent the next hour or so chatting. He discusses his job and he shows me how to work some of the machines. He's so interesting to listen to. Not just his words but the life that he puts behind them. He's cool and calm but he has a spark to him. *I could listen to him for days.*

At around midnight he says, "We should go. I have an idea." He takes my hand and I follow him as we lock up and go outside. He has his car and I have mine. "Follow me okay," he says as he walks me over to my car door. As I am about to open the car door, he pulls me in quickly against him and kisses me hard. Sparks are flying. The world around us is crumbling away. As far as I am concerned we are the only two people on the planet. All I can feel is the tingle throughout my body and my car door pushing against my back. Our kiss goes from passionate to tender to frenzied. My hands are wrapped around his strong back. His hands are in my hair. He pulls away gently and is now looking at me right in the eyes as he stretches out a single curl of my hair. We are both breathing hard as he whispers, "Curly...I think I like this even better," and he smiles a wickedly sexy smile.

I beam back and he slowly lets go of me and backs up. "Follow me," he whispers.

Standing there stunned, I watch him as he makes his way to his car, a beat up old Honda hatchback. I open the door to my car and sit down still in shock. I'm flustered and blushing, elated and aroused. As I turn on the car, the StoneTemple Pilots "Vaseline" blasts out of the speakers, startling me. I had forgotten to lower the volume after my one women show on the way here. I lower the volume and follow as Evan pulls out of the parking lot. I would pretty much follow him anywhere at this point. About a block down the road he pulls into a driveway. He parks his car, jumps out and gets into mine.

"Hi again," he says.

"Hi yourself," I make a lame attempt to be flirty.

"Is this your house?" I ask staring at a beautiful modern looking house with a lovely balcony over the garage."

"Yes, my dad is in construction. He designed and built the place himself."

"Impressive!" I say.

He laughs.

"What's so funny?" I say softly.

"You are." I frown and he continues on with, "You have this way of saying things that's so different.

So...uniquely you. It's not always what you say that surprises me but how you say it."

"What do you mean?"

"Oh, don't get me wrong, I like it. I like it a lot."

Not sure what to think, I change the topic. "Where are we going?"

"I thought maybe to play pool," he says.

"Oh," I raise my eyebrow and say, "are you going to show me a thing or two."

He laughs again, "See I wasn't expecting that, and yes, if things keep going the way they are, I think I'll be teaching all kinds of things." The idea sends a rush of energy through my body. He grabs my hand and gives it a squeeze as I pull out of the driveway and head toward the pool hall. I can't stop smiling the whole way there. As I'm driving he begins twirling one of my curls gently around his finger. The little hairs on the back of my neck are crying out at his touch.

I've played pool before, but I'm not great. The pool hall is a popular hangout. It's one of the few places to chill out at late at night. I'm not quite old enough to go to bars and the underage clubs...well...they stink, both literally and figuratively. So coffee shops, parks, friends' houses, and movie theaters are all good options.

We arrive at Club Billiard quickly. I've never been to this place before but it is similar to any other pool hall. Evan pulls open the heavy oak door. There's a long flight of stairs going up, it's covered in worn forest green carpet. The whole place smells like beer, smoke, and chicken wings. I reach the top of the stairs and turn to enter the dimly lit pool hall. There is a large bar and small eating area on my right. On my left there are about a dozen pool tables most of which are occupied. Evan motions for me to follow him over to the bar. I follow. Evan leans over the bar and whispers something to the bartender. The bartender points to the far corner of the place. Evan grabs my hand and leads me there.

There is a tall lanky waiter there. He is finishing up with a group of scantily clad middle aged women, cougars if you will. They are signing their bill and he's joking confidently with them. *He owns this tip.*

As we wait Evan puts his arm around me. I wrap my arms around his waist and rest my head against his chest. I fit perfectly against his body. It reminds me of the night we spent at Britta's house snuggling.

The waiter glances up at us, smiles and winks. Evan whispers to me, "That's Allan." I vaguely remember him telling me about his best friend Allan at Britta's house. It has got to be a good sign that he's introducing me to his best friend.

The cougars leave and we go over to the now empty table. Evan shakes Allan's hand and says, "Allan, this is

Emilia." I still love the way he says my name. It makes my knees weak.

"Emilia, it's nice to meet the girl that Evan won't shut-up about," he says. *Oh my word! Evan talks about me with his best friend. That has to be a good thing, right? I hope Allan's not simply saying that.* I blush.

"Really? I'm glad I've made an impression," I say as I shake Allan's hand, "and of course it's nice to meet you too."

"Now, let's get you two set up," Allan says as he grabs a tray of billiard balls and sets them down on the table. "Don't forget, the best games have something worth playing for." He finishes placing the balls in the triangle. I sense this is a line he uses with all his tables but I like the idea of making the game interesting. He gives Evan the white ball, winks once more in my direction and leaves to go tend to another table.

"Do you want to break?" he asks.

"No, you go ahead, but maybe Allan's right. Maybe we should make things interesting." I'm not exactly sure how to do that but, I feel naughty even suggesting it.

"Oh? What did you have in mind?" I knew he'd ask that. *Now what do I say?*

To buy me time I walk slowly over to a chair in the corner and take off Britta's jacket. I try to be as sexy as I can but I kind of fumble with the left sleeve. I get it off and place it on the chair. Then it comes to me. Before I can even think about the ramifications I say...

"How about we play for souvenirs?" I say.

"Souvenirs? What kind of souvenirs?" He sounds intrigued.

"I win, I get your unmentionables, you win, you get mine." I feel funny saying it. Unmentionables is the kind of word I would read about in one of the romance novels I use to sneak out of my Granny's extensive collection when I visited her over the summer. *I wonder if he knows it means bras, panties, and underwear?*

"Unmentionables...really?" His eyes light up. *Oh, he knows what it means.* "Which unmentionables are we talking about?" He smiles wickedly as he looks me over.

"Your choice, but, that's only if you win and frankly I'm not worried," I giggle.

"Oh is that right? Well, you have a deal baby." I melt. Usually I hate being called baby but right now, the way it makes me feel when his lips utter it, it is suddenly my favourite word in the English language. I finally get why every pop song ever written uses it.

He chalks his cue and hits the white ball hard. Balls scatter all over the table and a striped ball goes in. He quickly sinks three more. Then he finally misses, but only by a hair. I calmly walk over and bend down to eye my shot. As I do Evan walks behind me and discretely runs his finger along my hip, he follows the outside seam of my jeans. A rush of energy flows through my body, but I have motivation, so I stay focused. Taking the shot, I nail it.

"So you're not going to fight fair then?" I say.

"You were the one who told me that you never play fair," he says. I giggle. I had said that hadn't I. I still don't know why but right now I'm so glad I did. *This is going to be fun.* Getting lucky, I sink one more ball. Then, I miss by a mile as I feel his hands lightly touching my behind. *Now the real fun begins.*

He leans down to line up his shot and I lean over so that my flowing tank top reveals my cleavage right in his sightline. Just to throw him off I say, "See anything you like?"

He smiles, takes the shot, and misses. Then says, "Yes I do."

He walks around the table and kisses me just enough so that my head is swimming. Then he says, "Your shot, pretty girl." *Oh he is good.* Perhaps I'm beat at my own game. *I need to step it up.*

I take my shot and miss. Then I try a new approach. "So maybe if I knew what I was playing for I could keep my head in the game?" I ask innocently as he lines up his shot. "Like are we talking boxers, briefs, bikinis, or perhaps thong?" He breaks concentration for a second as he shoots but still makes the shot.

"Definitely not a thong," he smiles. "Is that what I'm playing for?" he adds.

"Oh a girl has to be able to keep some secrets; besides that surprise is one worth waiting for."

His pole cue connects and his intended target ricochets around missing the pocket. I think I have rattled his concentration. I feel a sense of sexual power, control. I like feeling desired in this way. As I line up my shot he leans over and pulls down his shirt-collar to line up his cleavage with my sightline. He says in a girly voice "See anything you like." I laugh and miss by a long shot.

He sinks two more balls quickly, leaving only the black ball, before I can come up with a plan. He motions to the corner he's aiming for. *He's so good at that motioning thing.* As a last-ditch effort I come up behind him as he is bent over and drape my body against his. Not caring that we are in a room full of other people I place my hands firmly on his behind. I fail miserably as the black ball annihilates the corner pocket. He spins around, wraps his arms around me, lifts me up off the ground and kisses me passionately. With this, I've never been so happy to lose a bet. He lowers me to the ground and puts his forehead against mine, looks into my eyes and says, "I believe you owe me a souvenir. He runs his hands along the shoulder strap of my bra.

I look down and say, "Is that your choice then?"

He shakes his head and says, "I wouldn't want to spoil a surprise that is worth waiting for."

Smiling, I say, "We should go. I'd like to give you your souvenir in private."

Evan puts money on the table and we leave quickly. Both of us are eager to be alone. We jump in the car and I start driving towards his house. He puts his hand on my thigh and tickles ever so gently. He is not working up my leg like the infamous Mister-Grab-Ass-Sleaze-Ball. He is slowly moving his hand in a very small circular motion in a specific section of my mid-thigh. It's so tender and attentive. I'm getting so aroused by this simple motion. I pull up outside his house and turn off the lights.

He leans over and kisses me. He has soft commanding lips. I'm following his lead like he is dancing me through a complicated waltz. It's magical. Every synapse in my body is firing at once. I gently push him back into his seat. When our lips part he groans ever so slightly. It's such a sexy sound. I push back into my own seat and undo the clasp on the back of my bra. I slowly grab the left strap and pull my arm out. I lead his hand to the top of my right shoulder and say, "Your souvenir sir." A smirk dances on his lips as he pulls ever so slowly on the dark blue strap. As he pulls my nipples become increasingly hard. He lets out another slight groan. Shivers quake throughout my body.

He looks at the lovely blue bra very intently and says, "I've never been a fan of souvenirs but now...I have to say, I wasn't envisioning blue."

"It's my favourite colour," I say shyly hoping he's not disappointed.

"I think it's my new favourite too." He turns and kisses me again. He takes his fingers and lightly brushes them down my side over my shirt ever so slightly touching the side of my breast. Instinctively, I arch my back towards his hand to intensify his touch. My fingers gravitate to his shirt feeling his sleek muscles underneath. The action acts as an open invitation for him to do the same. His hand cups my breast over the thin silky material of my tank top. His thumb begins teasing my nipple to a state of perky arousal. I'm so overwhelmed by the surge of feelings. Time is suspended as his tongue expertly intertwines and dances with mine. My hands are fisting handfuls of his hair, his are masterfully massaging my breasts. *How's this feeling even possible?*

A bolt of lightning. My brain kicks in. It's like Steph, Britta, and Sarah's warnings have fought their way through the surge of hormones dancing around my brain. *I'm one of many. This is our first date.* I try to shut my brain off and enjoy but I can't. Pushing Evan back into his seat. I fall back into mine. We're both sitting there breathing heavily staring straight ahead. *I totally want more, but I also want to leave him wanting more too.* After a minute or so of staring and breathing I break the silence.

"I had a really good time."

"Me too," he takes my hand in his.

"I better go. Steph will be waiting for me." I know this is the smart choice for a first date, but secretly I want him to flip down the seat and take me right here in the Tempest.

"I'll call you." He lifts my hand to his lips and kisses the back of it. *So chivalrous. Did that really happen?* He then opens his door and climbs out. Evan stands in the driveway and gives me a small brief wave as I back out. The whole way to Steph's I think about how I need a cold shower...an ice cold shower...badly. *So badly.*

6 Innocence Revealed

The next couple of days are blissful. During the day I daydream about Evan and at night he calls. Our conversations are easy. We flow from one topic to another. He's witty and smart, cool and charismatic. He has a way of listening to what I have to say that makes me feel all important, like I am the center of his universe. I desperately want to be. I really like him and can't wait to see him again.

It's Thursday night, I'm talking to Steph on the phone. I'm gushing over Evan as per usual. Steph is being her ever wary self. It's then that she asks the question I have been afraid to address with myself.

"So, have you told him you are a virgin yet?"

"Um...no, not yet."

"You are going to tell him then?"

"I don't know? I mean...I'm not sure."

"Well, it sounds like you really like him and Britta seems to think that if she hadn't come into Alex's room when she had, you would have already lost it."

I take a deep loud breath to demonstrate my annoyance with this line of questioning. I know Steph is only asking because she's worried I might be in over my head. Frankly, she's not entirely wrong. I haven't even told her about Sarah's warning. I suppose I want to continue living in my little fairytale. I try not to let Steph's concern bother me but it does make me hope that there are no wolves lurking in the woods.

"I'm just enjoying myself Steph. I'm not sure if I'm going to sleep with him, but I'm not ruling it out either."

"I thought you were saving yourself."

"I am, but I'm not saving myself for marriage. I just want it to be special and with someone I care about." I hear myself saying the words to Steph, I realize that *this IS what I'm saving myself for. I've never really defined it before, but there it is.*

"So, you can see why I worry when I hear that you're throwing yourself at a complete stranger in Alex's bedroom then."

"Yeah, I know, it wasn't my shining moment, but Steph, he's not just some guy. I really like him."

"I know you do. That scares me too. Britta's impression of him is very different from yours. I don't want you to get hurt."

"I know. I don't want to get hurt either but I'm invested now. Besides, I know you have my back."

"Always."

"Night, Steph."

"Goodnight, Em."

I lay in my bed thinking through the conversation. *I know I need to tell Evan I'm a virgin but after all the innuendoes...I'm just not sure how he will take the news.*

What if he thinks I'm some kind of tease? Shit! It might scare him off or worse; what if it makes him pursue me for the wrong reason, like I'm some kind of elusive conquest. Ugh. I don't want to think about it anymore. Maybe I should just tell him tonight and get it over with. He should be calling soon so I better get ready for bed.

I'm in bed filling out an application to be a camp councilor at a day camp. I'm interested in becoming a teacher and figure it will look good on my application for Teachers College next year. I'm about halfway through when the phone rings.

"Hello."

"Hi Emilia." He still calls me Emilia. I still love the way it sounds coming from him.

We talk for a little while about my application. He mentions that he's planning on being home for the summer but may be going away for school. My heart sinks, but since this is not yet a present reality, I choose not to dwell on the idea that he may be leaving.

After about an hour, I muster up the courage to have the talk about my virginity. I'm nervous as all hell, but I need to know what he thinks. I'm also curious about his history.

"So, um...I have something I kind of need to tell you." I suppose I could have waited for a natural segue in our conversation. *No turning back now.*

"What is it?" he sounds worried. I guess he hears the nervousness in my voice.

"Well, this is a little hard to share with you."

"What is it?" He says sounding more insistent this time.

"I'm a virgin." *There, it's out.*

There is silence for about ten-seconds. I'm waiting for him to say something. It feels like an eternity. I know that he needs a second to process this, but it's killing me.

Finally he says, "That's not what I was expecting you to say." I want to ask him what he was expecting but I need to keep my eye on the prize and gauge his reaction to my news.

"Are you okay with this?" I ask hoping to get him talking.

"I guess," he says, "but are you like waiting until your married or is it a religious thing or something?"

"No, nothing like that. I guess I'm just waiting for the right guy to come along. I want my first time to be, you know...special." It sounds super cheesy. I wish I had thought of a less sappy way to word it, but there it is.

"I get that. It's kind of sweet."

So he isn't running screaming for the hills. Maybe I should ask him about his history?

"What about you?" I whisper with trepidation, "What was your first time like?"

There is a pause and then he says, "I was sixteen. She was eighteen. We were hanging out after school and she kind of took the lead. I was totally awkward and it was less than special. I guess guys are a bit different you know." He sounds embarrassed about sharing this with me.

My nervousness gets the better of me and I joke. "Older woman, huh? Nice work."

He laughs, "Yeah, what can I say. I'm that good."

"You certainly are," I say as seductively as I can.

He laughs again.

"What about the other times? Are we talking hundreds of women here?" I think my lighter approach is working better so decide to stick with it.

"No, not hundreds."

"Tens?"

"Less than ten," he says.

"How many?" I cut to the chase.

"Six, I guess."

"Six," I repeat not knowing whether this is a good thing or not. *It's less than Britta and Steph have implied but it's six more than me. I wonder who they are? I wonder if I've met them? What if that girl Sarah was one of them? Yuck!* I can't ask who but I want to know more so I ask, "And were all six awkward and less than special?" I'm probably pushing my luck.

"No. I feel weird talking about this," he admits. I feel bad that I have pressed the issue so I offer up a reward for his honesty.

"Sorry, I just want to know what I have to look forward to." A little presumptuous I know, but hey.

"Oh, well in that case," he says, "not awkward at all. I think tantric would be a better description."

I laugh. "Really?" I say suggestively.

"But, seriously," he says, "most of the times that I've had sex it was in the heat of the moment. I've had one real girlfriend and that was a bit different, I guess more special. I don't know what to tell you Emilia. I like you, but this is a lot of pressure you know."

"I know."

I don't think I could sleep with anyone on a whim like that. I kind of always thought my first time would be with someone I love. I'd want to be in a relationship. I couldn't just be a 'conquest'. That would eat me up inside.

"A virgin? You really didn't seem like a virgin at Britta's house or in the car."

"I'm a virgin, not a saint. You don't have to treat me any differently and you don't have to feel any pressure either. We can just keep having fun and if anything more happens, well...I like you too and maybe it will just feel right sometime."

"Yeah well, I've gotta go," he says, "maybe I can see you on Saturday or something." He sounds weird – distant maybe. *Shit. What's going on in his head?*

"Call me tomorrow and we'll figure things out," I say realizing that I don't feel good ending our conversation this way. I try to figure out a way to make this uncomfortable feeling leave my body. "And...Evan."

"Yeah."

"Before you over-think this, could you do me a favour?"

"What?"

"Pull out your souvenir and remember how things were before this conversation."

There is a faint laugh and then he says, "Goodnight, Emilia."

"Goodnight, Evan."

7 Booty Calling

It's Friday night, and Steph and I are watching *Reality Bites* in the basement rec room for the hundredth time. We are eating our favourite foods – snacks that we can prepare in under five minutes: mini-pizzas, popcorn and of course chocolate. As a game, sometimes we even time ourselves. Steph's sprawled out on the couch and I'm sitting on the love seat closest to my room so that I can hear my phone ring when Evan calls.

Hours go by, the movie is over, and we are now flipping through the mindless drivel that's on T.V. Steph stops on a rerun of *90210*. It's the "Donna Martin Graduates" episode. Tori Spelling drank at a pre-prom party and now she won't graduate with her class. *Oh, boo hoo.* We giggle and make fun of the poorly acted apology scene.

As it ends, I realize that it's one o'clock and I still haven't heard from Evan. After our conversation last night I think that this can't be a good sign. Steph is asleep on the couch. I turn off the television, cover her up, and head to my room.

Feeling insecure and confused, thoughts fly through my head. Frustrated, I curl up under my duvet and try to sleep. An hour goes by and I'm still laying there trying not to overanalyze my situation.

<<BRING>> << BRING>>

I jump. It's my phone. I grab it quick, hoping not to wake Steph in the next room.

"Hello," I whisper.

"Emilia." It's Evan and he's unusually loud.

"Evan?"

"Hey, I'm sorry it's so late. I've been playing poker with the guys at Tom's all night."

"Oh, that's okay, I guess."

"Fuck off Tom," Evan says obviously not to me. "Sorry, Tom's just being, well, Tom."

"That's okay," I say again.

"I'm gonna go outside for a second. It's too loud in here."

"Okay."

"There, that's better," he says with his regular volume restored.

"I'm glad you called," I say because I am.

"Yeah well, there's just something about you. I don't know what it is," he says, and I immediately realize he has been drinking. *Advantage Emilia*, I think to myself.

"Oh yeah, what do you mean?" I probe.

"I just can't stop thinking about you."

I couldn't be happier. *He's opening up to me about his feelings.* I may combust.

I try to take a cooler approach. "I think about you a lot too." *If every waking moment counts as a lot.*

"You're just so different from other girls. So real."

There's that word again. I wish he said 'cool' or 'smart', 'sexy' or even 'amazing' would have worked. But nope, I get 'REAL' again.

"I like you too Evan," I say.

"When do I get to see your sexy body again?" he says and now I'm sure he's drunk. I play along, wanting to see where this will lead.

"When would you like to?"

"Now," he answers without hesitation. "I wanna kiss you so bad," he slurs.

I giggle and respond, "I'd like that."

"You should really come over," he says. At this point my Spidey senses are tingling. *This is quickly turning into a booty call.* I've got to turn this around quickly. *Abort, abort* I tell myself.

"Where are you taking me tomorrow?" I ask completely changing the subject.

"Where do you wanna go?" His voice is oozing sex. *Oh, he is no use in this state.*

"We'll figure it out tomorrow. I'll get you from work at eleven," I assert knowing that someone has to.

"Okay."

"Goodnight, Evan," I coo sweetly.

"Goodnight, my Emilia," he says.

'*My Emilia*' echoes in my brain and I have never wanted anything more. I lie in bed wide awake with thoughts swirling around my brain. *I do, I do want to be his Emilia. I hope that he really is thinking about me all the time, and that I really am different from the girls of his past. I wonder what they look like. Does Evan have a type? What if they all look like me? Right, like there are clones running around looking like me. What a weird thought. They probably don't look like me. Maybe they have killer legs or big boobs or something. Maybe he still hangs out with these perfect female specimens all the time. Crap, now I'm all self-conscious. No, no self-pity! The boy just gave you all kinds of reasons to feel good about yourself. Don't go and dream up supermodel ex-girlfriends.* I dismiss my deprecating thoughts and I try to push out of my mind the whole booty call notion. All I know is, *I am definitely in trouble when it comes to this boy.*

8 Parkette Romance

It's ten minutes to eleven and I'm on my way to The Coffee Bean. At a red light I glance in the mirror to check my make-up. This time I've gotten myself ready and I'm a little nervous without Britta's sense of style and skillful fussing. I'm wearing a fitted blue shirt and a short flowing skirt. I feel sort of trendy because this skirt just came in at the store this week; it's part of the new spring collection.

The weather is starting to warm up and I want to make use of it. In the back seat I have an emergency sweater, just in case I get cold. Hopefully, we are going some place cozy and I won't need it.

I pull up outside his work and he is waiting outside. I find him leaning up against his car like the lead in a John Hughes movie. He looks just as cool. I take one last peek at myself in the mirror, take a deep breath and open my car door. *Jake Ryan, here I come.*

"Hello, pretty girl." *John Hughes would approve.*

"Hi. I hope you weren't waiting long."

"Place was dead tonight so it was an easy close. Besides, I was excited about seeing you."

The smile on my face is making my cheeks hurt. *He likes me. He really likes me and he's being so sweet. This couldn't be going any better.*

"I'm excited about seeing you too. What are we going to do?"

"Well, I was thinking I could surprise you."

"Okay," I say, a bit wary about the prospect.

"We'll take my car," he says as he motions for me to get in.

I lock my car and jump in the passenger seat of his. Evan's car is old but it has an awesome sound system.

"What do you want to hear?" He says and as he hands me a large CD case. It has like fifty CDs in it. Flipping through I look for something to fit my elated mood. As I flip, I come across Mariah Carey. I laugh to myself.

"Find something amusing?" he asks.

"I didn't take you for a Mariah Carey fan," I say.

"I have eclectic taste and she can sing."

I smile and pop it into the CD player. Mariah's voice belts "Fantasy" out of the speaker and before I can even get used to the idea of Evan liking this, he begins belting right along with her. He knows all the words and the most surprising part is that he's good. I'm flabbergasted. He is carefree, totally confident, and full of emotion as he sings. It's like he has channeled the diva in Mariah. It's so endearing and a little funny too. I can't help but think back to when I first saw him, when he was the steering-wheel-drummer. He is completely himself in this moment. He's so entertaining...so engaging.

At the end of the song I turn down the volume and say, "Was that my surprise? 'Cause I loved that."

"No, I'm just getting warmed up," he says.

"Can't wait," I say because after that I am really looking forward to what comes next.

We turn onto a street with large, mansion-type houses. About half-way down the block we pull into the driveway of a large brick home. If the landscaping outside is any indication, this house is professionally maintained.

"This is Allan's place," he says. "I thought we could hang out with him and his girlfriend, Jen."

"Oh," I say, maybe a little disappointed that I'll have to share Evan with others but also pleased that he is comfortable bringing me here.

"I hope this is cool?"

"Yeah of course," I say, trying to sound more upbeat.

We walk along a curved brick pathway leading to a set of double front doors. Evan is holding my hand and I really feel like his girlfriend right now. Without even knocking Evan opens the door. This tells me that his relationship with Allan is very similar to mine and Steph's.

"Al," he yells. "Al, we're here."

Still holding his hand I follow Evan through a huge kitchen that has two separate eating areas. We walk toward a staircase that leads to the basement.

"Allan?" he says one more time as he begins his descent down the first three stairs towards a small landing that has a door to the backyard. Right when we reach the landing and are about to turn down the longer staircase into the basement we hear...

"Ev, wait no! Not a good time buddy."

I can also hear a girl squealing ever-so-slightly.

It's too late we're mid-way down the stairs before Allan's words register. We turn and see a black duvet on a king sized bed wriggling about with bodies under it. *Shit. We are most definitely interrupting.* Evan and I run back upstairs where we both look at each other snickering.

Evan motions for me to follow him into a living room area. This house is so fancy I feel like it's a show home. Evan sits on a large white leather couch and I sit down beside him. He envelops me under his arm, pulling my head onto his chest. My arm drapes across his body.

"So, that's Jen," he says with a laugh.

"Oh. Something tells me that she wasn't expecting us."

"Actually, they're always all over each other," he admits as he rubs my back gently. "They're part of the reason I wanted a girlfriend."

Girlfriend? Is he implying that I'm his girlfriend? Am I hearing him right?

"A girlfriend?" I whisper softly in hopes that he will continue and clarify without me having to ask the question.

"Yeah well, I just thought," he says but then pauses.

"You thought what?"

"You're gonna make me say it aren't you?"

"I'd like to hear it," I say in a flirty way.

As the words leave my mouth Allan comes bounding into the room. He has a guilty smile plastered on his face. He's full of energy, almost hyper. He says, "So that was awkward." By his expression I know he doesn't care that we walked in on him. *I hope Jen feels the same way.* "Jen will be up in a few," he says as he turns towards the kitchen and yells back at us, "What do you guys want to drink?"

"I'll grab a beer," Evan yells to Allan. "Where did your folks go this time?" He adds.

"Aspen I think," Allan says nonchalantly, as if that isn't over the top.

Then Evan turns to me and says, "I don't think he has those cooler things but he might have wine."

"I don't actually like those cooler things," I say. "I'll have a pop or something."

"My girlfriend will have a Coke," he yells into the kitchen.

I look up at him in awe and before I can say anything he plants a kiss on my lips. *I am... I am... I am his girlfriend!* Deepening the kiss I wrap my leg over his. Now, I am straddling him. I pull back so I can look into his eyes. I cannot contain my smile.

"So you like this idea?" he says absentmindedly playing with one of my curls.

"Very much so." I flop down on his chest and still straddling him, we hug.

"Uh hum." Allan clears his throat as he enters the room in an obvious attempt to make sure I am aware of his presence.

I slide off Evan's lap onto the white couch. Allan hands me my drink and Evan a beer. As he does, Jen emerges from the basement.

"Hi Ev," she says. "This must be Emilia."

Jen is a lovely blond girl. She has an athletic build and she dresses like a dancer. She seems totally unrattled by our earlier interruption. It's funny to me that she isn't embarrassed. She really has no reason to be, I guess. She and Allan have been together for like a year according to Evan. It's not like they were doing anything wrong. We were the ones who barged in. I kind of like her confidence, actually. Maybe someday I can embrace sex with such an easy-going, fun-loving way. Choosing not to apologize for interrupting them, we all casually pretend it never happened.

"So, girlfriend? That's cool," Allan says as he looks at me and winks. I guess winking is just his thing.

"What?" Jen says taking a second to clue in. "Oh, that's great. It's about time I had a girl to hang out with again," she adds.

"Come," she says and before I can even protest she has grabbed my hand, pulled me off of the couch, and I am sitting on the offending king-sized bed from earlier. I'm downstairs in Allan's bachelor pad of a room.

"So, you and Evan are making it official?" She says.

I am a bit confused *it sounds like we are getting married or something.*

"Yeah, I guess," I say.

"Evan's a great guy. I've known him for a long time and I don't think you have anything to worry about."

What does that mean? What is she implying? Maybe I should ask.

"What do you mean?" I'm nervous but I ask anyway.

"Oh...it's just...in the past he hasn't been good when it comes to being...you know...being committed and faithful."

"Oh," is all I can come up with. I feel like she hit me with a brick.

"Yeah, well I guess he wasn't really exclusive with the other girls...well except for Sarah."

"Sarah?" My jaw drops. "He said they were just friends." Jen's eyes light up and I know immediately that she is a gossiper to her core. She has me right where she wants me.

"They are just friends, now, but they dated for like three months awhile back."

The girlfriend that had the 'more special sex' with Evan was Sarah. No wonder she hates me. Now I need to know: Was her warning jealousy, or had he been cheating on her? "Why did they break up?" I ask the question, knowing full well that I'm feeding the gossip-monster.

"It depends on who you ask. She seems to think he was messing around with other girls throughout their entire relationship. He insists that Sarah's just paranoid and that she was his only girl until he broke it off."

"What do you think happened?" *Now maybe I'm the gossip-monster.*

"I don't know really. He is a flirt but I'm not sure if it went beyond that when they were together. One thing I am sure of, is that before Sarah, he was good at juggling."

I'm trying to wrap my head around all this new information. I must have a concerned look on my face because Jen adds, "He seems to really like you though, so I think you're probably fine."

Alarm bells are ringing in my head. Steph and Britta are warming up their 'I told you sos.' Ten minutes ago I was elated by my newly acquired 'girlfriend' status. Now I'm so conflicted.

He's good at juggling? What the hell am I supposed to do with that? Jen seems to be enjoying watching me squirm. Wait a minute? I can't let some girl I have known for like three seconds alter my bond with Evan. We have something special, I can feel it.

"I think we should go back upstairs to see the guys," I say.

We head upstairs. The guys have made snacks and set up the movie *Top Gun* for us to watch. We have all seen it before but it's a classic, so why not. Jen and I are sitting on the floor leaning against our boy's legs across from a giant big screen television. It is the epitome of a double date. Even after my gossip-monster got the better of me, I feel safe as Evan leans forward and rubs my shoulders while Goose goes down in flames.

After the movie, I realize how late it is, and that I should head to Steph's but Allan and Jen have gone to get their bathing suits on to go in the hot tub. *This house is unreal.* Now Evan and I are finally alone.

"I think it's time for your surprise now," Evan says to me.

"You mean this wasn't my surprise?" I ask.

"No," he smiles a wicked grin and takes me by the hand. He grabs a blanket off the couch as he leads me towards the back door. He flicks a light switch and we are standing in the backyard with white twinkling lights hanging over our heads in a large gazebo. *This house is seriously unreal!*

"It's beautiful," I gush.

"It is, but this isn't the surprise either." He is amused by my expression.

"What could better than this?" I say.

He leads me down a small set of stairs onto a cobble-stone path that weaves its way back into a dark portion of the yard. I'm a little chilly but too excited about my surprise to care. He opens a gate and we are standing in a breathtaking garden. It has little lights illuminating the cobble-stone path that continues to lead my eyes on a journey through the garden. I can hear the trickle of water from a little waterfall to our right. He lets go of my hand and says, "What do you think?"

"It's beautiful...magical," I say.

"It's even prettier later in the spring," he asserts.

"I find that hard to believe." I look down at the tulip buds which look like they are about to burst into a rainbow of colours. "I like it like this, full of potential."

"I'm glad you like it," I hear his voice walking away from me. I turn as he begins spreading out the blanket in a dark spot underneath a willow tree beside the little waterfall. My romance meter is through the roof.

"Like it? I love it. What is this place?"

"Allan calls it the Parkette. It's a park for the fifteen or so houses that back onto it. Al and I used to come out here to smoke pot but I always thought it would be nice to bring a girl here."

"You mean, I'm the first girl you have brought here," I say stunned.

"Well, yeah," he says quietly and I see him motion for me to join him.

Sitting on the blanket, I am totally smitten. All of the questions I have, all of my concerns have vanished from my mind. Overcome by my surroundings I can't speak anymore. I lean in and kiss him. We start slowly and I'm enjoying the tenderness of his lips. Then his lips become more commanding and passionate. I'm lost in the kiss as he lowers me to the blanket. I can feel the soft fleece against my bare legs as his hands begin making their way under my shirt. I arch my back as he unclasps my bra strap. I can barely hear the waterfall over our rapid breathing. He slowly brings me back to a sitting position and lifts my shirt over my head. In the dim shadow-cast light he is looking at me.

"You're beautiful," he whispers. I'm so lost in the moment I say nothing as he lifts his hand slowly towards my breasts. His fingers touch me on my stomach first. His touch is ever-so-slight. He uses the tips of his fingers as he slowly works his way up onto my breast. My nipples grow harder as he delicately circles them. Then he lowers his head and begins to tickle them with his tongue. I have never felt so aroused. I hear myself let out a loud "oh."

"Shh," he whispers but I can tell he is smiling at my noise.

I can now feel his hand moving up the outside of my thigh towards my behind. He lets his hand rest on me there all the while still teasing my breast with his tongue. I run my hands through his dark hair and rub his broad shoulders hoping he never stops. Grabbing a handful of his shirt I begin trying to pull it up. He pulls away for a second and takes it off. The faint light dances over his muscles. I run my finger down from his shoulder and over his pecs, down toward the sexy little trail of hair below his belly button. As I do, the hand that was resting on my butt begins slowly tugging on my panties. I reach my hands down to help him pull them off. I hear him gasp slightly with anticipation. I'm left only wearing my flowy skirt. I have goose bumps and I know he can feel them as he begins running his hands up my inner thighs. He stops suddenly and grabs his shirt. I think the worst for a brief second but then I realize he is giving me his shirt so I won't be cold. I put it on and he says under his breath, "Wearing my shirt reminds me of our first night together."

His hands are back on my inner thighs and I'm not cold anymore. I'm hot, very hot, and very wet. I'm so turned on I don't know what to do with myself. I want to be holding, kissing, and touching him, but instead, I am just laying here lost in my own pleasure as his fingers finally reach my sex.

That circular motion he has used in the past to ignite my body is now focused solely on my most sensitive area. I quiver with excitement. "We'll take this slow baby," he says quietly.

In my head I joke *'It's a little late for that.'*

He takes one finger and pushes steadily inside me. It's a strange unfamiliar sensation. I find myself moving into his hand to intensify the feeling. Evan begins moving his finger in and out rhythmically.

"How's that feel?" he asks with a husky 'I know you like it' tone.

"Oh..." is all I manage.

He takes his finger out and slides a second finger in with it. It feels rougher and I am more stretched by it. When he starts to move it I can't help but meet his rhythm. I feel the moisture on his hand as he works his magic. With his other hand he rubs my clit. It doesn't take long before I am overcome by the most exhilarating feeling that has ever possessed my body. I'm numb and electrified, relaxed and invigorated all at the same time. I relish ever second of the stimulation.

As I begin to regain my composure, Evan lays down beside me. He gently pushes a stray curl behind my ear.

"That was fun," he murmurs.

I smile back at him, unable to articulate.

A few moments later I regroup. *I can't believe that I just...we just...did that...here. I should be self-conscious or something, but instead I'm...I'm happy. I'm content. Something about being with Evan feels right.*

As he strokes my hair I snuggle into his body and I can feel his hard erection against me. My thoughts are invaded by an overwhelming urge to reciprocate. The problem is that I've never really done this kind of thing before. I mean, I've touched a penis before but it never really got to the point where I was manhandling it with any expectation of, you know. *Should I say something? No, I am just going to have to call my inner vixen out to play. I really hope I have one.*

I sit up slowly and straddle his thighs. I'm still not wearing any panties and his jeans are a little uncomfortable under me. He leans up on his elbows and I drag my fingers over his chest and down towards his jeans. I begin undoing his button, slowly unzipping his fly. I rise up on my knees and he helps me pull his pants down. He is wearing boxer briefs and I can see his erection pressing against the thin material. I can't resist a nervous joke "I was expecting a thong," I say thinking back to our pool game. He smiles.

I rub my hand over his erection on my way to the waistband of his boxers. I pull them down. His hard penis springs up as it's freed. I'm surprised by the size of it. I don't know what I was expecting but it seems really big. I reach down not sure what I am doing. I wrap my hand around it and begin stroking it in the same rhythmic fashion he had pleasured me. It feels different than I thought it would. It's really hard but the skin is soft as it shifts along the shaft with the motion of my hand. He lets out a satisfied sigh, which rewards my inner vixen and makes her more feisty. I lower my mouth to it and continue the same rhythm trying not to involve my teeth. He groans with delight and I pick up speed. I begin sucking and moving my tongue in a circular motion. He is rocking his hips to meet my mouth. It is so big and hard, I have trouble taking the whole thing in my mouth. I focus my attention on the tip and hope I'm doing it right.

He lets out a frantic statement, "I'm gonna cum." He tries to pull away but, I don't stop and in a couple seconds the salty substance hits my mouth. Not sure what to do. I swallow and gasp. Evan is letting out the most contented humming sound. I mentally give my vixen a high five and flop down beside him.

Holy shit. That just happened. I did that. I smirk at the thought. We lay there smiling and staring up into the willow tree for a while.

"A virgin?" He whispers.

"Yep."

"You don't do that like a virgin," he says.

"Beginners luck."

He smiles. "Really?"

"Really." I smile back.

"You are full of surprises, aren't you?"

"I could say the same about you."

I wish I could stay laying on this blanket forever. Of course, I might prefer to be wearing my own shirt and some panties. Eventually we get up and leave our enchanted-lustful-secret-garden. We say goodbye to Allan and Jen. Evan drives me to retrieve my car from The Coffee Bean's parking lot and I sneak into Steph's house at around four in the morning. All and all, a night filled with pleasurable surprises. I couldn't be happier!

9 Crushed

Over the next few weeks, we talk and hang out every free moment. School is back on and we're juggling work, classes, and late night phone calls. I've fallen hard for Evan. I know he likes me too, but somewhere deep inside I'm still afraid that I will awake from this perfect dream to find him in bed with another girl. It's probably the reason I haven't told Steph about Sarah's warning or Jen's gossip session. I know she would make me scrutinize my reality and I prefer to keep dreaming.

Steph has warmed up to Evan. I guess it was inevitable. All she hears about is how wonderful he is.

I've even told my parents that we're dating. My mom wants to have him over for dinner sometime.

I just love being Evan's girlfriend.

Today we're going to meet up at Tom's during our spare period. Tom lives between our two schools so it doesn't take long to drive there. He lives with his dad and brother. It's kind of a frat there, actually. Evan and Allan practically live there too. Tom's house is always open, even if no one is home. Everyone is welcome to come and go as they please. Small parties regularly spring up there out of the blue. I have received many a late night phone call from Tom's place recently.

Tom likes me because I am a good sport and he loves to mess with people. He and Britta still have this strange 'friends with benefits' kind of relationship going on. Unfortunately, I think Britta wants more. She pretends to play it cool with him, but the way she gushes over him when he is not around tells me another story. I really hope she doesn't get hurt.

Britta and I jump in the car and drive over to Tom's. When we get there we go inside to wait for the guys. I'm a little weirded out about being here without the guys, but they have assured me that Tom's dad is cool with us hanging out whenever. We're watching a rerun of the Fresh Prince. We've been here a while now and there is no sign of the boys. The phone rings.

"Should we answer it?" Britta asks.

"It could be the boys," I say as I stand up to get it.

"Or it could be for Tom's dad," Britta warns.

I stop and let the answering machine get it.

We hear Tom's dad's voice: "Hey, we're not in at the moment. Leave us a message and we will call you back. BEEP."

"Hi, ah...this message is for Tom. Tom, it's Sarah." She lets out a nervous giggle. "I'm just looking for Evan. If he's with you could you get him to give me a call?"

"What the hell does Sarah want with Evan?" Britta asks with a disgusted look on her face. Her mind has obviously gone to the same place mine has. *She is trying to hook up with my boyfriend.* What Britta doesn't know is that Sarah has already had 'more special sex' with him when they used to date. I know it, and it's the reason why my stomach is turning. The nausea is overwhelming. *So much for giving him the benefit of the doubt.* I'm steaming mad.

"I don't know," I say. I can hear the angry tone of my voice. "Let's get out of here." The credits for the Fresh Prince are flashing up on the T.V., which tells me that the boys are already half an hour late. "We're going to be late for our next class," I add in a softer tone to make it seem like the phone call is not our reason for leaving.

The rest of the day is an angry, confused blur. I've been stood up and possibly cheated on. My mind goes to dark places. I can't help visualizing Evan in all kinds of compromising positions with the weasel-faced Sarah bitch. Yeah that's right, I'm officially petty and mean.

I have to work tonight so I won't be able to even talk to Evan until ten. I'm not really sure if he's working, so it could be closer to twelve. *Ugh.*

I'm laying on my bed at ten thirty and the phone rings.

"Hey pretty girl," Evan says.

"Hey," I say back coldly. I've had all day to stew about this and I am not in a good head space.

"What's wrong?" He asks.

I start off small. "I thought we were meeting up at Tom's place during spare."

"Oh shit, I forgot," he says. "I'm sorry. I got busy at school, you know."

Nervously, I try to frame my next question in a manner that will not make me sound like the crazy-jealous-untrusting-girlfriend that I am. "Ah um, Tom got a call when we were there waiting for you."

"Oh yeah?"

"It was Sarah."

There is a long pause. A pause that makes me wonder *what the hell is going on in his head right now.*

"What did she want?" I hear nervousness in his voice.

"You...um...I mean to talk to you."

"Oh, did she talk to you?" he asks.

"No, why? She just left a message."

"Ah, she's in some of my classes. She probably just wanted help with something," he brushes it off.

"What kind of help are you giving her?" I can't help it; my voice is riddled with innuendo. The question just came out. Now I totally sound like the crazy-jealous-untrusting-girlfriend.

"What do you mean?" he says, but what he means is 'what are you implying?'

"Jen told me that she was your girlfriend," I say sounding like a gossip-monster and knowing that I'm getting Jen in shit.

"Yeah well, that was way before you."

"So why didn't you tell me? The night I met you, you made it seem like she was some crazy stalker. Then I find out that she was your girlfriend for several months."

"I don't know what you want from me here." He sounds frustrated.

"I just want to be able to trust you...that's all. Evan, I really like you and the idea of you...I don't know, being with someone else, with Sarah, totally freaks me out."

"Have I ever given you any reason not to trust me," he says and I feel small.

"No, but you weren't honest with me about your relationship with Sarah and it's just, well everyone keeps warning me about you."

"So you believe them. Emilia I can't believe this. I gotta go before I say something I'm gonna regret."

Click.

What the fuck just happened? I'm shaking all over, curled in a little ball under the covers on my bed. *What have I done? Are we, are we...still together?* A huge lump forms in my throat and I cry myself to sleep.

The next morning I look dreadful. I spend an extra twenty minutes getting ready to go to school just so I can feel human again. I drive to school and sit through my classes absorbing nothing. It's Friday and usually I would be excited about spending my weekend with Evan, but right now I'm trying not to cry on my chemistry textbook.

School's over and Britta says to me, "Are you and Evan going to Tom's party tonight?"

I didn't tell her about the fight Evan and I had. I was afraid I would be a blubbery mess or that it would fuel another round of her 'Evan's a player' deterrents. I don't want her to go there again.

"I don't know," I say and I add, "I'm pretty sure Evan is working tonight." He usually closes on a Friday and we hang out afterwards.

"Come with me then," Britta says. "I don't want to show up alone."

Maybe this is a good plan? I begin to plot out a scenario in my head. *Maybe I go to the party with Britta and when Evan shows up after work I can apologize and things can go back to normal?*

"Okay," I say to Britta, "can I borrow something to wear?" I add, knowing that looking drop dead gorgeous can only help the plan along.

We hang out at Britta's for a while. She plays little-miss-stylist. By the time we are ready to go I am a glammed-up version of myself. Like the Hollywood version of Emilia. I feel a little bit odd wearing Britta's heels but she assures me that it's cool to wear heels to a house party. We decide to take a cab because Britta convinces me that we're going to be drinking and living it up tonight.

The cab pulls up outside Tom's place at around 10. I figure I can get a few drinks in me before Evan arrives and I'll be in the right mood to apologize. We walk up the front steps and open the door. Tom, Allan, and Jen are in the front room with about five other people. The place is packed. Britta is in front of me and she makes her way into the room first.

"Hey!" Tom yells as he gets up to hug Britta. Then he looks at me and I see the panic in his eyes. I quickly look over at Allan and Jen. They are just as shocked at my presence. My heart begins to race as Allan leaps up and hurries through the living room out into the kitchen. I spin around to the doorway behind me. I can see him in the hallway as he turns to head up the stairs. I glance back at Jen who has an 'I am so sorry' look on her face. Without even thinking I run up the stairs after Allan. He's at the far end of the hall when I reach the top of the stairs. He's facing a door about to open it. He turns to me instead and says, "Em, what's up?" In a high pitched overly-excited loud manner as if to warn Evan of my presence before opening the door.

"Allan move!" I shove him to the side and turn to open the door.

Allan pulls gently on my shoulders and says, "Em...you don't want to go in there."

"The hell I don't!" I say full of conviction.

I turn the handle and there he is. Evan is laying on the bed with the top button of his jeans popped. His legs are spread and her hand is on his thigh as she kneels over him. Startled by my entry, the girl jumps up and it's her. It's Sarah, complete with an open blouse and boobs busting out of her lacy brassiere. Fuck! From this angle her boobs look huge. I kind of wonder how she can stand up with those things. I'm not entirely sure what is going on here, but one thing is clear, the intent in the room is pungent. *He's definitely surpassed the circling her ankles stage*, I think to myself. *Was she going to go...were they going to...ugh!* It is too horrible to think about. I'm enraged!

"What the fuck, Evan!" I seethe.

"EM!" Evan jumps up and clambers towards me.

"To think I was coming here to apologize to you for not trusting you."

"Em, it's not what you think. We didn't do anything," he pleads.

I glance at Sarah's boobs and say, "Evan. Are you kidding me? You're really going to play the innocent card here? Sarah you want him back so badly? You can have him!"

I turn and storm past Allan. It's hard to walk angrily in heels. I make my way downstairs barely holding myself together. I can see by the crowd at the bottom of the stairs that my outburst upstairs has not been a private one. Avoiding all eye contact I push the front door open and start walking down the street towards the main road where I can get a cab. *I'm sure Britta will find her own way home.*

I hear Evan's footsteps getting closer as he jogs behind me. *Damn heels* I think to myself.

"Em, wait!" he pleads.

"What?" I say as the tears begin to well up in my eyes.

He grabs my shoulders and says, obviously upset too, "I don't know what to say Emilia."

"How long?" I look him in the eye and search his face for the answer. "How long have you and Sarah been..." I can't finish. My words die in my grief stricken throat as I realize from the look on his face that this is not the first time he's been with Sarah since he and I started dating.

"Em, I...I don't know. I don't know what to say."

"How long, Evan?" *I need to know. Has he ever been mine? Have I meant anything to him? Has anything been real? What does she have that I don't? I guess giant boobs. Is that what this is about? Boobs? He couldn't be that superficial, could he? I also thought he cared about me but obviously, I was wrong about that. Maybe he IS nothing but a player?*

"It's complicated," he says lowering his head so that he's not looking at me. "Sarah and I have always had this weird, physical relationship. We even dated for a while but it didn't work. Then I met you and you were so awesome. I didn't want to be with her anymore. I told her we couldn't be together anymore. Ever since, she's been very persistent, very persuasive. She's always around. Tonight I had a few beers and I was just so messed up after our conversation last night that I...FUCK! I don't know what to say, Em."

And for once, "Neither do I."

I wrap my arms around myself covering my heart, concealing my pitiful excuse for breasts. *How could he do this? Does he have no control over his penis? Was our relationship not physical enough for him? Fuck! I'm so glad I didn't sleep with him. That doesn't change the ache strangling my heart right now though.*

"Don't cry," he says as he wraps his arms around me.

I cry harder. I can smell his natural scent. It makes me sadder because I know this is the last time I will.

"NO!" I say and I push him away. "Just go." I sound defeated.

I turn and continue towards the corner. He is still following me but he keeps his distance now. I stand there on the corner for what seems like an eternity, but I know it's only about a minute. I hail a cab, get in, and don't look back.

Arriving home at around eleven, I walk in and my mom says, "Hi honey!" from the other room. I take Britta's shoes off. I'm holding them in one hand as I flop to the floor and sob. My mom comes running down the stairs to the landing at the front door. She hugs me close and says, "What happened? Are you okay?"

"We broke up," is all I can muster between sobs.

"Oh, honey," she says sounding sympathetic but somewhat relieved. My mom helps me up and we sit on the stairs together. At first she rubs my back and says nothing. A few minutes go by and the hurt is still excruciating. I can't believe how much my heart physically hurts.

"It's going to be okay, Em. I know it doesn't seem like it now but you'll be okay." Mom reassures me. I know she is trying to help but I just can't deal right now.

I can hear my phone ringing my room. *It's probably Britta or Steph.* Britta must have figured out I left by now and I'm sure she's called Steph in as reinforcement.

For now I'm utterly broken. I pull myself together enough to give my mom a hug and say, "I'm going go to bed." The empathy is oozing out of her as she watches me walk downstairs to my room.

I call Steph and say, "I'm okay," totally lying and "I don't want to talk right now, I'll call you tomorrow."

She wants to help but my heart is broken and there is nothing she can do to mend it. Besides, she and Britta were right all along and I chose to ignore them. *Why didn't I listen to them?* I lay on my bed fully dressed crying for a while. I feel pathetic and naive.

There is a faint knock on my bedroom door. My dad slowly opens the door. "Your mom told me what happened," he says in a gentle 'I'm speaking to a wounded animal' kind of voice. "Are you okay?"

"I'll be okay, Dad," I say and immediately begin sobbing harder, disbelieving my own words.

He walks over to me, grabs the blanket from the end of my bed, and covers me. He proceeds to lay down on the floor beside my bed. He cradles his head in his hand and looks up at my broken-self and says quite simply, "I'm here if you need me." His words resonate in me. My sobbing subsides a little. It's as though his presence takes away some of the hurt. There are good men the world. I lay there and listen to my dad's breathing.

"Thanks, Dad," I say genuinely appreciating his support. I'm not sure how long he stays because I eventually drift off to sleep.

The next few weeks are unbearably sad. I find I'm numb to the world. It's easier this way. I can't listen to music. Every song brings my heartache to the forefront. I'm not hungry. I can't sleep and when I can, I can't wake up.

Evan calls a couple times and leaves messages but I cannot bring myself to call him back. I secretly save one of the messages though and I listen to it a couple times a day. It says, "Hey, Emilia. I just wanted to talk. I miss you."

I'm glad he misses me. At first I was glad because I wanted him to realize he made a monumental mistake. Now I am glad because it means I'm not the only one missing the way we were.

A month goes by and I'm starting to feel a bit more like myself. Britta is still doing the fuck-buddy thing with Tom. She says Evan is moping around but I think she's just trying to be nice to my fragile ego.

Tom asked Britta to his prom. She can't stop talking about him. Steph is seeing Nick, that 'annoying guy' from the pool. So I have been flying solo lately. My grades have never been so high and I'm picking up extra shifts at work all the time. This Saturday is my birthday and I am going out with my girls. I'm totally looking forward to letting loose.

10 Unwanted Souvenir

"You look smokin', Em." Britta says as she finishes straightening my hair. I glance at the mirror and admit that I do look good. Ever since the Sarah thing I've been more self-conscious about my body and appearance. I guess when your boyfriend cheats it's only natural to feel like you're lack something. The fact that Sarah has a massive rack has definitely caused me to fixate on my perky shortcomings. I adjust my bra so that my small bosom offers a hint of cleavage in the low neckline on my sparkly tank top.

"Thanks Britta. You've outdone yourself."

"Here Steph. Try this red one," Britta says as she hands Steph a tight red dress.

"I don't know about this?" Steph says, but I know that Britta will have her way in the end, and it's no use fighting it.

We're dressed and ready. We head out to a fancy restaurant. It's my nineteenth birthday and I can officially drink legally! I order a cosmopolitan off the drink menu. The waitress smiles a 'oh isn't she cute' smile at me. We're having a great time. It's so awesome listening to Steph and Britta fawn over their boys. They are so happy and I'm happy for them. It does highlight my single status though. By the time dessert hits the table, I've consumed two cosmos and my third is arriving.

As we get up from the table the alcohol hits me in a wave. I'm feeling carefree and happy. *I may be over Evan*, I think to myself. We get in the cab to go to the club and Britta leans over to me. "I hope you don't mind that I told Tom where we're going."

Happy carefree me says, "No, of course not, that's cool."

We get to the club and we're on the guest list so we breeze past the line. We walk in. I start seeing all kinds of friends and acquaintances from school. Even the girls from work are here. I look at Britta and Steph; they are beaming. I yell loudly over a retro ABBA tribute that is blaring: "What did you guys do?"

"We knew you were in a funk, so we invited everyone we could think of to cheer you up. Happy Birthday, Em!" I hug Steph and Britta. I feel so special.

Someone hands me a drink. I think it is a screwdriver; it's good. Everyone is dancing. I'm full of energy. Normally, I don't dance. I usually shuffle my feet a little and maybe swing my arms. Tonight however, I am on fire! I feel the beat running through my hips perfectly. *I am owning this dance floor.*

Britta rushes past me. I turn to see her throw her arms around Tom. Then, I see Steph behind her. She is obviously angry with someone. Her face is serious and she is pointing and shouting. The music is too loud to hear what she is saying, but as I move towards the commotion, I see the target of Steph's venom.

Evan. Evan is standing there just looking at Steph as she berates him. He's not saying anything. He is wearing a white somewhat fitted dress shirt untucked. It hurts to admit it to myself but *he looks really hot.* In my somewhat inebriated state, I approach Evan and Steph, and I decide to take control.

"It's okay Steph," I say as I walk in between the two of them and look directly into Evan's eyes. Part of me wants to kiss him, but I know that's not a good idea. I take his hand and pull him into the stairwell that leads down to the bathroom. I can see Steph looking at me with an angry 'what are you thinking' look on her face. Waving my hand at her to go, I mouth, "I'll be fine."

"It's quieter in here," I say even though I can still here the base of Nine Inch Nails "Closer" pounding through the wall beside me.

"Emilia," he says almost shyly, like he's afraid he's in trouble, "Happy Birthday." He reaches into his pocket and pulls out my bra.

I grab it. I'm not sure what it means. *Is it the 'We are broken up so here's your stuff thing' or does he have another angle?*

"You don't have a use for souvenirs anymore?" I say.

"I don't want a souvenir to remember you by," he says, "I only want you." With that he picks me up and kisses me. I'm not sure if it is the alcohol or his words or the kiss, but my world is spinning. I'm lost for a moment. His kiss sends shock waves throughout my being. I feel my nipples respond in an instant. *Traitor nipples.*

He's feeling it too. I can feel his erection pressing against my body. *Snap out of it, Em. Have some resolve.* It's a whirlwind of emotions. I'm so enthralled with his touch, but the heartache he has caused me... My brain jumps back into my body and I push him back.

"You can't just do this," I say, not sure what I mean. "You can't break my heart and then kiss me and make everything better." *Oh, that's what I mean.*

"Emilia, I'm sorry. Sarah doesn't mean anything to me. I'm not going to lie to you. I was making a play. I don't really know why. I wasn't even interested in her. Things were so simple with her. I didn't have feelings for her. I was, I don't know, afraid of what I was feeling for you."

I'm hurt and softened by his words at the same time. The fact remains though that I can't trust him. "What, so you liked me so much you needed to sleep with someone else. That's fucking fantastic!" I say sarcastically.

"Emilia, all I know is that I'm miserable without you. I wish this wasn't the case. I wish I could erase that whole night or move on, but the fact is that since you left, I can't look at another girl without comparing her to you. No one stacks up."

"Evan," I say calmly, "how am I supposed to believe you? My vision of our relationship is so tainted. I'm not sure if you ever really liked me or if you were just playing me the whole time. Was I always one of many? How do I know that a set of boobs isn't going to walk by right now and catch your eye?"

"I don't know," he says and he looks defeated. "You weren't one of many. You aren't. I know it's hard to believe me but I really care about you – more than I have ever cared about a girl. I want to start over, to earn your trust. I want it to be like it was before I screwed everything up."

"I want to believe you, but, I'm not sure I can go back, Evan. I just don't know."

"I'll wait," he says. I am confused by his response.

"What do you mean?"

"I'll wait for you to be ready. I have no choice. You're all I think about." The alcohol dissolves my resolve and I find myself draping my arms around his neck. He pulls me tight against his chest into his embrace.

"What if I can't?" I say under my breath into his ear.

"You will," he whispers back. "I will just have to be patient."

"And trustworthy," I add. "Let's go before Steph gets you thrown out or something," I say and usher him out of the stairwell and onto the dance floor.

He breaks away for a second and hands the D.J. something; I think it's money. Mariah Carey's remixed version of "Fantasy" with O.D.B. belts out of the speakers around me. I know he is trying to make me remember when things were good. He smiles and dances to the song with me and my girls. Steph and Britta are shooting him daggers. If looks could kill. But, neither of them stop dancing. They know that he's still important to me so they suck up whatever they need to and continue dancing.

It's hard not to be drawn in by Evan, especially after all the drinks that I've had and the kiss that has my blood still boiling. He's so hot and his fluid movements on the dance floor make my mind wander to dirty places. He puts his hand on my lower back and says in my ear "I'm over at the bar if you need me, pretty girl." As he leaves to sit at the bar with Tom, his hand drags slowly across my back. My body tingles in a way that only he can make it. While I dance, I can feel his eyes following my body as I move. It makes me feel wanted. It makes me feel sexy. Perhaps it's the alcohol but my insecurities about myself fade away as I become one with the music. Even though I know we are far from back together, I feel like there's a glimmer of hope.

11 Tell Me How You Really Feel

As we wait for a cab outside the bar, Evan moves in from behind and wraps his arms around me. The alcohol is coursing through me, making all the lights have pretty trails as I spin around to meet his gaze.

"You okay pretty girl?" he says in the tender familiar voice that pulls on my heart strings.

"I am now," I slur and lift my head to kiss him.

Our lips barely graze one another when I'm being ripped away into a cab by a very unimpressed Steph. As my ass hits the vinyl seat, she rips into me.

"What the fuck was that! That douche bag cheats on you, turns you into a depressed hermit for weeks, and then you practically throw yourself at him the first chance you get. What the hell, Em!"

"Steph, it's not like that." *Actually, it's exactly like that, but I have no will power against his charms. In all other areas of life I am so level-head, so rational. But when I'm with him I'm different: carefree and driven, physically and emotionally, in a way I've never known before.* The ideas whirl around my head but in my inebriated state I can only defend myself to Steph by saying. "I don't know what to tell you Steph. I feel different around him. I can't help it."

"Well try! He's bad news, Em. He's already fucked you over once. What makes you think things will be any different this time?"

"We're not back together," I say and it sounds like bullshit even to me as it comes out, "I told him I didn't think I could trust him again. He said he wants to earn my trust."

Steph is blabbing away about how gullible I am but the alcohol and the movement of the cab are overwhelming me. I rest my head on her lap and she strokes my hair. I try to gain control of my world as it rapidly spins around sloshing in my cosmo-soaked grey-matter. "Em, this guy doesn't deserve you."

"Steph, I don't know what I'm doing, but I need you in my corner, you know? I'm probably gonna fuck this up one way or another. But, I need you."

"I wish you could move on, find someone new. I don't want that asshole to wreck you." I give her a pouty face and she shakes her head as she continues running her fingers through my hair.

"Okay, you have me. No matter what, you have me." I fall asleep on her lap with a relieved, comfortable smile etched on my face.

12 Misgivings and Everything After

Over the next couple of weeks Evan is super attentive. He calls me regularly. He comes to my school to hang out. He meets me at my work and takes me out for coffee, or should I say cream and sugar. I'm still trying my best to keep my bitterness to a minimum. He even comes by my house and meets my parents briefly. They're polite but guarded with him. It's probably hard for them knowing that he's the one that broke my heart only a little over a month ago. I never told them why we broke up. It's bad enough that Steph and Britta know.

Sometimes I think both Steph and Britta look down on me for letting Evan back into my life. It's hard not to feel insecure about getting back together with Evan for so many reasons: my friends' opinions, my trust issues with Evan, and my desire for self-preservation. Evan has been fantastic but I still have so many reservations. I really don't want to risk being hurt again.

We're kissing and flirting like before but so far that's all I can handle. My fear takes over when he tries to go further. He says he understands. He says he's willing to wait for me to be ready for more. I hope we can get past this somehow. *How will I ever be sure he feels the way I do?*

My phone rings. It's late and I'm in that place between sleep and awake. I startle and answer the phone in a panicked tone: "Hello."

"Hi Emilia...Sorry. Did I wake you?" Evan's voice is smooth and low. *Maybe I'm still dreaming?*

"Yeah, I mean no, I mean, I don't..."

He doesn't let me finish. "I have something to ask and I can't wait until tomorrow."

Now I'm fully wake. "What?"

"Well, you know prom is next week and I was wondering if you would go with me." His voice is still mellow.

My immediate reaction is to dance around the room and yell YES! YES! YES! Something stops me. I'm silently contemplating the whole 'Prom Night' thing.

"Emilia?" he says checking that I'm still on the phone because I haven't responded.

"I'm here," I say. "I'm just thinking."

"Thinking about what?" he asks calmly.

"Evan, I'm not sure. I mean I would love to go with you, but it's just so soon. I haven't even really figured out what we are doing yet."

"Emilia, I want you to be my girlfriend. I want to be your boyfriend. I don't want anyone else, just you Emilia, just you."

"I want to say yes Evan, I really do...it's...the hurt is so fresh and the prom – well everyone knows what prom night is all about."

"Emilia, that's not why I'm asking you to the prom. I'm asking you because I'd like to take my girlfriend on a romantic date and show her off to all my friends."

How ridiculous. "Show me off?" I giggle. "All right, I'd love to be your date, but no funny business," I warn jokingly.

"See, that wasn't so hard was it?" I can tell he is pleased with himself.

"Night you," I say.

"Good night, Emilia." His soft tone returns.

Prom night comes and goes. We have a great time drinking and dancing with all of Evan's friends. He introduces me as his girlfriend to everyone and anyone who will listen. I can't help noticing Sarah lip-locking/dry-humping some dude all over the dance floor. I'm glad Britta's here. She even seems to be more accepting of Evan. And, true to his word, no sexcapades happen. Too be completely honest, it's actually a little disappointing. He looks so hot in his Tux, my body wouldn't mind taking it off him. *Who's stupid idea was the 'no funny business' anyway?* I know he's trying to prove to me that he is a man of honour. So, the Tux stays on.

I'm feeling better about us and it's getting easier to trust him. Now that school has wrapped up, the carefree days of summer are upon us. I'm working full-time at a day camp. Evan is working for his dad's construction company. Things are good. We're still moving slowly but I'm happy with our progress.

When Evan plans a weekend away with our friends at his cottage, I'm excited about spending more time with him. Evan and I will leave with Steph and Nick on Friday night after Evan's shift at The Coffee Bean. Britta and Tom will leave on Saturday after work. Allan and Jen can't make it.

I finish packing, load a bag and a small cooler into my trunk, and head over to Steph's to pick her and Nick up. I'm surprised she's agreed to come. She's still very cold to Evan. I think she may be coming just to keep an eye on me. As I walk into Steph's place, I find her in the middle of an argument with her mom. I've never heard them argue; it's weird. I'm not even sure what they're arguing about but I feel totally uncomfortable. I decide to wait outside on the porch. About ten minutes go by before Steph emerges from the house, slamming the door behind her.

"What's up Steph?" I say concerned.

"I can't go to the cottage."

Totally confused I say, "Why not?"

"My mom keeps saying we have a family commitment, but she won't tell me what it is."

I can feel her frustration. Her hippy parents have never told her what she can and can't do. She is a grown-up. She can do whatever she wants, but as she recounts the argument I know that tonight, for whatever reason, she's staying home. We talk for about an hour and decide that she will come up tomorrow after her family thing.

Now that I'm behind schedule, I rush to pick up Evan. I pull up in front of his house and see him standing outside waiting for me with a bag, a case of beer, and a liquor store bag.

"Hey, pretty girl," he says.

"Hi, you," I say. "So, I went to pick up Steph and she can't come until tomorrow."

"Oh yeah? Why's that?"

"She's got some family thing. I don't know. It's weird."

"So, I have you all to myself then." He smiles a wicked smile.

Until the words came out of his mouth, it hadn't occurred to me. Before I can think about it Evan says, "Let's take my car then, better tunes."

I transfer my stuff from the trunk and we're off. I'm excited about going to Evan's cottage. His dad created it from the ground up. If it is anything like his house, it's going to be amazing. Evan speaks very highly of the place. His mom used to take Evan and his brother, Edward, to spend their summers there. Evan's eyes light up whenever he talks about fishing at the lake, catching frogs, and building forts in the woods. The thought of little Evan running around the forest and jumping off a dock warms my heart.

"How long will it take us to get there?" I ask.

"About two hours," he says as he pops a CD in.

Etta James' killer voice comes flying out of the speakers. "Summertime" is the perfect song choice for this moment.

I roll down my window and let the rush of warm humid air flow in. I breathe in the freshness and feel relaxed. I look over at Evan as he drives the car. He's beautiful. The wind blowing his dark hair gently, his blue eyes picking up the flashes of light from the street lights, his strong physique is so...

A moment of clarity washes over me. *Evan's worth the risk. Sure he fucked things up for us before, but he's trying so hard. It's been a while now and he has gone out of his way to reassure me that he's committed to me. It's my fear that is holding us back. He will hurt me and I will probably hurt him too, but in the meantime...I need to give in and admit to myself that I love him. Admitting it to myself is weird. I was probably in love with him before the whole Sarah thing. That's why it hurt so much. All I know is that I've never felt this way about another person. When I'm not with Evan, I'm thinking about him. When I am with him, I'm emotionally connected to him in a way that I can't even comprehend.*

The song ends and Ella Fitzgerald chimes in. "Where'd you get this CD?" I ask.

"Oh, I like to listen to old music on the way to the cottage. It puts me in the right mood. We have an old record player there that plays all this great jazz, classical music, the Beatles, the Stones, the Carpenters...pretty much anything my parents liked once upon a time."

"That's awesome I can't wait to get my hands on it," I say as I reach over and put my hand on his thigh.

"Hands on what-now?" he jokes.

"The record player, of course," I say coyly as I move my hand further up his thigh.

"Oh, I see." He shifts in his seat. *I'm having an effect.*

Two hours cannot go by fast enough. By the time we get there I'm peaking with anticipation. I'm not sure what's going to happen. All I know is that I am in. My trepidations, and fear have subsided. I'm ready to be Evan's girlfriend wholeheartedly.

We turn down a dark winding road and then another. We're the only car on the road. We finally come to rest in front of a large wooden A-frame cottage. Evan leaves the headlights on and hops out of the car. I wait in the passenger seat as he unlocks the door and turns the power on in the cottage. The light's glow stretches out of the windows and illuminates the forest around us.

I turn off the headlights and get out. It's so peaceful. I can hear frogs chattering at the lake's edge and even a loon call in the distance. The crickets chirp loudly at my feet. I take a deep breath. The air is so fantastically fragrant.

I walk slowly past Evan towards the screen door. He's on his way out to collect our things from the car. The screen door makes the most amazing sound as it smacks back.

I step inside and it is stunning. It is truly architecture at its finest. Ahead of me is an entire wall of windows. On my left there is a cozy galley kitchen with a breakfast island that opens into the large dining area. There is a lovely red wood fireplace in the middle of the room. On my right there's a quaint living room.

"There is a loft up those stairs with two bedrooms, and there are two more down here," Evan tells me as he brings my cooler into the kitchen. "This is the bathroom over here. I just turned on the hot water so it'll take a while to warm up."

"It's beautiful. I love the smell of the wood. What is it?" The whole cottage is covered from floor to ceiling in tongue and groove boards. I love the diagonal cuts that make up the A-frame roof best. I've made my way to the couch and I'm sitting down staring at the ceiling. The dim light from the table lamps bounces off of it so perfectly.

"It's all pine. The walls are natural. That's why it has that great smell. I'm glad you like it. It's one of my favourite things." He mucks about in the kitchen. I hear him pouring something and mixing away. When he emerges, he's holding a large wine glass filled with the reddest wine I've ever seen.

"What is this?" I ask as he hands it to me.

"It's vodka and cranberry juice. I think you will like it. It's way better than the wine coolers you like so much."

I'm about to correct him when I realize he's joking. As I bring the glass up to my lips I hear the ice cubes jingle against the side of the glass. The cottage is so quiet and peaceful that it is a surprisingly loud sound. If we were anywhere else, it would've gone unnoticed. The sweet yet bitter taste of the cranberry juice awakens my taste buds. It's delicious.

I put my feet up on the couch and get cozy in the arm of the overstuffed corner cushions. Evan grabs a knitted blanket and covers my legs. Then, he makes his way over to the record player, and puts on some classical music. "This is my favourite. It's Bach," he says.

It starts off very soft and slow. The sound fills the space. I can feel the record's sound in a way that CDs don't really compare. The odd crackle of the needle on the record is an unexpected delight. The notes begin dancing and joining together to make a symphony of sound. Evan sits down opposite me on the couch. I close my eyes and breathe in the music as I rest my head back on the cushion.

Evan begins circling my ankles with his fingers. I smile a little and let out a quiet but audible moan. Taking notice of the moan he takes a chance and moves further up my legs. His touch is so steady, yet light. I'm tingling in all the right places. He moves closer, picks up my right leg kisses my ankle, my knee, my thigh, my inner thigh... I'm reeling with anticipation. He lowers my leg pinning it between the cushions of the couch and his body. Then he turns his attention to my left leg. This time he drags his finger along my ankle, my knee, my thigh, my inner thigh, and then brushes it over my panties.

"Oh," I moan. Wanting so much more, I pull him up on top of me and press his lips to mine. It's a soft, passionate, weak-in-the-knees, stop-time kind of kiss. I'm lost in the electricity that is pulsing through my body. I lift his shirt over his head and rub my hands on his chest dying to feel all of him. He pulls back and looks at me. He studies my face as if he is asking if I am okay. I smile and run my hands through his hair. Reassured, he works his magic. He lifts my shirt up running his hands quickly up my body and begins kissing me just below my ear on my neck. His heavy breathing combined with the tender teasing touch on my neck is mind blowing. He works his way down my neck on to my chest. *It feels so right.* He stops at my bra and smiles up at me and says, "My favourite souvenir."

It is a lovely pink lace bra not the infamous blue one, so I respond..."Maybe after tonight it will be."

He pulls the cup of the bra down exposing my breast and begins kissing, sucking, licking my hard nipple. I squirm with desire under him. I see a smirk appear on his lips. He stands up abruptly and motions for me to follow. Dizzy with pleasure, I don't move. Before I know it, he's back in front of me. With one quick motion he lifts me up over his shoulder. He proceeds to carry me up the long flight of stairs to the loft. He lowers me down on the bed. Bach is still playing, but the song is now fast and commanding.

He switches on a small light beside the bed. The light shimmers off his chest. I pull him closer and begin undoing his jeans. I start by loosening his belt and pulling on the buckle. I make quick work of his button. He is hard beneath his fly and it makes it difficult to unzip him in a smooth manner. I lower his jeans to the floor, slowly running my fingers up along his muscular legs. I rub my hand over the growing bulge in his underwear and then slip my hand under the material and grab his hard penis. Gripping it in my hand, I begin stroking it. He puts his head back and groans. I pull down the boxer briefs and take him in my mouth. I follow the rhythm of the music and massage his testicles with my hand. He puts his hands in my hair and matches my rhythm.

"No, it's too good" he says. I know what that means, but I don't want this to end so I ease back and stand up.

"Do you have a condom?" I say.

"What? Really?" he says. After the last few weeks, I guess this wasn't what he was expecting. "Yeah, I mean, are you sure?"

"I'm sure," I say, because I am.

He reaches down to his jeans grabs his wallet out the back pocket and fishes through it. He pulls out a shiny silver package and says, "Let's play some more first. I think it's your turn."

He starts by undoing the clasp of my bra and then he removes my skirt. I'm wearing fancy underwear. I'm so glad Britta talked me in to buying them. They're pink, lace, bikini-cut panties.

"I was wrong. These are my favourite souvenir. Definitely worth waiting for." I giggle as he looks me over. He takes his time pulling my panties to the floor. The anticipation is killing me. He lowers me onto the bed. He lays beside me with his head on my shoulder. I can feel his nakedness pressed up against mine and every fibre of my being is aroused. I want him so badly. With one hand he begins massaging my breast while the other reaches down. His finger is circling my clit. It's heavenly. I cannot help but rock my hips and press against his touch. Ecstasy. I'm entirely physically driven at this point.

I roll over on top of him, taking him by surprise. "I need you," I say. I can feel his erection pressing into my stomach. He lifts me back so I am straddling his legs, rips open the silver packet, and unrolls the condom around his penis. I watch with bated breath. I'm not nervous; I am SO ready.

"We need to make you wet first," he says.

"I think we've already taken care of that," I say in a sultry voice.

I move over him and he holds his penis up so I can lower myself onto it. It is uncomfortable at first as it goes inside of me. I stop briefly to let my body get used to the size of it. Then I continue until he's filling me. It hurts, but in a good way. I begin to move…to rock my hips back and forth. My sex rubs on the skin around the base of his penis and I can feel his balls hitting against my butt. The sensations are overwhelming. I begin to move on top of him, bring his penis in and out of me quickly, and then slowly, and then quickly again. He groans underneath me.

He flips me over and begins forcing himself in and out of me in a smooth controlled manner. The feeling is, is… His movements, the pressure against me is so, so necessary. As he moves into me, I become increasingly aware that this is the only thing that will satisfy my deep carnal need. It's everything I ever thought it would be. *It feels so fucking incredible!* I'm, I'm, I'm…I'm quivering, writhing. I climax under him. After a few more quick thrusts, he releases in me. I feel him pulse within me.

"Oh, Emilia!" He exclaims from somewhere in his core.

We lay there, him still inside me for several minutes listening to our breath. Our heartbeats slowly return to normal. Finally he gets up and kisses me gently.

He presses his forehead against mine and looks me directly in the eyes. "You okay?" he asks, trying to assess my mood.

"Mmmm," I hum contentedly, unable to really think or speak.

I kiss him again as reassurance. He gets up slowly and heads downstairs to the bathroom. I lie in the bed trying to collect my thoughts and contain my grin. I look around for my panties and opt to grab a blanket. I wrap myself in it. The fleece feels good on my skin and I'm reminded of our night at the Parkette. I walk downstairs. Evan is wearing only a pair of track pants. The light accentuates his chiseled abs. *Yum.* I watch as he looks through the extensive record collection in search of a song that fits this moment. *He's so, so perfect.*

"Tough act to follow?" I joke as I pick up his shirt of the floor and put it on. The scent reminds me of the night we met.

"Sure is," he grins, "but I know what I am looking for," he adds. "Ah, here it is."

He flashes me the Beatles' *Revolver* album. My parents were big fans so I've seen it before. He motions for me to come over to the record player. The record makes a slight scratchy noise as he places the needle down. Evan pulls me close to dance and he begins to sing along with the song "Here, There and Everywhere". I listen as his voice hugs the Beatles melodic song. The warmth of his body and the relaxed rhythm with which he directs me across the floor is enchanting. I try to make sense of the lyrics. *Is he trying to tell me something or is this just a song he likes to dance to?* I try not to read too much into anything, but my heart is so invested and I can help clinging to the hope that his is too.

Tears are welling up in my eyes. As the song ends, I know that no dance has ever affected me as deeply as ours has. I'm elated, moved. Emotional ecstasy exists. Resting my head on Evan's shoulder he stretches out one of my curls and we continue to dance during the pause between songs as if it doesn't exist. The next song begins and I can't help but giggle. The most romantic moment of my life is currently being punctuated by "Yellow Submarine".

"I do love you," he whispers in my ear over the music. His revelation takes me by surprise. Not that he loves me, although I wasn't completely confident about that, but that he has actually said it.

I look up at him and kiss his lips gently. I pull back so we are nose to nose. "I love you too Evan." "Yellow submarine" drifts into the background of my consciousness.

13 Shacking Up

"Emilia," I feel a kiss on the back of my neck. Evan is crawling back into the bed. "Morning beautiful," he says as he wraps himself around me. "I made you breakfast. I hope you like bacon and eggs."

I smile at the thought of Evan puttering in the kitchen. I let out a little hum sound. It is a relaxed, happy sound. Opening my eyes, I look out the window of the second story loft. The view is breathtaking. It's as though I'm perched high in a grand oak tree. Leaves frame my view of the crystal blue lake. Right in front of me, in the middle of the small bay, is the cutest island I have ever seen. It is small, very small. It only has a handful of young trees on it. The leaves on the silver birch tree seem to dance in the wind and match the shimmer of the sun on the lake.

I dress quickly and walk down the stairs towards the kitchen. I see the cottage in the light of the day for the first time. The craftsmanship is exquisite. The decor is nautical and warm. I can't wait to curl up with a good book in the overstuffed, navy chair with white piping around the armrests.

Evan is plating breakfast in the kitchen. "Hi you," I say. Ever since last night's dance I've had a perma-smile plastered on my face. It's the kind of smile you have when you know a secret that everyone else is trying to figure out. I keep replaying the tune of 'Here, There and Everywhere' in my mind.

"You look happy this morning," he says with a devilish grin. *He knows the secret too.*

"Thanks for breakfast. It smells amazing," I say as I head over to the record collection to select some morning tunes. I select *The Best of the Jackson 5*. I've never heard the Jackson 5 on a record before. I'm excited about it. Plus, I think it's upbeat enough to justify my goofy grin.

We both take turns singing along. There's something about watching Evan try to hit Michael's high notes that is so endearing. As we sit, sing, and chat, I feel completely at ease. The thought occurs to me that *I had sex for the first time ever last night and here I am, no regrets, no awkward feelings. If this were a movie, I would be pregnant, have a STD (yuck), he would be totally uninterested in me by now, I would feel ashamed, and my world would be falling apart. I'm so glad I don't live in the movies!*

After breakfast, I head to the bathroom to take a shower. The water comes streaming out of the shower head. I hear the door open. "Could you use some company?" Evan asks.

"Sure, I have a spot here that's hard to reach."

He opens the shower door. He is already naked. "Oh yeah?" he smiles. "Where?" I glance down at my naked body and before I can even say anything he is in the shower kissing me. "I think I can figure it out," he murmurs between kisses.

The water is dripping down our naked bodies as we hold each other close. He moves down and begins licking and suckling my nipple. His hand is working its way up my thigh. He pushes me back so I am pinned up against the cold tiled wall. He pushes my legs apart and puts his tongue on my sex. My arms are now stretched out bracing me against the glass. Between the movement of his hands on my behind, his tongue on my sex, and the feel of the water dripping down my breasts, my body is in a state of absolute euphoria. I'm a tingling, quivering mess. Now that I've had a taste of sex, I want him inside me so badly. I have a need that only sex can satisfy. I push his head back. He looks up at me. I pull him up and proceed to go down myself. I'm now pinning him against the glass side of the shower as I take his penis in my mouth. I pull and suck. I move in and out, sometimes slow and sometimes fast. I pay particular attention to the head. I swirl my tongue around it a few times. I look up at him. "Do you have any more condoms?" I ask.

"I was hoping you would want to play again," he coos as he reaches to open the shower door a crack. He reaches his hand out and pats the floor several times before finally grabbing a condom and pulling it into the shower.

"Aren't you presumptuous? How many condoms do you carry around with you?" I joke.

"Hopeful. Not presumptuous," he clarifies.

He rolls it onto his penis. "Turn around," he says in a soft commanding tone.

I turn around and he grabs my hips and pulls them back. He puts his hand between my legs and sticks two fingers inside me. I let out a loud moan.

"Oh, you're ready," he says gruffly as he removes his fingers and glides his penis inside me – slowly at first to get me good and wet. I press both my hands against the tiled wall and push back against him. He begins to fuck me hard. His penis is filling me. It hurts and feels amazing all at the same time. He is slamming against me. Harder, harder, it's so hard. I can't get enough. I...I...I...I'm going to cum. I begin releasing around him. He continues pumping into me and the sensations are overwhelming. Moments later, I feel him pulse inside me. He groans loudly and pulls out of me.

I turn and throw my arms around his neck. I'm woozy and need to support myself. We stand there trying to catch our breath as the water continues running over us. It begins to feel cooler. I realize we are out of hot water. For the first time ever I feel dirtier having showered.

The rest of the morning goes by in a blissful haze. We sit out on the deck and have tea. We walk down to the dock and dip our feet in. We even attempt to skip rocks on the water. He has had a great deal of practice and has them jumping four or five times. Mine seem more driven by gravity. By lunch I'm curled up with my book in the comfortable navy chair, with my feet resting on a make shift ottoman made from a stool with blankets piled on top of it. I am about to get to a juicy part when the phone rings. *It must be Britta and Tom* I think to myself. *I bet they're lost.*

Evan gets the phone. "Hello." He looks shocked. "Yes, it's me." He listens for a long time to the person on the other end of the phone. His face is one of confusion and disappointment. "Yes, she's here. I realize how this looks, but I assure you that is not what's happening here." Now I'm really worried. "Mrs. Somerville please..." *Fuck it's my mom and for whatever reason she is freaking out on Evan.* I grab the phone from Evan whose face is now pale.

"Mom," I say shocked.

"Emilia Jane Somerville, what on earth do you think you are doing?" she scolds.

"What do you mean Mom?" *She can't possibly know, can she?*

"Stephanie's mother called me this morning. It seems she and Steph's dad are splitting up and she wanted you to be there when she told Stephanie." I'm stunned. *Poor Steph. That is why her mom wanted her to stay home.* My heart is in my throat as my mom continues to talk. "You told me Stephanie was going away with you." Her tone is very accusatory. "But, NO! You're too busy shacking up with your boyfriend behind my back to help Stephanie through this ordeal."

'Shacking up,' really? Are those really the words that came out of my mom's mouth? "Mom it's not like that," I say sounding guilty as hell.

"What is it like? Your friend Britta, who was also supposed to be cottaging, according to you, just called to see if you heard about Stephanie. So, you tell me, what is it like?"

"Mom, Steph was supposed to come with me last night. I went to pick her up but her mom said she couldn't come. Britta was coming today."

"Emilia, your father and I are so disappointed in you...in your choices. This is the same boy that only weeks ago had you crying on my shoulder and moping around here; and now you are having some sort of romantic getaway with him?"

"Mom, I'm sorry I'm disappointing you. I hadn't planned on 'having a romantic getaway' and I feel bad that you think I'm lying to you. Had I known Steph's parents were going to drop this on her, I would have stayed with her last night."

"The fact is, Emilia, when you found out that Stephanie wasn't going to the cottage, you should have stayed anyway."

"No, Mom, the fact is, I'm not a little girl anymore and I'm going to make decisions that you may not agree with." As I hear the words leaving my mouth I know I'm hurting her. I know that she only has my interests at heart and that she only wants to protect me. But the words are out in the universe now. I have said them and I know they're true.

Growing up, my mom was always talked about how I needed to take responsibility for my own actions. She and my dad were always trying to help us make 'good choices.' They said that they were preparing me for life. As a kid, I hated hearing, 'Emilia I'm trusting you to make a responsible choice.' It was the worst. In reality, they were the ultimate puppet masters. Whenever they said something like that, I would just think really hard about what I *thought* they wanted me to do, and I would do that. Here, in this moment, I realize I'm my own person. What my parents think is the responsible choice here isn't the choice I feel in my heart. This time I'm making the choice. The puppet masters are not going to like this.

"Mom, I'm a smart girl. You've taught me well. I'm not going to do anything stupid. I am, however, going to make grown up decisions on my own. You're going to have to trust me."

"I..." there is a long pause and I fear she is about to break out in tears. "I know you're growing up. I fear you may be in over your head here, though. I don't want to see you hurt again."

"I know Mom. I don't want to get hurt either. Hopefully, I won't." I look over at Evan. He is sitting on a bar stool at the counter top in the kitchen. His back is to me and he's running his hands through his hair. I know he's been listening to my entire conversation and I guess I'm looking to him for reassurance. He's not even looking at me. A larger lump forms in my throat.

"Are you coming home?" she asks.

"I'm gonna go to Steph's. If she's okay, I'll come home," I say.

"Emilia."

"Yeah, Mom."

"Your father is very upset. I will try to reason with him, but, it could take a while before um..." She trails off.

"Let me deal with Steph first, then I'll worry about Dad." Her words hurt. I try to put the idea that my dad is disappointed in me out of my head.

"Bye, Mom."

"Bye, Em."

Evan is still sitting with his hands raking through his hair. I walk up behind him and drape my body against his back desperate for a contact. "You okay?" I ask.

"Your mom hates me," he says still facing forward.

"She doesn't hate you. She just doesn't like the idea that you are here alone having your way with me. What did she call it? Oh yeah, 'shacking up' with me."

He lets out a small laugh and wheels his stool around to face me. He put his arms around my middle and hugs me. His head is on my chest. "I'm sorry I hurt you back then."

"I know."

"I don't know why I was such an ass. I'm never going to do anything like that again."

"I know," I say stroking his hair.

"You know I was miserable when you stormed off. I hated myself for doing that to you. I think I'll always have that image of you standing in the doorway of Tom's place in your sexy heels, looking so perfect, and calling me on my shit. No one had ever done that to me before."

"Surely Sarah accused you of cheating." As it comes out, I regret saying it. On his face I can see I'm wounding him.

"No. Well, maybe. But, she was so, so needy and clingy that I never had to worry about her leaving me. You, you were...are so much stronger than that. You made me beg you to take me back."

I pull back, bend down, and kiss him.

"Watching you hail that cab, tears in your eyes, knowing that I did that to you...that was the hardest moment of my life," he divulges. "Promise me you won't ever leave again."

"Promise me you'll never give me a reason to," I say.

14 Facing the Music

The drive home is long. My mind is on Steph. I tried calling before we left but I got her answering machine. I didn't leave a message. I didn't know what to say. I have two hours to figure it out.

Steph's mom is a lively, funny, smart lady. She works for a non-profit organization that helps provide support for families that have a child or children with special needs. I really want to be a teacher someday and so I love talking to her about her work with the kids. We get along very well, and I genuinely enjoy her carefree approach to life.

Steph's dad is also cool. He can't drive at all, but that never stopped him from driving us to school before I got my license. Every time he drove us, my life would flash before my eyes – not because he was a speed demon; he was an extremely slow driver. It was more because he was completely oblivious to the fact that anyone else was on the road with us. He would leave his turning signal on for the entire drive, swerve into other lanes, and even occasionally stop at green lights. That's kind of the way he is in life too. He travels at his own speed, not worried about what others are doing, simply getting from one place to another. He is a sweetheart, really. I find it particularly funny that sometimes when Steph and I are coming home really late, he is still up, snacking and typing on his computer.

Last year, I went with Steph to celebrate her parent's 25th wedding anniversary. They renewed their vows in a beautiful park by a river. Friends and family were all there. It was kinda cheesy but also very sweet. I can still picture them doing the cake thing, where they feed each other a small piece and then smush it onto one another's faces. They seemed so happy. *Divorce? Why would they want to get divorced?* I can't wrap my brain around the idea.

First, we go to Evan's place to pick up my car. Then, I head straight to Steph's. I walk up the front steps and take a deep breath and open the door. My eyes meet Steph's dad's and all I see is pain. He steps towards me and throws his arms around me. *This is way worse than I thought.* He is sobbing on my shoulder. I pat his back like I am soothing a tired baby.

"Thank you for coming," he says as he lets me go. "She's in her room. She won't come out."

I nod sympathetically and make my way up the stairs. Steph's room is in the attic of the house. They converted it to a bedroom and a bathroom when Steph was very little. As I enter the room, I see Britta. She looks at me with sad eyes and shakes her head slowly. I walk in and, lying on the bed in a heap, is Steph. I think she's asleep. I look back at Britta and whisper, "Is she sleeping?"

She nods and stands up. I follow her into the tiny bathroom. "It's bad," she whispers.

"What happened?" I ask quietly.

"Her mom left. She's moving in with some guy that she met at work. She told them some shit about being 'ready to live again.' Apparently she hasn't been happy for a long time."

"I can't believe it! Never in a million years would I have thought...another man? Crazy!" *This explains my greeting downstairs.* "How's she doing?"

"She isn't saying much; she's cried a lot. I think she's still in shock. Now that you're here, I'm going to head home for a bit. It's been a long night." I feel pangs of guilt. *While Steph was dealing with this catastrophe I was enjoying my romantic rendezvous.*

I sit and watch her sleep for a while. After an hour or so, she stirs. "Hey," she says.

"Hey," I say back. "You okay?"

"A bit better I guess. It fucking sucks though."

"Yeah I know. I'm shocked," I say.

"Yeah...I guess I kind of knew that things weren't perfect, but it's not like they were fighting or anything. They were just, like, not really involved in each other's shit anymore. My dad would do his computer stuff. My mom was always saving the less fortunate. I don't know. It's shitty you know?" She cries a little.

"I know," I cry a little too.

A few hours go by and we are sitting eating ice cream, watching *Pretty Woman*. Steph pauses it and asks, "How was the cottage?"

"You really want to talk about this now?" I ask.

"Of course. Besides it'll distract me."

"Well...it happened."

"NO?"

"YES! On the way up I realized that I totally love him and I need to stop worrying about getting hurt and just live."

"Love him? Really?"

"Yeah, but wait...it gets better. So, we get there and he starts playing this romantic classical music."

"Classical? Really?"

"Shut up. It was romantic. We start making out and he carries me upstairs to the bedroom."

"No way."

"Yeah. It was so hot. We fooled around for a bit, and then I just asked him if he had a condom."

"Safety first. I like it," She laughs.

"I'm a safety girl," I giggle, sounding like Julia Roberts from the movie. "I was nervous but it felt so right somehow."

"Did it hurt?" Steph asks.

"A little, but it also felt incredible."

"Did you..." she asks implying the question, 'Did you orgasm?' Steph has had sex a few times but she has never really been impressed. Twice she has described it as 'okay' and 'alright, I guess.' That was probably another reason why I wanted to wait.

"Yes. Once that night and once in the shower in the morning." *I'm glad I waited*, I think to myself.

"The shower?"

"So good."

"You're happy then? No regrets?"

"I am. He even told me he loved me and not in the heat of the moment either."

"I'm happy too, then. Just be careful though. Keep being you. I like you. I wouldn't want you to go changing on me or anything."

"Promise. I think I'm more me now than I have ever been. I even did my geeky Michael Jackson impression in front of him and he still likes me."

"That must be love." She pokes me.

"Shut up and turn the movie back on you jerk." I poke her back.

Steph is dealing with enough right now. I decide to spare her the news that her parents' divorce has also sparked my emancipation from mine. Driving home from Steph's, my thoughts are only on my parents' disappointment. I'm dreading the look on my dad's face. My mom, I know after our conversation, is going to be okay. I know it will take some time for her to get used to the idea of me as a grown up, but she will. My dad however, I'm not so sure. Something about disappointing my dad brings me to a childlike state. I want to curl up in the fetal position and cry at the thought. He has always been a quiet, loving support in my life and I hate the idea that I have damaged our bond. As I pull into the driveway I am overcome by emotion. I sit in my car crying. I'm not sure if it is the Steph thing, my conversation with my mom, or the impending conversation with my dad. Whatever it is has me sobbing on my steering wheel.

I need to pull myself together so I turn up the radio. The song "Round Here" by the Counting Crowes starts. I sit, listen, and breathe. By the middle of the song, I am singing along. It ends. I feel marginally better. I turn the car off and go in to face a different kind of music.

"Hey, I'm home," I call as I walk through the door.

"Hi Em. I'm in the kitchen," my mom calls.

I head upstairs. She is making spaghetti sauce.

"Your brother's coming home to stay for a couple nights," she says. No mention of my 'shacking up.'

"Cool" I say not really caring, but Jay's presence might help with the whole dad thing.

"Where's Dad?" I ask.

"He's watching golf downstairs, but I am not sure you want to talk to him right now. He's still upset. I am too, but I'm trying to give you the benefit of the doubt."

"Thanks Mom." I walk over to her hug her and then head downstairs.

"Hey Dad," I say as I enter the rec room.

He says nothing. He stares straight ahead.

"Dad?"

Still nothing.

"So what, you're not talking to me now?"

"I'm not sure what to say to you."

"I'm sorry if you think I was deliberately lying to you. I wasn't."

"I guess I thought you weren't the kind of girl who, you know, gets with the first boy who pays attention to her," he says.

I'm pissed off immediately but I'm somehow rational enough to realize that I have hurt him and he is just trying to hurt me back. Before I snap back, I pause. I give his words a second to hang in the air – a second for him to hear them and realize that they are not true. Then I say very calmly, "Dad, I'm sorry if I hurt you but this weekend was not like that."

"I trusted you to make good decisions. Trust is a hard thing to earn and now...well...I don't know," he says.

"I know you don't think that I've made a good decision. I get that it's hard for you to see me as a grown up woman. I'm almost twenty years old, Dad. I'm going to have to live with my decisions, not you." That is probably the most grown-up comment I have ever made. I'm not sure how I'm so level-headed, so rational, but man I hope I can keep it up, because the look on his face is killing me.

"What about the next time you come crying through that door? What am I supposed to do then?" he asks frustrated.

"What you have always done. Support me. Love me. Fix me and send me back into the world again." No, that is officially my most grown-up statement. It's like I am channeling Oprah or something.

He gets up of the couch, walks over to me, and bear hugs me. I feel like a child inside his strong arms. It would be nice to stay here, but I need to grow up. He lets me go and as he does, he says, "No car except for work for a month."

I could continue to argue my point about being a grown up, but frankly, it is his car, and I do still live in his house, so I will give him this. Besides, it will make Evan have to work on our relationship a little bit more if he has to be the one with the wheels for a while.

15 You Decide

I have been trying to decide where to take my university undergrad. There are three teacher's college programs I am interested in. One is three hours north of the city. Another is in British Columbia, and the last is just downtown. Each has its pluses and minuses. The program north of the city is probably the best in terms of academic quality and my future hire-ability. Steph has decided to get the fuck out of Dodge, I guess, because of her parent's situation. She is going to BC. If I go with her, I know I won't be disappointed. Then there is the whole Evan thing.

Evan has been living downtown in a condo with Allan and Tom. He chose to go to business school and stay in the city. I don't fool myself into thinking that I'm the reason he stayed, but I like to think that maybe I was a small factor. I'm super happy with him but, like Britta, I'm worried that I'm more into us than he is.

Britta and Tom had been doing their 'friends with benefits' thing for almost two years when she finally broke it off. She says that she realized she was more invested than he was, and it was starting to make her feel like shit. She wanted to be more, but Tom wasn't into that so they split. Things have been a bit awkward ever since.

I have questions about my future with Evan too, but I'm not even sure what they are myself. At twenty-years-old, it is not like I even feel comfortable talking about marriage and stuff. So, what? I don't think I want to move in with him. I like having my freedom during the week. I don't know. Maybe going away to school is an important step for me. The thought hurts my heart. I guess I need to discuss the options with all the players involved.

"So, um, I'm trying to figure out what to do about school. I need to reply to the acceptances I received."

"Well, you know how I feel," Evan says. But I don't.

"Not really."

"I love you Emilia. I would like to have you all to myself, but I understand this is a choice you need to make about your future and you're the only one who can decide what's best for you."

"I don't know what that is."

"Em, I think we're good. Going away is a big deal, though. I'm not sure what that would mean for us."

"So what you are saying is you love me and if I stay here we're good, but if I go away we're not going to make it."

"It's not that simple. I'd like to say we'll be together forever, regardless of your choice. The reality is that if you go away, it'll be very hard to maintain the intensity of the relationship that we have. I just don't want you to fool yourself."

"I get it. I'm not happy about your candor, but I get it."

The rest of the night I'm cold towards Evan. I'm upset that he didn't make me feel like he would walk to the end of the earth to be with me. I guess I either wanted him to beg me to stay or, at the very least, to tell me that time and space won't tear us apart. *Perhaps my conversation with Steph will be more to my liking?*

"So I talked to Evan and he wants me to make my own choice. He did, however, tell me that he doesn't know what will happen to us if I choose to go away."

"I get that," Steph says. "He can't make any guarantees. I think it's cool that he is telling you to make your own choice. At least he isn't being a possessive ass."

That's one way to think about it, I guess. "What do you think I should do?"

"Oh, so you want me to be a possessive ass and say I want you to come with me. I'm not going to do it, Em. You need to decide what's best for your life."

Great, now Steph is leaving me hanging. Frustrating.

16 Lettin' Go

The guys have decided that they want to play poker this weekend. Since Evan is busy and Britta and Steph are newly single, we decide to make a girl's night out of it. I pick Britta up at around nine and head to Steph's dad's apartment. We arrive to find Steph drinking without us.

"You know what's fucked up?" Steph says as we walk through the door. "Tonight I went out for dinner with my mom and she brought that douche-bag boyfriend of hers. She didn't even think to tell me he was coming. Come to think of it, if she had, I wouldn't have gone."

I still can't believe Steph's mom is so incredibly selfish. Doesn't she realize the impact her actions have on her family?

"That sucks, Steph," I empathize. "Are you okay?"

"Yeah. I mean no. I mean, I don't freakin' know. It's not even like he's that bad a guy. I just fuckin' hate him though, you know?"

"Did you have dinner with them?" Britta asks.

"I had several drinks and some pizza before splitting. I just sat there the whole time, not even really talking, just being mad – really, really fuckin' mad! She acts like such a child around him. It's sickening!"

"What can I do? You want me to key his car or something?" I joke as a lame attempt to lighten the mood.

"No, let's just go out tonight and forget about it," she says.

Britta hands us a Vodka cooler each and says, "To forgetting about shit." I think she is still having trouble getting over the Tom thing. He's the only boy I've ever seen her upset over. Even though they were never officially together, Britta hasn't been with anyone else for the past year and a half. She pretended, for Tom, that their relationship was only casual, but it's been clear to me for a while now that she was more serious about him than any other guy – ever.

"To forgetting about shit," we say in unison as we raise our bottles. Clink.

Two hours later and three more drinks in, we call a cab. We head to a bar that has a drag show at midnight. I've never been, but Britta swears it's always a good time. It will also help with the forgetting because tons of straight guys go there too. They're there to prey on all the girls that go for the show, I suppose.

It's elevenish when we arrive. I head to the bar and order shots for my ladies. It's the least I can do to help them forget. Down go the Jello shooters and out come the dance moves. We are having a blast. I haven't seen Britta or Steph as carefree as they are right now. The club has a Spanish flare to it. I'm trying to pick up the hip shaking thing. I'm failing miserably but having so much fun in the process.

Britta hands me her new cell phone. It's one of those cool new flip phones that have just come out. She says, "Do me a favour. Hold this. I don't want to get desperate and call Tom."

I slip it into my back pocket and continue my lame excuse for Salsa. Steph brings another round of drinks and to my surprise, she has a handsome stranger accompanying her. He has dark hair and is tall like Steph. He has a tight, white, v-necked T-shirt hugging his muscular chest. I immediately think, *well done Steph!* He does the shots with us and then begins dancing all over Steph. She's having an awesome time. She is totally going for it. I love seeing her living in the moment.

I turn to see Britta dancing with a tall blond guy. She's less into it than Steph and I realize she needs a save. I move between them to prevent him from gyrating all over her. He turns and begins focusing on the girl behind us. Britta and I walk over to the bar. From there we can get some air while watching Steph with her man.

"Two cherry Jello shots!" I yell to the bartender. As I do, the music grinds to a halt. Lights start flashing and three overly dolled-up drag queens, if that is possible, enter the dance floor. They look like Vegas show girls and I'm envious of their abs and legs. They own the dance floor. They start singing and dancing right in the middle of the bar. Before I know it, one of them has grabbed my hand and I am spinning around the dance floor. I look over to Britta for help only to see that she's being sashayed around herself. I feel stiff and self-conscious. My queen pulls me in close and says in my ear, "Honey, just let go and enjoy." He/she spins me out and then back into him, I mean her. I close my eyes, listen to the music, and let go. We dance like I have never danced before. I am exhilarated and captivated by the rush of energy that flows through my body. It's freeing! It's fun! When I think it cannot get any better my partner pulls me in, grabs both my hips, and flips me right over. It is the craziest thing I have ever done on a dance floor. For a brief moment I'm completely upside down. The song ends and I am sent spiraling back into the crowd. Another girl begins dancing and I am left clapping on the sidelines with everyone else. Steph and Britta come running over. We laugh and randomly talk over one another as we try to make sense of our collective experience.

I'm on such an incredible adrenaline high. I have the uncontrollable urge to call Evan. I leave Britta, Steph, and her mystery man and head to the bathroom. I grab Britta's cool phone out of my pocket and call Evan.

"Hey, you," I say to Evan.

"Emilia, is that you?" Evan asks.

"You're never going to believe what happened to me tonight," I say.

"Are you drunk, Em?" I must be slurring or something.

"This man, I mean woman, I mean queen, told me to let go and I did. It was the most incredible feeling. I went completely upside down."

"Emilia, are you okay? You sound...you aren't making any sense," he says.

"I'm fine. I couldn't be better. Steph's with some guy. She seems happy and Britta, well, she gave me her phone so she won't call Tom."

"Emilia, where are you? I'm coming to get you."

"Evan, I'm fine. I'm having such a great time."

"Emilia, I'm worried about you. Please tell me where you are?"

"Oh shit, there's a guy in the bathroom. He's dressed as a girl but he is still a guy, you know?" I whisper into the phone. I have never seen a guy in the girl's bathroom before. I think it is worth noting.

"Emilia, where are you?"

"Evan, I'm fine. I'll see you tomorrow or maybe I'll sneak into your place late tonight. I looove you!" I slur. Click. I hang up.

I head back to Britta and Steph. Britta and I continue to dance once the show is over. Steph is busy making out with her stallion in a booth by the bathroom.

"I'm really glad we did this," I say to Britta.

"Me too," Britta says, and then I see her cheeks blush with colour as she spots something behind me. I turn just as

Evan grabs me by the shoulders. He looks me up and down. He hugs me and says, "I was so worried." Still consumed by Evan's hug I see Tom and Britta standing in front of one another. I can't hear what they are saying and I look to Britta to gauge her reaction to him. I can't tell if she is excited or upset. She turns away and storms off towards the bathroom. *That can't be good.* Tom follows her.

I pull back from Evan's hug and say, "What are you doing here? I told you I was fine. How did you even know where I was?" He looks out of place. Ever since he started business school he has lost a bit of his edge. He has more of a tailored haircut and his clothes have less of a rocker-vibe to them.

"Emilia, you didn't sound fine, and it wasn't hard to find you; Britta's always talking about this place." He hugs me tighter. "Em, I was so worried about you. If anything ever happened to you...I just love you so much."

"Not enough to make me stay here for school," I say. The alcohol has made me brave.

"Emilia, is that what you think?" I try to avoid eye contact but his hold on my shoulders makes it impossible. "Em, the idea of you going away is killing me. I don't want to stand in the way of your future." There's a brief pause. "What am I going to do when you call in a drunken stupor from hundreds of miles away? How will I come to your rescue then?" He pulls me into his chest.

"Who says I need rescuing?" I push away.

"Fuck Emilia, what do you want me to say?"

"I want you to tell me to stay!" Until I said the words, I didn't know that is what I wanted, but here I am with my new-found drag queen wisdom 'letting go.'

He looks at me so intently, my knees want to buckle. "I want you to choose me. I want you to stay." He picks me up off the ground and kisses me. A new rush of energy flows through me. I wrap my legs around him and we continue to kiss like we are the only ones in the room.

Someone dancing bumps into us and I'm forced back to reality. I see that Allan and Wonderwall-Stoner, I mean Jeff are here too. They look completely out of place. It's comical to watch them try to act macho as they lean against the bar between Cher and a Flamenco Dancer. I remember that Britta and Tom have stormed off and I tell Evan that I'm going to go check on them. I pass by Steph and Rico Suave who are still making out.

Tom is standing outside the girl's bathroom. There's no sign of Britta.

"Everything okay?" I ask Tom. Clearly, because he is out here alone, things are not going well.

"Em, I don't know what to say," he says with his eyes full of hurt.

After my earlier success with my new mantra I say, "Honey, just let go."

Not feeling the mantra quite the way I am, he says, "What's that supposed to mean?"

"Don't over think it. Do what you feel."

"I can't stop thinking about her, Em. But, I have never been the kind of guy that dates or calls, you know?"

"Don't over think it," I repeat. "Just let go."

"Can you get her out here?" he says.

"Go get her yourself," I smile. "This place is very flexible on bathroom genders."

I grab his hand before he can protest and pull him into the 'ladies' room'.

Britta is standing in front of the mirror trying to fix her make-up so that it doesn't look like she has been crying.

I push open a stall and close the door behind me leaving Tom standing with Britta. I feel funny hiding out in the stall but it was my quickest exit and I didn't know what else to do. I stand behind the door and listen.

"What are you even doing in here?" Britta snaps. Their conversation before was obviously heated.

"I'm here for you," he says and my heart melts a little.

"Tom, we've been through this. I'm not some piece of ass you can have whenever you want to. I like you. I really like you and I'm tired of being with you like that."

"Britta, I like you too. I like you a lot. I want to try. I've never done the boyfriend thing before and I'm not sure

I'm going to be any good at it, but I'm not going to over think it. Let's just..."

Let's just what? I can't hear anything. I peek out of the line between the stall and the door to see Britta and Tom kissing. Drag queens have all the answers. I discreetly open the door and sneak past Britta and Tom who are now getting hot and heavy against the wall of the 'ladies' room'.

17 Preemptive Strike

Staying at home for my undergrad is very routine and at times mundane. During the week, I go to classes, study, write papers, work, and watch a lot of *Law and Order*. On weekends, I head to Evan's condo. We usually go to a bar close by and stumble home to have crazy drunken sex. It's fun, but the predictability of it all leaves me feeling like perhaps I'm missing out. Steph's always calling to tell me about this crazy adventure or that frat party. I guess I wonder what life would have been like if I had chosen differently.

School's not easy, but I'm tenacious and I put my head down. I study and write. My grades are good, I guess. I just completed my third year of a five year program when Evan announces to me that he's going to take six months off to travel before starting a job with the bank.

"What do you mean you're going to Europe? What does this mean for us?" I ask. Evan is the only entertaining aspect of my life. I love him. He's my security. I have aligned my future with his. Although I've never said it to him, I envision marriage and babies. I see those things. The rug is being ripped out from under me. We have been together for a little over four years. I have stayed in town for University to be with him and now he's leaving. *What the fuck?*

"Emilia, we're good, but I want to travel the world before I start my career path. I need to get out, explore, and find out what I really want, you know?"

I know. I get it. I question my own choices too, but, my worst fear is that what he wants doesn't involve me. "I get that you want to see the world. I do too. It just scares me that you're doing this without me." Then I have a horrible thought. *Maybe it's us he wants a break from.* My heart's in my throat as I ask the dreaded question, "Are we breaking up?"

"No, babe, it's not like that. I love you so much...I just..." The pause is too long. The pain wells up in me. He is saying one thing but I know what he's doing. I can feel what's coming next in the pit of my stomach. "I guess I want to be free to travel without feeling like a part of me is tied to my life back here."

I want to snap back and say, 'What, I'm tying you down?' but instead I weep a little.

"Oh come on, Em. Don't cry. I'm not even leaving for a month. We don't have to decide anything right now. Emilia, I love you and I have a great time with you. Let's forget about this whole thing for now. We can talk about it later. We've got time."

This is the craziest idea I have ever heard of. Was I just dumped in advance? I have never even considered the concept. So, we will date, fuck, pretend everything is normal and one month from now he will go away and be free to do whatever the hell he wants while he's 'finding himself' like an asshole. Is that honestly what he's proposing? What the fuck am I supposed to do with that? "You know what, Ev. I think I am going to go home now. I'm having a little trouble with the idea that I've been preemptively dumped."

"I'm not dumping you. This is NOT about you, Em. I just need to take some time to be, to decide what I want to be."

Mad. Hurt. Devastated. Crushed. I say, "You can start now. I can't be with someone whose want for the future doesn't include me."

"Em, I know this is a lot to take in but seriously...let's just relax."

"Evan...I don't know what to say. You are choosing the 'what if' over the 'what is.' I have chosen the 'what is' all along. Good fuckin' luck with your 'what if'." I am not entirely sure what I'm saying, but it's all I can come up with in the moment. I end strongly with a firm, "I'm done." I grab my coat, slip on my shoes, and slam the door shut.

On the other side of the door I am overcome by emotion. I frantically push the elevator button hoping that the doors will open before Evan comes after me. I know that if he opens that door I won't have the resolve to go through with this. I hear his footsteps on the floor on the other side of the door. The elevator door opens. Rushing inside, I push the *close door* button. I see Evan's face for a split second before the doors close and the elevator whisks me away.

Fuck! When I arrived, everything was status quo. And now, now I broke up with my best friend. What the fuck am I doing? Who the fuck am I kidding? I cut him loose before he could officially dump me for Europe.

I go home. I'm upset but surprisingly holding it together. *Perhaps my preemptive strike has made me feel a little more in control of the situation. I need to talk to Steph or Britta to really get a handle on my feelings.*

"Hey, you've reached Steph and Shelley we can't come to the phone. Leave us a message and we'll call you back. BEEP." *Shit. Her answering machine. That's not going to help me. It's only going to make me think about how that machine could have said, 'You've reached Steph and Em...' if I had chosen to go to school with Steph years ago. Instead, here I am: no Steph and no Evan, stuck in my fuckin' mundane existence.*

"Steph it's me. Call me when you get a chance." *I sound like I've been crying...I guess because I am slightly.*

I try Britta. "Britta, hey, it's me. Ev and I...we um...we broke up." As the words leave my mouth I begin sobbing. *So I am really upset; good to know.*

"Oh shit, Em. What happened? He didn't?" I know what she is thinking so I cut her off.

"No. He is going to Europe next month and he wants to be free to explore without being tied down." *It sounds even shittier when I say it.*

"So, he broke up with you now?" She sounds confused.

"No, he wanted us to stay together until he leaves. But, I can't stick around knowing that there is an expiration date, you know?"

"You broke up with him?" She sounds shocked.

"Yeah, preemptively."

"Ballsy!" Now she sounds impressed.

"What do you mean, 'ballsy'?"

"Brilliant, actually."

"What? Britta, you're not making any sense."

"Em, the last time you walked out on him you had him wrapped around your little finger. He went from being a player to a boyfriend so fast he may have gotten whiplash along the way."

"Your point?"

"Em, you know that he loves you right?"

"Yeah." *I do know that.*

"So, making him come back to you is your only real move here. He's gonna realize that you're what he wants. If you wait for him like a pathetic sap while he's gallivanting around Europe, he is going to do what he pleases, because he'll know that when he comes home you will fall into his arms. What you're doing is, you're forcing him to actually lose you."

"How is this a good thing?"

"Don't you see? Once he realizes that he's lost you he'll do everything in his power to get you back. Just like last time." *I like the way Britta can spin anything. No wonder she's going into marketing.*

"Britta, but what if he doesn't?" I feel nauseous.

"Em. This is your only real move." *Maybe she's right?*

"Britta, I'm really tired. I've gotta think about this. I'll call you tomorrow."

"Night, Em. Be strong okay?"

"I'll try." Click.

I check my messages before I go to sleep.

"Emilia, I don't know why you are being like this. I'm not breaking up with you. You're being ridiculous. When you get home, call me...I love you." His last words ring in my ears. *Does he really love me? I know he cares for me, but would he be cutting his ties with me to gallivant around Europe if that were true? And, the 'ridiculous' comment...that just makes me fucking mad. Like it's preposterous that I wouldn't want to stick around only to be kicked to the curb in a month. The more I think about it, the angrier I get.* I decide not to call him back. I pull the covers over my head and pass out.

I awake with the phone ringing. It's late. It's three am. My heart's racing from being startled awake.

"Hey, Emmm" Evan slurs.

"Evan?"

"I don't know what flew up your ass tonight. Like you are gonna break up with me," he says, like the notion is unfathomable.

"Evan, have you been drinking? We can talk about this tomorrow," I say giving him an out.

"Em, why don't you come over now. We can have really great make-up sex," he says trying to entice me, but all I hear is a drunken booty call.

"Evan," I say very matter-of-factly, "you are going to Europe with the intention of figuring out life. For you, this doesn't include me. In fact, you have decided you want to free yourself from our relationship to do so. I am NOT being ridiculous. I'm NOT coming over to fuck you and I'm NOT some pathetic groupie who is going to pine for you while you sow your wild oats. I love you Evan and as much as it hurts, I have to do this..."

"Emilia, come on this is crazy. I'm only going for six months. You can't let me go and have some fun?"

"That's just it Evan. Your fun should never involve other women. That's not cool with me. The fact that you don't realize that you're putting us in jeopardy really fucks me up."

"Em, it's not like I am going to Europe to get laid. I just don't want to always be worried about you, calling you and stuff."

"Well Ev, this way you won't have too. Goodbye, Evan."

"Em..." CLICK. I hang up because I don't want to hear anymore bullshit justifications. For the first time I feel like I am making the right decision. *I guess Britta's right. This is my only move. He's expecting me to pine for him and take him back guilt-free after he has had his fill of European pussy. Ugh!* The thought is revolting. I lay awake and consider the possibility of life without Evan. It's a foreign thought.

18 Ugly Cry

Evan has been a huge part of my life for four years now. Suddenly, is dawns on me that cutting him out of my life is crazy. Everything reminds me of him. This morning, I find myself bawling my eyes out as I put my jeans on because I have just found a movie stub from *High Fidelity* in the pocket. We saw it together a couple weeks ago. My tears actually cause the ink to run on the crinkled up scrap of paper because it reminds me of how Evan and I love mixing peanut M&M's into our big vat of popcorn at the theatre. It's something stupid and meaningless, I know, but to me, it's the kind of thing we wouldn't do with anyone else. It's our thing. *Now...we don't have a thing anymore. I miss him. I miss 'us'. Sniff, sniff.*

I have to strip the bulletin board above the desk in my room. I can't bare to see the photos of us posing at prom, lounging on the dock at the cottage or in Allan's hot tub. The hardest one to put away, though, is the picture where I am sitting with my back nestled against Evan's chest, his arms draped casually around me, and he is looking over my shoulder with such love in his eyes. It captures the Evan I adore.

It's strange, as I put the photo into to the desk drawer, I think about the fact that Evan has changed so much since it was taken. *He isn't the same edgy, confidence-oozing boy anymore. Now, he seems so grown up. He's all about making his way in the business world. Maybe he has lost himself a little. Maybe he does need to find himself? Why does he think he has to do it in Europe, though? Why does he have to do it without me? I don't want to do anything without him.*

A few weeks pass. I feel like I have no life. It's so difficult to plan a night out with anyone because after four years Evan and I share all the same friends; not that I'd be good company anyway. So, I stay in and bond with my oversized white duvet.

I know that I may run into him before he leaves, but I have already decided that I can handle it. I can be strong. I've listened to Cake's version of "I Will Survive" probably a thousand times. It's my new mantra.

Working at the camp helps. The kids are great and I think the experience is really preparing me for teaching. My courses at university feel so far removed from the real world. The camp gives me a chance to get down on the floor with the little ones and really find out what makes them tick. I like that I can draw from their interests and we can really learn together. Thank goodness for this opportunity because otherwise I would spend twenty-four seven wallowing. Plus, I am so tired after work that I don't have too much trouble sleeping.

Evan keeps leaving messages, but none of them say what I want to hear.

It's the week before Evan is scheduled to leave for Europe and I've managed to stay away from him for three whole weeks. It has taken all of my will power and several pep talks from Britta and Steph.

After the end of my shift at work, I walk through the parking lot towards my car, like always. Only this time is different, I see him – Evan is there in the parking lot. He is standing beside my car. *Fuck. I want to run to him, throw my arms around him, and tell him not to go. I want him to hold me, kiss me, and love me, only me forever.*

I take a deep breath, clear the lump from my throat, and walk with my head held high to the car.

"What are you doing here?" I ask.

"You won't answer any of my calls."

"Evan, I can't do this."

"I know, Emilia. It wasn't fair of me to put you in the position I did. It has taken me a while to see that but I didn't want to go knowing things between us are shitty." I want to hug him. I feel the tears welling up in my eyes, but I know I have to stand my ground. I hear Cake's "I Will Survive" start up in my head and I muster some strength.

"When do you leave?" I ask as I look down at my feet trying to avoid eye contact.

"Thursday" he says. *That's just three days from now.* "I miss you, Emilia."

"I miss you too, Evan."

He reaches out and pulls gently at one of my curls. I close my eyes and try to hold on to the feeling. *This may well be the last time I feel the slight tug.* I can't help myself. I throw my arms around him and bury my head into his chest. Tears stream down my face, but I don't make a sound. I sniff his natural scent, trying desperately to somehow keep it with me. He kisses the top of my head like you would a small child, and I become aware that he is really letting me go. *He is embracing his trip and trying to find closure before he leaves.* The thought is devastating. *Britta's plan had not accounted for him wanting to be free and me making it easier on him.*

I take a deep breath, wipe my tears with my hand, look up at Evan, and say with all the sincerity I can muster, "I hope you find what you are looking for."

"Thanks, Em. You're gonna be fine, you know. I love you so much. I have to do this for me." He opens my car door and motions for me to get in. I am still struck by his ability to quietly and commandingly motion his will upon me. I climb in. He leans in and kisses me lightly on the lips. He closes the door. I feel a warm tear fall down my cheek and roll under my chin. I put the key in the ignition, blink slowly, trying to will myself to drive away. Turning the key, I put the car in drive and pull out. I can see Evan growing smaller in my side mirror as I pull away. I turn right out of the parking lot and immediately make the next right so I am onto a residential street.

I pull over and sob. I cry the ugly cry; the sniffly, boogery cry of an inconsolable woman. *I have lost him. I have lost Evan.* It's like something out of a movie. As I sit there Greenday's "Goodriddance" a.k.a. "Time of Your Life" comes on the radio. I hadn't even noticed the radio was on and until now. It's as if the D.J. from the radio station is customizing a soundtrack for my life. The words dig a bigger cavity in my heart. The physical pain is insurmountable. I sit there for what seems like an eternity. My eyes are bloodshot and swollen. They sting as I begin the drive home. I pull right into the garage and enter directly into the basement of the house. I deliberately avoid seeing anyone, heading right to bed to stay there. It's days before I surface for anything more than basic life necessities: food, water, and bathroom breaks. I call in sick to work. I'm no use to anyone anyway.

19 What's Stopping Me

The next week is marginally easier, not much, but easier. The week after that, I even smile once or twice. After the first month, I am numb but functioning. Going back to school helps, but I find myself comparing everyone to Evan. Random things happen at school and I automatically want to tell Evan. I miss him but I am okay. *I'm okay, I guess.*

While in the computer lab researching something for my thesis, an email pops up in my inbox:

evan@notmail.com ~ Subject: Shark!!!

Hey Emilia,

I am in the South of France visiting my cousin and the most amazing thing happened. The fishermen down at the pier were teaching me how to catch an octopus. While I was trying, a large shark started swimming around me. I froze when I saw his dorsal fin. He circled me for a minute or two, grabbed a fish, and swam off. I have never been so scared or felt so exhilarated before in my life. It was so crazy. I wish you were here to see it. Emilia, this place is beautiful. The internet café, however costs a fortune.

Talk soon <3 Ev

I read the email a hundred times. 'I wish you were here to see it.' I'm not sure what to think. I craft my reply.

emilia@notmail.com ~ Subject: Evan Crusoe

Ev,

You in shark infested water? I would love to see that. I am so glad you are enjoying yourself.

Life here is good. I am going to try some new things myself. I'm actually going to a university pub crawl this weekend for the first time. I guess you could say I am the only fourth year frosh.

Hope you are having a great adventure :). Where are you headed next?

<3Em

It was about a week later when I received a reply. I must have checked my emails a hundred times a day in between.

evan@notmail.com ~ Subject: Pub crawling?

Em,

I hope you didn't have too much fun living it up frosh-style. I am crazy jealous thinking about all those first year shits rubbing up against you on the dance floor.

I have been on a train overnight so I am exhausted. I am in Rome. Everything here has so much history. It is really cool. I am hanging out with a couple of other guys who are passing through as well. I have to say I am enjoying the freedom of backpacking around, but, it can be lonely too.

Love, Ev

He's jealous, hanging out with guys (not girls), and lonely? I have to say, this is not what I was expecting. I need to reply.

emilia@notmail.com ~ Subject: Trip Envy

Ev,

I would love to see Rome. I hope you are taking all kinds of pictures. Are you doing the touristy museum, chapel, cathedral thing or are you living amongst the Romans?

I am glad you are enjoying the sights and that you have found some friends to explore with. Over the last few weeks I have been branching out too. Having you gone has forced me to socialize with people at school for the first time. They're nice, but I get what you mean about being lonely too.

Love, Em

evan@notmail.com ~ Subject: Thinking about you

Em,

I have been hanging out in Prague for the last week. I love it here but I finally realized why I have been feeling so isolated. I miss you. I am with two really good traveling friends but I can't shake the sense that I want to share all of this with you. I love you Emilia.

Your Evan

Ah! I am not sure what to think. I read the email again and again. The smile on my face is goofy. I can't seem to stop smiling, though. I'm happy, truly happy for the first time in months. *Should I be happy? He did leave me for the prospect of something better. Just because he didn't find it, am I supposed to leap back to his side? Probably not, but it is all I want to do.* I begin to respond to the email. It takes me two days to come up with:

emilia@notmail.com ~ Subject: re: My Evan

I miss you too.

Love, your Emilia

evan@notmail.com ~ Subject: Xmas break

Emilia,

I need to see you, pretty girl! When is your Xmas break? Can you meet me in Europe? There is so much I want to show you. Please say you'll come. I will help with expenses. You name the place, I will be there.

On my knees here,

Evan

P.S. I would love to show you Monaco.

I have never wanted to do anything more. It has been four months since we have been together. I thought by now I would have moved on, or at least be thinking about other possibilities. I have been out to pub crawls, to a frat party, on two dates (Britta fix-ups). I have not so much as kissed another guy though. I didn't want to. None of them made me feel anything close to the way I feel when I'm with Evan.

Our time apart has shown me that I really wasn't missing anything. *Life with him is far better than life without him. And fuck, I have never been to Europe. What's stopping me?*

I try to figure out how to reply. *I don't want to seem too desperate. I am taking a huge risk jumping on a plane for him.* I decide to be guarded with my feelings...to reply more as a friend than a girlfriend.

emilia@notmail.com ~ Subject: Monaco Dec. 10th

Evan,

I would like to see you too! My last exam is the 9th. I can leave on the 10th, but I have to be back by the 24th to spend Christmas with my family. Can we swing Paris too?

<3 Em

evan@notmail.com ~ Subject: Paris, I am in!!!

I can't wait to see you, mi amore! I will call you tomorrow, five pm your time. I want to hear your voice so badly. We can make plans then. Look into flights if you get a chance.

LOVING YOU!!! Ev

I was at school when I got the email. I think, based on time zones, that he means he is going to call me tonight. He probably sent the email late last night. I go directly to the travel agency at school and find two potential flights. I also find myself doing silly things all day in anticipation of his call.

I put on make-up and buy a new shirt. Rationally, I know he cannot see me over the phone but for some reason I feel the need to make myself presentable. Maybe I'm just trying to make the time tick by faster.

Five o'clock rolls around and I am staring at the phone. I am willing it to ring. After about ten minutes, it finally does.

"Hello?"

"Hello, Emilia." My heart races as his husky tone massages my name.

"Evan, I'm so excited about traveling around France," I say, because I am.

"I can't believe you're coming. You're amazing, you know that?" He strokes my ego.

"I've always wanted to explore Europe." I decide not to stroke his ego back.

"You're going to love Monaco. My cousin has a place for us to stay. It is unlike any other place I have seen. I stayed there for almost a month so I know all the ins and outs."

We talk about details for several minutes and then it becomes apparent that his calling card is running out of money.

"Em, I've gotta run but I want you to know. I'm sorry and I want us to be us again."

"Evan...(I pause to think)...let's see how we feel when we see each other."

"I love you Emilia," he says and I melt a little.

"I love you too, Evan," I say with 100% honesty. *I'm not quite sure if that will be enough this time. I was so broken by him. Maybe I will be too guarded to let him back into my life. I want to try.* I am afraid though.

Over the next couple of weeks, I decide that I need to keep an open mind and heart. My parents are not thrilled with the idea of me taking off to Europe and I suppose convincing them that I am making a good decision is convincing me as well. I want so badly for my happily ever after to be with Evan. I'm a realist though. I only want it if it feels right.

20 Not Every Girl Can Work a Towel

I am standing at the baggage carousel in Nice, waiting for my tattered old red suitcase. I borrowed it from my mom. It has seen many worldly adventures. I've packed every classy outfit I own into the small pathetic looking bag. I'm all too aware that I am not going to fit into the opulent lifestyle associated with the South of France. I feel like a bit of an impostor even attempting to dress up for the trip, but I don't want to stand out. Plus, I want to make an effort for my reunion with Evan. Wearing my only pair of designer jeans, a white tee shirt, and a leather jacket I borrowed from Britta, I become increasingly nervous standing here. I watch as several other passengers collect their belongings. Suddenly, I have Evan's familiar hands covering my eyes.

"Guess who," he says playfully.

"Pierre?" I say giggling.

He drops his hands spins me around, hugs me, and says in a gruff playful tone, "Who's this Pierre?"

I pull out of his hug to see his face. He has a scruffy stubble. It's so hot! His eyes pierce into me as a smirk hits his lips. He pulls me close again back into his arms. His embrace is so comforting. I fit so perfectly against him. My senses are alive. I can feel his heart beating against me. His Evan-scent is intoxicating. I try desperately to capture all aspects of this moment. Everything about him is so captivating. I'm at ease and self-conscious all at once. His touch is invigorating. I missed it so much. Still hugging, I feel his hand move lower so it lightly caresses my lower back and sends a tingle that travels throughout my body.

Out of the corner of my eye I see my red suitcase circling the carousel. Reluctantly, I pull away and grab it before it disappears through a small luggage shoot in the wall.

"Is that all you have?" Evan asks.

"Yep, this is it," I say.

"Great, let's go!" He grabs my bag and motions for me to follow him. Man, have I missed his motioning. This is the first chance I have had to really look at him. He looks so trendy, put together even, in his white dress shirt and grey wool pants. They hang off his body like they were made for him. Except for his scruffy stubble beard, he is polished. I like European-Evan.

We get outside. It is late and the moon is high in the sky. There is a fancy red sports car waiting for us. A very British looking guy jumps out of the driver's seat and throws his arms around me.

"It's great to meet you, Emilia. Evan has told me all about you. He would not stop talking about you, quite frankly," he jests.

I am totally at a disadvantage because I know almost nothing about this guy. I know he is Evan's cousin and that he lives here, but I am struggling to remember if Evan has even told me his name.

"I am so glad to meet you too. Thank you so much for picking me up and setting us up with a place to stay." I skillfully avoid using this name.

"Nigel's the best!" Evan says as he stows my luggage in the trunk.

Nigel...Nigel. How am I going to remember that? I try to commit it to memory.

Evan holds the door open for me and I clamber into the back. It is a beautiful car but the backseat is perhaps better suited for a small child. I find my knees are uncomfortably close to my chin. In no time, we speed down a highway headed for Monaco. The road is winding and Nigel is driving like a Formula One racer. I'm seriously afraid for my life, crammed in the back of this little rocket, as they chit chat in the front. I can't help thinking – *Didn't Grace Kelly fly off one of these cliffs?* – as we weave through the mountains. As we approach Monaco, the traffic is minimal and I ease up on the handle of the car that I have been white knuckling the whole ride.

Evan reaches his hand back discretely and finds my ankle. He begins a slow circling assault on my senses. I can't help but remember our first night together. It is magical the way his fingers can entrance me. I sit perfectly still and focus all my attention on the couple of inches he is masterfully igniting. *Oh, how I have missed him. How have I gone without this feeling? How have I gone without him?*

A pang of emotional pain hits me in the chest. I am elated to be here with him, but the hurt of his choice to come here 'sans' me was just so devastating. I'm torn by my pleasurable reaction to his touch and my haunting memories of the misery he has put me through. My uncertainty about this trip comes to the forefront of my brain. *What am I doing?*

"This is us," Evan croons from the front seat as he pulls his hand away from my leg. 'Us'. The word resonates with me. The absence of his touch is immediately mourned by my skin. Cold air surrounds my freshly charged ankle.

Nigel pulls up outside a closed bakery. He stops the car and we get out. My body is relieved. I stretch unconsciously. Across the street, I can see a little café on the water and a few sailboats in the port. The moonlight shimmers off the ripples of the Mediterranean Sea. It's beautiful and utterly peaceful. I can hear the water lapping against the concrete of the port. I take a deep breath of the cool crisp air and try to shake off some of the exhaustion from my flight. My nerves made sleeping impossible last night and the time difference is starting to mess with me. I need to pull myself together.

Evan lifts my bag from the trunk and then man-hugs his cousin.

"Thanks again for the ride," I say.

Nigel peels away. Evan motions for me to follow him. The street is empty. It is December. It is cold, but not overly so. I'm Canadian after all. We approach a door beside the bakery. It's glass except for the lock. Evan inserts his key and we are standing in an extravagantly decorated, but extremely small, marble or maybe granite lobby. There is a small table with a vase of beautiful fresh white flowers, mailboxes, an elevator, and that's about it. The intoxicating smell of the flowers, lilies I think, is distracting. It is so odd to see such lovely spring blossoms at this time of year. Evan gives me a devilish grin and I immediately know what he is up to.

"I should warn you," he says as we wait for the elevator. "These condos are tax havens. Nigel's buddy owns this one. It is worth millions but only because of its ability to save the owners millions. The one we are going to stay in is ridiculously small. You'll see. I kind of like the idea of being in very close quarters with you though." His devilish grin returns.

"Behave," I scold, totally kidding.

"Not a chance," he quips back.

Everything about the building is small but nothing, not even his warning, prepares me for how small the condo unit is. It is one room with a murphy-bed that folds out of the cupboard on the wall. The other cupboard is deceiving as well. It is actually the kitchen, if you could call it that. It is a stove, sink, and fridge in a closet. I could cook breakfast from bed in this place. The bathroom is nothing to write home about either. I'm amazed that my expectation of opulence is not at all being realized. This place is a facade. But, as I head out onto the practically non-existent balcony, I feel suddenly at home. Evan comes behind me and puts his arms around my waist. Looking down I realize that there are small coins covering the balcony. I look over onto the neighbouring balcony. It's covered in them too.

"What's with all the coins?" I ask.

"They're pence. They are worth about half a penny. Nobody really uses them here," he explains.

"So people just throw money out?" I ask.

"I guess so," he says. "Sometimes people don't know the value of what they have and they carelessly throw it away."

"Is that so?" I say knowingly.

Oh, my. That look on his face is so...he spins me around and kisses me like his life depends on it. His lips are softer then I remember. Opening my mouth his tongue slips in and teases mine. My insides are on fire. It has been so long that everything feels new. His hands are powerful and commanding as they stroke my back and head. His stubble is rough and foreign to me. I love the way it hurts a bit. My breasts press against his chest. I feel my nipples perking up. He pushes me against the railing and the metal presses into me. His erection is now hard against me. He kisses my neck and I let out a lustful moan. I push him in through the open door into our 'opulent suite.' We fumble, not wanting to stop touching each other as we lower ourselves onto the bed. He lets go of me as my back hits the bed.

He is watching me so intently, his fixation is arousing. He kneels on the bed in front of me as he removes his shirt. His muscles are exposed. I run my hand down his pecs. He groans and I respond by tossing my white shirt on the floor. He nuzzles my boobs as he reaches back and unfastens my bra. Seductively, I pull one strap off and then the other, and flip it to the side of the bed. He takes my nipple in his mouth, suckles, and nips. It instantly perks up even more. His tongue circles. He pulls away leaving me wanting more, and then as I am about to protest, he begins again. *It's part of his game. He's toying with me.*

His hand skims my skin as he lowers it and begins undoing my jeans. He climbs down the bed and kisses on top of my underwear as he removes my pants. He begins to take off my panties. They give him some trouble so he takes them in both hands and tears them apart. He is so forceful in this moment, I've never seen him like this. It is incredible! His tongue starts frantically and skillfully caressing my sex. His stubble brushes against my thighs. I rock gently against him. My hips take on a life of their own. His fingers thrust into me. I feel my juices well up. I am all of a sudden driven by an overwhelming urge to have him inside me.

"Oh please, Evan," I beg as I try to bring him up on top of me.

"Not so fast, you," he says as he intensifies the pressure on my clit. The pressure...the sensation...there is nothing that equals this state of being! I arch my back and "OOOOHHH...aaahhh."

"That's my girl," he murmurs oozing with pride.

He slides up beside me on the bed and begins kissing me. It only occurs to me now that he is still wearing his grey pants. *Oops, perhaps I should have taken care of them earlier.* Still kissing me, I begin to pull his pants off; then, each sock in turn. I slow my actions to tease him a little – to build the intensity of his anticipation. Feeling brave, I roll him on his back and straddle him. Mockingly I pretend to tear his boxers off. He laughs and purrs, "I hope you packed more of those."

I remove his boxers and begin fondling his cock. It is bigger than I remember. I let my tongue touch the tip. He is leering expectantly at me. I lick around the tip focusing my attention on the head of the penis. He closes his eyes and hums slightly. I take the whole thing in my mouth and suck, at first lightly, and then I increase my force. I put my hand on his balls and massage gently to compliment his blow job. I am all powerful in this instant. I'm seductive, controlling, calm, and calculating. It's a rush unto itself. Just as I feel him about to burst, he sits up and raises me up. He grabs his pants from the floor and pulls out a condom. He rolls it onto his dick. I straddle him and lower myself on top of him. He is so deep inside me. We fuck. Harder and harder. In and out, in and out, in and...out. When he is all the way inside me, he hits a spot that craves attention. I ache to be driven and the pounding is the only thing that satisfies me. I begin quivering. This time my release has a more relaxing intensity. My euphoria is followed instantly with a sense of utter calm. I feel him cum and I fall to his chest. We lay there, neither of us able to articulate. Several minutes go by and I feel him slipping out of me. I roll off him and head for the bathroom.

I grab a towel and wrap it around me. Staring into the bathroom mirror, I am flushed and I have that unmistakable I-have-just-been-fucked-hair. As I freshen up, questions bombard my brain. *What does this mean? Shouldn't we have had an intimate conversation before hopping into bed? Am I setting myself up for heartache? Has he been fucking around this whole trip? Now that he's coming home, am I playing into his hand?* My last question makes him seem so sinister. Before our break up I wouldn't have thought of Evan as conniving. But, now...well I guess I am wary. *He used to be a major player and there was nothing holding him back here. What have I done? How can I do this? But, it's*

Evan. How can I not? Does this make me some kind of doormat? Am I official one of those pathetic women who allow themselves to be used? I'm stronger than that aren't I? I feel sick. As I examine my teeth in the mirror, I decide that a conversation is necessary. I tuck a crazy tendril of hair behind my ear and head for the bedroom. Well, I guess it is technically the bedroom, living room, and the kitchen, but whatever.

Evan is lying in bed. His smile is contagious as he motions for me to join him. He pats the pillow. I crawl up the bed and sit beside him. For the first time, I'm having difficulty looking him in the eye. In my peripheral vision I can see him trying to focus my gaze, but I continue to look down at the towel that is covering me. I'm nervous and my body language must convey it.

"What's wrong?" he says in a gentle prodding tone.

"Nothing," I lie, not sure how to bring up the conversation.

"Emilia, I know you. What is it? You want to say something but you are afraid how I'll react right?" he says and then his tone changes to one of concern and shock. "You didn't...with someone else when we weren't together?"

"No," I reassure him. "I went out on a couple of dates and stuff – you know Britta – but no, nothing really happened."

"Oh," he says sounding relieved.

"What about you?" I put it out there trepidatiously.

"Em, I'm not going to lie. I had several opportunities to 'hang out' with other girls. But, when it came down to it, something was always lacking. Sure, it could have been fun. But the truth is, I didn't feel the same spark I feel when I am with you."

I grimace at the thought of him having 'fun' with other girls. He grabs my chin and turns my face to meet his. Looking intently at me he says, "Emilia, I love you. You are the one I want to be with."

He kisses me and plays with a curl. *I want so badly to buy in. I want to be reassured but something from within is nagging. Maybe time will help? Maybe I will have a clearer perspective in the light of day?* I rest my head on his chest and drift off to the sound of his breathing while he strokes my hair.

The morning comes quickly. The time difference thing is still messing with me a bit. Light fills the room and the starkness of the room becomes evident. There's no room for furniture. There isn't even a picture on the wall. I realize that other than the bed, there is no place to sit down. I don't think I have ever been in an apartment that didn't have a chair before. Evan is sitting on the bed. He's dressed and looks as if he has been up for a while.

I'm lying here covered only by a blanket, completely naked. My towel is in a little ball buried in the covers. I use my feet to shimmy the towel up to a point where I can grab it with my hands. I bashfully attempt to wrap it around myself while I'm still hidden under the duvet. Evan smirks like he thinks I'm funny. I guess he's seen it all before, but in this harsh light, I would prefer to keep it under wraps. I fumble out of bed and make my way to my beat-up suitcase. I grab it with one hand and re-enforce the security of my towel with the other. Looking less than graceful I head for the bathroom. Evan's eyes are glued to me.

"You are...I just love you so much," he laughs. I must look more ridiculous than I thought.

"Yah, well, not every girl can work a towel," I quip as I close the door.

I spend longer than usually prepping myself. I put on a tight v-necked blue sweater and my designer jeans. I even take the time to add blush and mascara. When I come out of the bathroom Evan is gone. In his place, there is a ripped piece of paper. I read the note.

Look across the street.

The café on the water.

I will be waiting with a Parisian Cocoa.

Love, Evan

I open the balcony door and spy the café. The view is gorgeous. The port is quiet. It must be the off season this close to Christmas. There is something marvelous about the idea of having the place to ourselves. I grab my passport/money holder thingy, put on my/Britta's leather jacket and head out.

The café is exactly as I would picture it. The man behind the counter is weathered and speaks only French. It's the kind of place that has been handed down in his family for generations. This is not only a café, it is his second home. It has pictures and framed newspaper clippings all over the walls. Multiple jars and tins house numerous teas and coffees. Freshly made biscotti are spread out on the counter. Evan is conversing with the old man fluently. I have always known that he went through French immersion in school but I have never heard him speak French before. There is something so intoxicating about it. When his eyes meet mine I make out that he is introducing me.

"C'est la fille que je vous ai parlé. Mon Emilia. Elle est l'amour de ma vie." The words dance melodically in the air. *I wish I knew what he was saying.*

"Elle est une fille très belle. Vous êtes un homme chanceux. Ne la laissez pas s'échapper Monsieur Evan," the man replies. The words are less magical from his lips.

"Vous êtes très sage Etienne," Evan says, and now I am getting kind of annoyed. I am starting to feel completely left out.

I nod and smile at the man. Evan takes my hand and leads me to a table facing the water.

"What were you two saying?" I ask.

"We were just agreeing that I shouldn't let you get away."

"Oh," I blush.

We sit and talk about Evan's travels. He tries to paint me a picture of this place bustling with tourists, of the harbour full of extravagant yachts, and of fisherman camping out for hours along the water's edge. There is such life in his voice as he recounts his shark adventure. This is the Evan I adore. Europe has restored his confidence. He isn't edgy the way he once was, but he has a carefree relaxed style that's so attractive. He seems so comfortable in his own skin. It's easy to get lost in his charisma. We sit for hours talking and sipping away at the most incredible, thickest hot chocolate I have ever tasted. I'm enthralled and delighted by the ease of our interaction. There is no awkwardness. *We are us.* It is so familiar and comforting. *We are us*, I think again and I know that regardless of my misgivings, I'm in this. *I am Evan's once more.*

We leave the café and head out for a walk. It's cold, but with Evan's arm around me, I am warmed in a deeply satisfying way. We walk along the water's edge and then up the hill. Everything seems uphill. He shows me the palace. It's massive. Its light, creamy colour seems so inviting. We get a lady to take a picture of us standing in front of its arched architecture. I love the intricate cobblestones everywhere. The buildings facing the palace are gorgeous as well. The scale of everything is intimidating. *I bet the owners of these places can't make breakfast from their beds. Actually they probably hire a Michelin-starred chef to make them breakfast.* These places scream wealth and opulence beyond my wildest imagination. It starts to snow lightly and we meander along some small sidewalks towards a little restaurant that Evan frequented during his stay. He insists I try the nicoise salad. It's délicieux!

     We continue to weave our way through the city. It's quite the leg work out. He takes me to a strip of high-end boutiques. Evan wants to go in one of the stores, but I'm anxious to get back to our little suite. Monaco itself is lovely, but being here with Evan is what makes it epic for me.

21 Nous Aurons Toujours Paris

Monaco is quiet and relaxing. All the little quirks that make me love Evan are only intensified by our constant close quarters. I'm utterly smitten.

Today we travel to Nice to take the train to Paris. I'm so excited. We arrive in Nice at noon and we purchase tickets for an overnight train ride to Paris. This will save us one night's accommodations. Neither of us has any real money to speak of, so any savings is worthwhile. It is the week before Christmas and everything is decorated beautifully. By early evening we find ourselves in a park near the train station. It's surrounded on all sides by the hustle and bustle of the busy city's traffic. It is like a whimsical paradise amongst the grind of the real world. To make it even more extraordinary, every tree is covered in Christmas lights. The little twinkling gems are enchanting. I grab Evan's hand and take him into a small grocery store. We stock up on baguettes, soft mozzarella, jam, and wine. We head back to the park and have an impromptu picnic. We camp out on a bench, right beside a small bridge over a frozen stream. We watch as couples stroll hand in hand past us. It feels like a dream. It's romance defined as I lean against his shoulder. We pass a bottle of Merlot between us. The faint sound of a street performer playing the violin in the distance becomes the pinnacle of our ambience. *If only we could freeze time and stay in this moment forever.*

The train ride is long and uncomfortable. I doze off briefly, but for the most part it's a restless night. Evan seems quite at home on the train. He did this night traveling thing a lot during his trip.

We arrive as the sun is starting to appear on the horizon. The red hues of the sun rising in the sky make the empty Paris streets seem enchanted somehow. We use our travel guide to navigate our way to a little hostel in the middle of the city. We figure we will be able to travel to all the major attractions easily from here.

We check in. Evan pays extra for a private room with a bath tub. He knows me too well. I have always preferred baths and the place in Monaco only had a shower. I've been craving a tub for days. We make our way up the spiral staircase to our room. It's lovely. It has a pretty window with two chairs facing it. It opens onto the street below. It will be a fantastic spot to have tea and croissants in the morning. We will be able to watch the comings and goings of the world below.

Standing at the window admiring the view, I hear Evan break out into gales of laughter in the bathroom. I rush over to see what's so funny. He is sitting fully dressed with his knees pressed up against his chin in the smallest bath tub I have ever seen. "I'm glad I paid extra for this," he chuckles.

"It's the thought that counts." I giggle at the sight of him.

He grabs my hand and pulls me on top of him. We are a mass of limbs trying to vie for space as he plants a kiss on my lips. I begin to kiss him back and his hands take me by surprise. He begins tickling me frantically. I erupt into a hysterical fit of laugher. I try to fight back but he is much stronger and I'm quickly overpowered. He lifts me out of the tub. I am a ball of giggles as he puts me down on the bed. He has both of my hands tightly gripped together with one of his. His free hand continues its tickle-assault.

"No...please...Evan...please!" I squeal totally at his mercy.

"Please, Evan, what?" He toys with me.

"Stop...Evan...stop, please."

Still rendering my hands useless with his, he pins my arms over my head and fervently kisses me. My gales of laughter are squelched by its intensity. The extremes of tactile sensation are overwhelming. A warm rush flows through me. I melt into his movements. I feverishly pull against his restraining grip but give in to the constant pressure as his free hand finds its way inside my pants. His legs pin mine as his fingers dip down under my panties. His kiss, my arms over my head, his fingers, my...so many things...*oh my.*

He releases my hands, his lips still pressed firmly against mine. I run my hands down his back as he makes quick work of removing my pants. Our lips part, he removes his pants and shirt in an instant. As I am bringing my shirt over my head, he pulls at my sock, running his hand firmly down my instep and resuming his fiendish tickling. I squirm as he peels the other sock off and prepare for the unbearable sensation on my foot. I sit up and try to get a couple pokes into him myself, my hands pawing at his torso. He smirks and seizes my hands once more. This time his nakedness is restraining my entire body.

"Ah...Evan...plea..se," I struggle.

"Shhh," he whispers in my ear and gently feathers kisses from my ear to my mouth. His tongue invades. I welcome it. He shifts and continues the gentle caressing of his lips down my neck to my breasts. It feels incredible. As he makes his way down, my nipples perk up to greet him. He lets go of my hands. I stretch them out first and then traipse my fingers over his muscular shoulders. He groans and trails his kisses along my stomach over my belly button. Lower still. I am pulling at his hair as his fingers brush over my thighs and meet his mouth at my apex. His tongue flicking my clitoris and his fingers pressing in past my folds.

"Mmmm," he hums and I echo his sentiment.

All thoughts have vanished from me. My synapses are otherwise occupied. He knows exactly how I work, where to touch, how much pressure to exert, when to push, when to pull. I feel the closeness of my orgasm as sensation builds. He knows too.

He stops abruptly. I'm reeling, but I don't have to wait long. In a flash, Evan has a condom on and is inside me. His rhythm is building me right back up, even higher this time.

"Emilia...yes," he exclaims loudly.

The sound of his pleasure rising is my undoing. I explode under him, quaking. Three final thrusts and he joins me, his weight, once again, pinning me to the bed. Now however, there is no fight left in either of us. I shift my weight to the side and he rolls off of me. Our breathing is ragged. A goofy grin is etched across my face. *I am so his.*

We settle in and decide that the rest of today will be a sleepy relaxing day and our real tourist adventures will begin tomorrow. Over the next few days we visit the Louvre and a couple smaller art galleries. We eat as many Nutella and banana street crepes as humanly possible. We go to a special church-service to hear the bells of Notre Dame.

My favourite by far, is the ice skating beside the Cathedral. The romance of it all is unbelievable as a light dusting of snow fills the air. We circle the rink for hours holding hands. The cold stings my cheeks but I am so captivated by Evan in this moment that nothing could spoil the allure of it all.

It's our last full day in Paris. It is December 22nd and life awaits us back home. I wake up and Evan is nowhere to be seen. We had planned to get up early to travel to the Eiffel Tower, and then to walk along the Champs-Élysées to see the shops and the Arc de Triomphe. I'm surprised that he's not here. While I'm getting myself ready, I hear Evan enter the room.

"Hey you, where were you?" I ask.

"I picked up some breakfast and I had some things to take care of," he says.

Intrigued I inquire, "What kind of things?"

"Oh, it was nothing," he says, but I sense he's hiding something. He is acting kind of strange, a bit fidgety. Now I am really intrigued, but I decide to drop it and investigate further later. I'm eager to see the Eiffel Tower.

We take the subway. It is a pretty cool transit system, very complex compared to what I'm used to, but we manage. My anticipation builds as we head toward the tower. I have seen photos of it all my life and I've always wanted to see it firsthand. On our approach I'm faced with a sad reality. It is covered on one side with scaffolding and a giant electronic billboard advertising some radio station. Apparently it is being cleaned. *I guess this is the Eiffel Tower's off season too.* I am thoroughly disappointed. Evan seems even more fidgety. *What's with him?*

"This isn't what I was expecting," I say. "I've always wanted to see the Eiffel Tower." I look up at the giant steel icon. "I don't know what I thought it would be like, but I'm kind of disappointed. I mean, I didn't think it would be so commercialized, and all that shit," I say pointing to the scaffolding, "makes it lose some of its majesty."

Evan seems even more disappointed but he says, "Maybe we should go up and see if that restores your vision."

We decide to walk the stairs. Both of us are young and it feels like the best way to really experience the landmark. After walking the 300 stairs to the first level, I began to question whether the lift would have been just as rewarding. I'm probably still a bit sore from all the uphill trekking in Monaco. Evan seems fine, so I suck it up. I huff and puff all the way to the top of the second level. The view is breathtaking. My vision is somewhat restored as Evan stands behind me with his arms wrapped around my waist. We stare out onto the Parisian landscape below. The sky is overcast so Seine River is an interesting shade of grey-blue. The buildings below all seem to be the same muted tones. A light dusting of snow covers the roofs below. I think I should feel exhilarated, over-come by emotion. I don't though. Evan's hug is warm and romantic, but the tower itself is still lacking, it's not really doing it for me.

"What do you think?" Evan asks. He sounds nervous. *Maybe he's afraid of heights* I think to myself.

"It's beautiful, but I guess after a lifetime of anticipation I thought it would be different."

"Oh," he sounds disappointed again.

"Don't get me wrong. I love being here with you. It is totally not you...it's...I don't know, the majesty of it is somewhat lacking for me. I'm not sure what I thought I would feel like here, but I just don't feel, you know, moved."

"Let's go then," he says as he grabs my hand.

"Can we go there?" I ask pointing a Ferris wheel at the end of the long street before us.

"Sure, babe," he says with a sad tone.

On the way down, Evan is not himself. He is all business. *I must have really ruined this adventure for him.* I feel bad.

We visit the Arc de Triomphe. Evan's very quiet the whole time. We take a few pictures. He seems distant and I feel worse. The day wears on as we walk down the Champs-Élysées towards the giant Ferris wheel called the Grande Roue de Paris.

We climb onto one of the Grande Roue de Paris' saucer-shaped gondolas. It hangs down below a large umbrella and looks like something out of Alice and

Wonderland. By now the sky is darkening and the blue hue of the lights on the Ferris wheel makes everything take on an air of whimsy. I look at Evan. He is nervously fiddling with his hands. *Funny, I never pegged him for a fear of heights. Sharks I know, but heights? This is new.*

"I am sorry if I ruined the Eiffel Tower for you," I say hoping to take his mind off our ascent. The lights in the city begin to dazzle me and I see the tower in the distance.

"Oh, no it isn't that," Evan says. "Emilia," he takes on a serious tone and I begin to panic inside, "this trip has made me realize many things about myself." My brain is in overdrive. *What is going on here? Oh shit, he's been acting weird all day. Is he...no...is he trying to tell me something...is he trying to break up with me? No, he can't, he wouldn't.* My heart constricts. "I wanted to explore, to see what I want out of life." Blood is pounding in my ears. "What I found out was that you are what I want." I breathe for the first time since he started talking. "I love you, Emilia. I have always known that. You leaving me, me traveling on my own, has just made it clearer to me. The past couple weeks have been the most incredible of my whole trip. You're funny, charming, beautiful, smart, and what's more, I feel more alive around you than anyone I have ever met. I cannot imagine my life without you."

"Ev," I begin but he puts his finger quickly against my lips.

"Shush," he says gently as he undoes his seatbelt. He lowers himself to the floor and grabs my hand. Our gondola rocks back and forth and he struggles to get down on one knee. My heart is beating out of my chest. It is only now, high above the Paris skyline, that it dawns on me what is going on. I'm completely overwhelmed by my emotions. The moment feels surreal, out of body even. "Emilia Jane Somerville, I love you. Will you marry me?"

The intensity in his eyes is unparalleled. His hands are holding mine and he's shaking like a leaf. Adrenaline is coursing rapidly to every part of me. I feel tears welling up in my eyes.

"Oh Evan, yes!" I say, having never even let a thought enter my brain but knowing wholeheartedly that this is what I want.

He kisses my hand first than wraps his arms around me. The saucer swings wildly with our movement. We kiss an adrenaline fueled passionate kiss. I am dizzy with euphoria.

He pulls back and with a huge grin he reaches into his pocket and says, "I should have given this to you when I asked, but I got caught up in the moment." He pulls a small folded piece of tissue paper from his pocket and proceeds to unwrap it. Between his finger and thumb he holds out a dainty silver ring with a stunning blue stone, *sapphire* I think.

"I know it's not a diamond, but when I saw it I thought of you. It is unique, brilliant, commanding, and I think it is incredibly beautiful."

I'm speechless. A tear rolls down my cheek as he slips it on my ring finger. I stare at it on my hand. We head up to the top of the Ferris wheel again and I honestly feel like I might take flight. I can see the now illuminated Eiffel tower in the distance and its majesty is completely restored. Perhaps some things are better when we appreciate them from a distance. Surrounded by the stars above and the twinkling city lights below, this is the single most romantic moment of my life. And, this moment I do not want to appreciate from a distance. I try desperately to regain my composure. I want to feel it all.

"I love it, Evan. I love you. Thank you."

"I called your dad this morning to ask for your hand. I'm not entirely sure he's ready to let you go, but he agreed. I was going to do it at the top of the Eiffel Tower but..."

"I can't imagine a more romantic place than this," I say looking out over Paris as we wheel around one final time. "Evan, I can't believe this...it feels like a divine dream. I'm so incredibly happy!"

22 Only Me

Christmas with my family is a blur. Having Evan home makes everything fantastic. We're inseparable. I'm even able to fool myself into believing that everyone is as happy about the proposal as I am. My parents' worried expressions and my friend's jaw-dropping responses don't faze me. *Sure twenty-three is young and we weren't exactly together before he left, but I know I want this and it feels right. Besides, it's not like we're in a rush to get married right away.* I can handle my parents' and friends' apprehensions. The prospect of spending New Year's with Evan's family is what has me on edge.

I have been to Evan's cottage several times throughout the five and a bit years we've been together. We have taken friends there and even spent a couple weekends with Evan's brother, Edward, and some of his rotating girlfriends. This weekend is different. Edward is bringing a new girl named Melissa. But that is not what concerns me. We will be spending the whole weekend with Evan's parents. I know Evan's parents are great but I haven't spent very much time with them and this feels like some kind of test.

Normally we would spend New Year's Eve drinking and partying with friends. Steph's back from school and here I am going away. *It sucks!*

When we announced our engagement, Mrs. Roseblade, or should I say Louise – *I have to get used to calling her that* – arranged this whole family trip thing. She was very nice about it. She called personally to invite me. There's no way I could say no to that. She's very sweet, but I can't help feeling intimidated by her. Evan's her little boy. I really want her to like me. It bugs me that I'm so nervous.

Traffic is horrible. We are still forty-five minutes away and we're already late.

"My parents aren't gonna care if we are late. Stop biting your nails." Evan grabs may hand from my lips, brings it down to my lap, and holds it there.

I watch as he weaves in and out of traffic trying to edge closer to the cottage.

"Why are you so nervous, anyway?" *Is it that obvious?* "My parents love you."

"I don't know. I really want this weekend to be perfect."

"Relax. Everything is going to be great!" I take a deep breath and Evan slides in a CD. Coldplay's "Yellow" surrounds me and I'm consumed by its melody. Singing along, I forget about my apprehensions for a while.

About an hour later we turn onto the cottage road. There is a light dusting of snow on the ground and the trees look like someone has methodically covered each branch with an inch of fresh powder. *It's breathtaking.* Evan and I are greeted at the door by his mom. Evan heads straight into the living room to see his dad and I'm left in the entryway with his mom.

Evan is a good mix of his mom and dad. His mom is an attractive lady. She has fiery auburn hair and a feisty personality to accompany it. In the past, watching her interact with other people, she always seems so vivacious, a true extravert. I can see where Evan gets his spark. With me however, she is quite reserved. She goes out of her way to make me feel attended to. She is always calling me 'dear' and initiating conversations about my interests. It's sweet, but it creeps me out a little. I'm not sure how to behave around her.

"Hello Mrs. Roseblade, it's so nice of you to invite us up for the weekend."

"Please, Emilia call me Louise. We are family for Pete's sake." *Damn-it! Why can't I call her Louise? I sound as if I'm five when I address her.* "Let me see your ring, dear."

I flash my sapphire and we talk about Evan's romantic proposal. She leads me upstairs to the loft. I feel funny because she is taking me to the room where Evan and I always stay. It's awkward knowing that this room has seen a lot of action over the years. I blush at the thought as she flicks on the light.

"We have made some changes to the space."

I look around at the freshly painted pale blue walls and beautiful new bay window. It is gorgeous but I can't help feeling a pang of sadness over the loss of our quaint love nest.

We head downstairs to see Evan's dad, John. He is busy reading the newspaper. He looks up and as his eyes meet mine I'm reminded that he is the source of Evan's stunning blue eyes. When he smiles, crows-feet frame them in a rugged attractive way. Looking at him, it is easy to see that Evan is going to age well. His dad congratulates us just as Edward and Melissa arrive.

Melissa seems nice. Edward always chooses very bright, artsy types and she definitely fits the bill. Their relationship is very new and Edward is consumed by her. I try to have a conversation with them, but I end up feeling awkward.

I turn my attention to Evan and John who are having a debate about how to best invest money or something. It's great seeing Evan so in his element. They're so animated in their conversation. It's fun to watch.

So far so good. Everything seems to be going smoothly. I make my way into the kitchen to help Evan's mom with dinner. I reach for a colander on the wall and something bright pink catches my eye. That is when I see them. There on the bulletin board in the kitchen pinned up with a thumb tack, is the most embarrassing thing I could ever imagine: my pink, lace underwear. I recognize them immediately as the very pair I wore my first time here at the cottage. *My first time ever,* my subconscious reminds me. *That was over five years ago. What the fuck!* I avert my eyes. I don't want Evan's mom to see me looking at them. *Why are they here? More importantly, why are they there, pinned to the wall? Who pins underwear to the wall anyway?*

Evan's mom starts asking me questions about our plans for the wedding and I am a complete imbecile. I'm unable to drag my mind from my unmentionables on display.

"So, when are you thinking you might get married?"

"Huh, um...ah...I don't know?" *Does she know my panties are inches away from her head right now?* She seems oblivious as she stirs the gravy.

"I guess you haven't had much time to talk with Evan about it, with Christmas and all?" she replies politely to my brain fart.

That isn't true. Evan and I have already agreed to wait until I've graduated and until we've saved enough to buy a small place of our own. We figure it will probably take us three years or so.

In this moment, however, none of that is articulated because my brain is being overwhelmed with the offending pink lace. There is a grocery list posted to the right of my skivvies. *It would be laughable, if they weren't mine. Have they been up there for years? Is there some on-going Roseblade family panty joke that I don't know about? I mean seriously, what the hell are they doing there?*

"Is everything alright, Emilia? You look a little...queasy."

"I'm fine," I lie. I am in full-fledged panic mode. "I think the holidays are catching up with me." *Sounds believable enough. Should I say they're mine and take them off the wall? They're so clearly sex-panties though. Fuck!*

"Can I give you a hand?" Melissa peeks her head into the kitchen. *Maybe I should point out the underwear...ask what they are doing there to throw people off my trail? Am I seriously coming up with conniving plans now? Maybe Melissa will say something? Should I deny they're mine if she does? Should I own up?*

"You can carry this to the table Melissa." Evan's mom hands her a bowl of mashed potatoes and says, "Dinner's ready everyone."

We head to the dining area and I'm relieved that my panties are not visible from the table. I push my food around the plate and say barely anything the entire meal. I listen to Evan and Edward joke around about summers at the lake. Evan's dad enjoys changing records throughout the meal. He seems to be working his way through his jazz collection. It would be a wonderful evening if my lacy-drawers weren't posted up in the other room.

As dinner ends, Evan's father begins clearing the table. He starts heading for the kitchen. I leap up.

"Evan and I can do that." I practically knock over my chair clambering from the table. I DO NOT want Evan's dad washing dishes with my undies right there. I nudge Evan in the shoulder, trying to urge him up quickly. He is mid-conversation with his brother. It's actually quite rude of me, but I don't care as I continue to dart for the stack of plates in his dad's hands and make for the kitchen. His dad says something about us not having to do the dishes because we're guests, but I'm insistent.

Evan reluctantly follows me to the kitchen. We are in plain view and within earshot of everyone else.

"What was that all about?" Evan asks, because for all he knows I'm just being super weird about wanting to do dishes.

I know the others can hear me so I say, "Dinner was so good. It must have taken your mom hours to prepare. This is the least we can do."

Evan starts washing and I pull a towel off the rack to dry with. The buzz of conversation around the table picks up. I can hear Edward and Melissa asking Evan's parents if they can book a weekend to bring their friends here in the spring. Hoping that everyone is focused on that conversation, I alert Evan to my panties.

I gesture with the cup that I'm drying. A puzzled expression comes across his face immediately. Then, as his gaze turns to me, I nod confirming what his thinking. I mouth, "They're mine."

"I remember," he whispers back with a wicked smirk on his face.

I give him my best 'shut-up' face and punch him softly in the arm. I feign that I'm reaching for another plate and whisper, "What are they doing there?"

He shrugs and laughs a little. "Apparently my favourite souvenir has found a place of honour." I punch him a little harder in the shoulder. *He wouldn't have, would he? No?*

"You didn't?"

"What me? No." He laughs some more.

"What should I do?" My hushed whisper sounds desperate.

"Mom, Dad!" Evan yells into the dining room. I turn beet red and start frantically shaking my head and grabbing at his arm. "What are Emilia's underwear doing up on the wall?" I could die of embarrassment.

Evan's dad starts laughing. His mom turns to him and says, "Pay up!"

"Your mom bet me five dollars that they were hers. We found them behind the bed when we were painting the loft," his dad explains. The room erupts with laugher as I reach over and pull out the thumb tack releasing my panties. I slip them in my pocket and take an exaggerated curtsy for everyone.

"And you thought she would be too shy to own up even if they were hers," Evan's mom addresses his dad. Then she turns to me and says, "You survived your hazing my dear." She heads straight for me in the kitchen and throws her arms around me. My flushed face is buried in her genuine embrace as she whispers in my ear, "Welcome to the family."

In one fell swoop all my tension is lifted. The rest of the weekend goes by with ease. I enjoy talking over our plans for a long engagement with Louise, and for the first time, I feel like she is more like a friend than Evan's mom. She likes that I'm so driven to get my career in order and buy a house before we get married. *Who knew panties and a push pin could change the whole dynamic of my relationship with Evan's parents?*

Part Two: Happily Ever After?

23 Just Getting Started

"I can't believe we're finally getting married." I'm shaking as Steph and Britta fuss with my dress. It's been four years since Evan proposed. Many things have changed in the world. In our personal lives, Evan and I have really focused on our careers. I am finally a permanent teacher. I have a job teaching children in Grade One at a small public school close to home. Evan has been promoted to Branch Manager at the bank.

We also bought a small house and have even adopted a fluff-ball of a dog named Maggie. We got her when she was five months old from the local humane society. She has big beautiful brown eyes that look at us with such adoration. And, the feeling is mutual. Evan and I couldn't be happier with our waggy little pup.

It has taken me a long time but my fairytale life is in full swing.

"All rise." I hear as the music changes. My new sister in-law Charlotte begins playing Bach's "Air on the G String" on the violin. My dad tucks his arm around mine and squeezes my hand a little. My eyes meet his and I feel my tears well up. The emotion of it all is overwhelming. A lump forms in my throat as we begin to walk down the steps. I see everyone that is important to me.

Jeff, Wonderwall-Stoner himself, is in the back row. He flashes me an exuberant smile. On the other side of the aisle, my eyes meet Allan's. He winks his approval. As I make my way past the rows of cameras flashing, I see my mom in the front row. The pride in her smile is immense. The tears in my eyes run down my cheeks. I turn and face my dad. He smiles softly, lifts his hand, and dries my tears. He kisses my forehead and releases my hand, giving it to Evan. For the first time during the long walk, I see Evan. He's gorgeous. His finely crafted tuxedo hugs his shoulders so well. Never have I seen him so polished and stately. I want to wrap myself around him right here. He kisses my hand and escorts me to the arbor.

We are standing in front of the most beautiful natural backdrop. Up here on the patio we are overlooking the pond, a small forest, and the expansive greenery of the golf course below. I glance out briefly and I'm struck by the sight of two beautiful swans swimming side by side. *Wow, the on-site wedding planner is good,* I think to myself. I feel someone pulling at my dress. I look back and see Steph fixing my train. *I love how she has always taken care of me.* I feel overwhelmed in the moment. I look to Evan for strength not to fall apart as we stand here as the center of attention. He nods ever so slightly and I take a breath.

"Ladies and gentlemen, we are gathered here today to witness the marriage of Emilia Somerville and Evan

Roseblade. Patience is a virtue, and one that both Emilia and Evan, as well as all of their friends and family, have had to possess in spades to bring us to this day. It is my understanding that this lovely couple has been together for almost ten years. It is my pleasure to unite them today for the rest of their days."

The ceremony is lovely. I am so thankful that the priest is providing me with the words I need to say. I have never understood the necessity of this custom before today, but in this moment so many thoughts and so much emotion has me dumfounded. I feel a gentle mist starting to fall from the sky as I sign the registry. I look out at our family and friends; they are being covered in a light rain. All dressed in their finest clothing, they sit here as the rain begins to fall.

"By the power vested in me, I now pronounce you husband and wife. You may kiss your bride." Evan's lips are perfect as they press up against mine. In one quick motion, he scoops me up and carries me to the covered terrace for shelter. The guests quickly clamber up after us to get out of the rain as well. The wonderfully clear day is now filled with sheets of rain. Friends with formerly pristine hair keep coming up to congratulate us. The rain has taken a rather comical toll on everyone's appearance. "Rain is good luck," everyone keeps toting. In all honesty, I'm so elated by this day that there could be a hurricane out there and I wouldn't care. The experience of walking hand-in-hand with

Evan through a sea of well-wishers is far better than I had ever imagined. Seeing all the people that are closest to me in one room, enjoying each others' company is extraordinary. I want to bottle this feeling.

Cocktails and photos fly by. A perma-smile is glued to my face. I give Britta a big hug as we get ready to sit down at the head table. I squeeze her hand, and take my seat next to Evan, and listen to our parents' heart-warming speeches.

Evan's parents take the mic, brimming with pride. Evan's mom begins, "Fornication..." the room erupts with laugher. She waits for everyone to stop. "For an occasion such as this..." she enunciates ever word precisely this time. The room chuckles again. She breaks herself slightly and laughs too. "I am so honoured to be here to witness the marriage of my baby boy to such a lovely, sophisticated woman. Evan has been a constant source of joy and humour in our lives. He has a commanding, confident presence that has always made his father and I proud."

"Evan and Emilia have been together for a long time now, which has allowed us the opportunity to really get to know Emilia. We would like to thank her wholeheartedly for her patience and strength of character. We are so pleased Emilia is joining our family...officially."

"There was a time I wasn't sure that Evan was the marrying kind. When Evan was in Kindergarten, he had many girlfriends. Every day, he would come home and tell me that his girlfriend was Julie or Maria or Vanessa or...well, you get the point. So one day his father asked 'Evan why do you have so many girlfriends?' To which Evan replied 'Dad, they are only my girlfriends when they are nice to me...when they are not nice, I get another girlfriend.' His dad thought this idea was genius. I am pleased to say that with Emilia's help, Evan has learned that the best girlfriends are the ones who challenge you to be a better person and stick with you even when you are not. Here is to Emilia, Evan's forever girlfriend."

Evan envelops his mom and dad, in a hug. I hug them too and sit back down in my seat. I'm more than a little relieved that Evan's mom didn't bring up the cottage underwear story during her speech.

I watch as a waiter pours wine into my brother Jay's glass at another table. I find my mind wandering a little. I guess the overly emotional day is beginning to take a toll on my mental state. I take a deep breath and sip my wine as Evan puts his arm around me and pulls me in so that I am resting on his shoulder. It is such a reassuring gesture. I feel so at home here, looking out at table after table of loved ones.

My mom and dad make their way to the front of the room. I can tell my mom is nervous. She's got her 'I am all business' look on her face. My dad seems more relaxed.

My dad starts "Emilia, Em...what can we say? She is our little girl. As a child, she was utterly perfect. She owes this description in part to her brother Jay who came before her and gave us a run for our money. He kept us up all night, broke all our prized possessions, and generally tested our patience time and time again. So, when Emilia came along, she was perfect...by comparison. She slept when she should, was neat and organized, and except for brief periods – about three dark years in her early teens – she rarely tested our patience. Then Evan came along..." He pauses for dramatic flare.

My mom proceeds: "I knew Evan was a big deal when Emilia came home one night blubbering. She was heartbroken over some menial thing or other. It was hard to tell because as anyone who has raised teenagers knows, every minor thing is the end of the world. Well, this was the first time Emilia had ever really been distraught over a boy. I remember saying, 'He is just some boy. I am sure in a week she will have moved onto some other crisis.'"

My dad cuts in, "I knew better. I told her that 'there is something different about this boy. She really likes him I don't think we've seen the last of him.'"

"Ten years later and..." he motions with his hands in our direction and then my dad continues, "Evan, I would like to welcome you to the family, to ask you to continue to care for my perfect daughter, and to thank you for allowing me the opportunity to say to my lovely wife in front of all of our closest friends and family, 'I told you so.'" There are some laughs around the room.

"But, on a serious note," my mom adds, "Evan and Emilia have grown up together. They have already shared good times and bad." She snuggles into my dad's shoulder and rubs her hand over his heart. "We have always felt that as long as we go through life together, the good times will always better and the bad times won't be so hard. I only hope that you two can enhance one another's highs and cushion each other's lows. Here is to my beautiful daughter and her wonderful husband."

I made it through the whole speech without crying, but my mother's hug starts the water works. My dad's embrace makes them worse. I compose myself and sit back down as the wait-staff begin bringing the third course. It is only then that I realize I haven't eaten anything yet. I nibble on the chicken and mashed potatoes. I chat with Steph and Allan. It is all lovely.

It isn't long before Steph is addressing the room. "Hi, I'm Steph. Emilia and I have been best friends since our first year in high school. We have always shared a love of music, cheesy romantic comedies, and anything that can be cooked in under five minutes. So, when I missed ONE party in high school and she fell in love with this stranger from another school, I was not entirely on-board. I was certain that her fascination with romantic comedies had caused some kind of psychosis when she told me that he was a bit of a rebel with a bad reputation, but that she thought he could change."

"I was surprised when I met Evan for the first time that he didn't look like Ethan Hawk circa 1995. He seemed like a nice guy, but, as the heroine's-side-kick I had to give him a hard time. As those of you who knew me during the beginning of Em and Ev's relationship will attest, I was not a supporter of Evan. Emilia's happiness was my main concern. After a while, I began to see the spark in Emilia's eye as she described her many adventures with Evan, and I started to come around. Perhaps, this handsome charismatic guy wasn't so bad? I was also worried about Emilia when I went away to school, but I began to realize that Evan was there for her. It was clear that I had to get used to the idea of sharing my best friend."

"When I finally let my guard down, I discovered that Evan was also a music fan and that he too enjoyed snacks prepared in under five minutes. The movies were not his favourite, but he was a good sport."

"Over the past ten years, not only have I had the greatest best friend, but I have also had the pleasure of watching, first hand, her own romantic comedy unfold." She turns to us and says, "The Ev and Em Fairytale is my favourite, hands down. So, I would like you all to raise your glasses, in pure rom-com style, and join me as we toast my favourite couple...'Here's to your happily ever after.'"

The room echoes, "To your happily ever after."

I throw my arms around Steph and she whispers "I'm so happy for you. I love ya so much!" Evan hugs her and I hear her say, "Sorry I gave you such a hard time in the beginning."

Evan smiles back, "No, you're not."

"Okay, I'm not. But, I am glad everything worked out for you guys."

"That, I believe." He smirks again.

Allan begins his speech: "Hello everyone. I'm Allan. Evan and I have known each other since Grade One. Not many of you in this room can say that you've been friends with someone since you were six. I have also had the pleasure of knowing Emilia for the past ten years, which means I definitely have some stories worth noting." He shoots a wink our way. "But, since I would like to remain friends with the happy couple, I will keep this very PG and tell you my favourite recent story about these two."

"Evan called me up about a year ago to tell me they had bought a house together and they needed a hand moving. I was thrilled that they bought the place, but less than excited about the prospect of lugging their stuff around on my Saturday. Now, when Evan and I moved into our condo in University, between the two of us, we had maybe twenty moving boxes total, including the Ikea furniture we needed to assemble. We were far from organized and I still think one of the boxes I moved into that apartment is unopened in my current closet. So, when they called me up, I was expecting to pop by for an hour and then have some beer with Evan after we set up the television."

"To my surprise, when I arrived to help, there was a giant moving truck with armoires, boxes piled high and dining room furniture. When I was living with Evan, our dining room furniture consisted of three bikes and an old drum set."

"The lovely Emilia, as always, was meticulously organized. Boxes were colour-coded according to the room they were to be taken to, and every glass item had been carefully bubble-wrapped. I diligently carried shit...oh, I mean stuff...sorry...for a couple hours. Emilia was a machine: cleaning, unpacking, setting up furniture. And, to my amazement, I watched Evan make quick work of assembling a bed, unpacking clothes, and setting up all the electronics."

"At our condo, the T.V. and Play Station were the only things set up for at least a month. I am not sure we ever got the coffee maker working. We just went to Tim Horton's all the time."

"But, by the end of the day at their new house, everything had been put away and all the furniture had been placed aesthetically just so. It honestly looked like they had lived in the house for years. They even had pictures on the wall," Allan says with sarcastic disbelief in his voice.

"Emilia and Evan were so eager and happy. When everything was done, I sat down on the couch with Evan to enjoy some pizza and beer and said to him, 'Evan you have come a long way since the days when we lived together. I can't believe you and Emilia are so grown up.' To which he replied, 'This stuff...this house...it doesn't make us grown-ups. Em and I just want everything to be ready so we can really start our life together.'

"I thought it was pretty awesome that after dating for almost a decade, that they felt like they were just starting their life together. I get it though, because Evan and I have known each other for over two decades now and I too feel like we're just getting started." An audible 'aw' can be heard from the crowd. Evan gets up and gives Allan a manly bro-hug. They whisper something to one another and Allan turns back to the microphone. "To Evan and Emilia..." he winks at me and raises his glass, "just getting started."

The rest of the evening flies by. The dance with my dad, tossing the bouquet, shots at the bar, cutting the cake, busting a move on the dance floor...it's a whirlwind of carefree joy. It's an incredible feeling, watching Evan as he interacts with our loved ones, all the while giving me a knowing smile that we finally did it.

Emilia Roseblade. I like the sound of it, but it is going to take some getting used to.

24 Beautiful and Resourceful

Evan literally whisks me off my feet for the second time today. This time we're alone, and the action is earnest and full of intent. I stare intensely into his blue eyes as he effortlessly carries me over the threshold of the inn and up a small flight of stairs. He fumbles as he reaches into his pocket for the key card while still holding me in his arms. He manages to open the door and places me on the bed.

The room is small and decorated in a Victorian style. There are flowers on the wallpaper and duvet. All the paintings depict some kind of quaint rural scenery. The overhead light is harsh. It's not exactly the type of magical venue that I envisioned for my wedding night. It is the only inn around for miles, so here I am on the bed in my gorgeous wedding gown, staring at my handsome husband.

"You look breathtaking," Evan says.

"You are quite captivating yourself," I reply. "I'm going to need some help getting out of this dress."

"With pleasure." He reaches for the lamp on the nightstand and in a flash he also quickly turns off the offending ceiling light. "That's better."

I turn away from him and lift my hair up to reveal the nape of my neck where the buttons of my dress begin. He makes a pleasant humming sound that causes a smile to explode across my face. As he starts to fiddle with first button he bends down and kisses my neck. It is gentle and endearing. I glance back at him and he is also wearing a smirk from ear to ear. His fingers are twisting and turning, desperately trying to finagle the top button. I giggle at the thought that there must be fifty more trailing down my back and he's stuck on the first one. "Delayed gratification at its finest," I jest.

"How much do you actually like this dress?" He quips back.

I reach into my hair which was expertly swept up by Britta into an elegant wispy mass of curl. I pull a bobby pin out and pass it to him.

"Beautiful and resourceful," he mutters. He slides the little metal clip in the loop that surrounds the top button and aptly pulls the tiny round iridescent bobble out, freeing it. He kisses the newly exposed skin and continues to work his way down my back, unbuttoning and kissing as he goes. Slowly unwrapping me like a precious package, and revealing my lacy corset underneath. I squirm with anticipation as Evan reaches the silvery beads on the delicate waistband of the gown. My lower back tingles as he plants a light kiss on the skin between my corset and my panties.

"I like," he purrs.

I lower the straps of the dress and try my damnedest to sexily slide out of the dress. I watch his eyes ignite as the mass of white fabric hits the floor. I feel slightly uncomfortable in this lacy lingerie, complete with thigh high stockings and garters holding them up. Britta and Steph bought them to shock me at my bachelorette party. I've never worn anything this risqué. The shocked, excited look on his face eases my discomfort and my inner Victoria Secret model emerges.

"Whoa," he utters. He looks as though he's memorizing my form.

I turn my attention to undressing him. He had already thrown his jacket on the chair when we entered. He is wearing a black vest with the silver grey tie I bought him for the wedding. He's so handsome, it is almost a shame to remove this dapper exterior, but remove it I will. Now standing in front of him, I make quick work of the three buttons on his vest. He helps me peel it off. I grab his tie and pull him in to kiss me. His hands caress my behind and push me against his hard body. I release my grasp on his tie and force him back onto the bed. I straddle him while I untie his tie. He raises his eyebrow ever so slightly. It begs me for more. I begin the process of undoing his buttons. I mirror his technique, unbuttoning and kissing all the way down. His eyes are burning, fixated on my every move. A euphoric rush of adrenaline, maybe hormones, surges through me. I am caught in a wave of emotions, overcome by the day's events. All my energy is raw and carnal.

Making quick work of his belt, I go for his pants and he turns the tables on me. All of a sudden, I find myself on my back as his pants and briefs fall to the floor. He crawls on top of me, pinning me against the bed under his weight. The boning in the corset pushes into my skin in a painful yet exciting way.

"Aren't you going to get me out of this thing," I say.

"Not a chance...we have all night pretty girl." The statement holds so much promise. He reaches down and pushes my panties to the side. I can feel the lace against my thigh as he pushes his erection deep inside me. The action pushes me up hard on the bed and the force of it causes me to yell out a foreign sound. Before I can even get my bearings, he wraps his arms under my back and holds onto my shoulders, simultaneously thrusting into me and pulling me into him. It is so primal so...so needed. I can't help but be consumed by the myriad of sensations that are enveloping my body. My hands madly prod at his back, up into his hair. Kissing...rubbing...feeling...it is so pure...so passionate. The repetitive, hard in and out motion builds in intensity. He knows my body so well. His skillful hips thrust perfectly, invigorating my sensation. I lower my pelvis ever so slightly and all of a sudden he is hitting a spot that is beyond words. "Oh, right there...yeah more..." My back arches. I claw at the sheets. The feeling is overwhelming as it continues to build. I twitch uncontrollably as my sweet,

sweet orgasm finds its release. Dizzy and blissful, I relax as I feel his climax inside me.

He flops down on top of me and then shifts so that we are both more comfortable. His head is on my shoulder and his body draped on my side. A few minutes pass as we listen to our breath return from its feverish pace.

"Well, Mr. Roseblade, that hit the spot," I purr.

"Certainly seems that way, Mrs. Roseblade," Evan says as he kisses my shoulder.

"Now, maybe you can help me out of this contraption," I say referring to the corset.

"Do I have too? It's so...unexpected...and hot," he runs his finger along my lacy bust line.

"I'm glad you approve, but I really want to curl up with you skin to skin right now."

"Sold," he says as he pulls on the dainty ribbon that weaves its way between my breasts. Strange that such a small pretty, satin thread is so integral to the structural support of the garment. A couple quick tugs and the two sides part freely, exposing my breasts. My chest is covered in light red pressure marks from the lace and boning. I see Evan's sad expression as he gazes upon the marks.

"Babe, are you okay? Did this thing hurt you?" he says as he kisses the darkest marks from my waist to my breast.

"I'm fine, but don't stop kissing me better."

I reach down and begin pulling off the garter, panties, and thigh highs. Evan watches as I toss the rolled up stockings across the room. They land on a desk by the window.

"Ah, that's better," I say.

"It certainly is." He wraps himself around me, and as he does, I notice that he is still wearing his black socks. The spectacle of it makes me start giggling.

"What?" he says as my giggle grows into a full out laugh.

"You...heheheh...you are still wearing your...heheheh..." I point to his socks.

"Oh shit, I guess I am," and he joins in on my laughing fit. I'm not even sure why it's so funny, but as we are lying on the bed in our post-coital state of bliss, he is undoubtedly, wearing long black business socks. Perhaps we're delirious from lack of sleep, high on emotions from our wedding day, a little tipsy from the shots, or maybe it was the sex that has made us giddy...whatever it is, the sight of Evan completely naked, except for his black socks, has caused me now to break into hysterical laughter to the point where tears are running down my cheeks. Relishing in my reaction, he begins strutting around the room showing them off. He proceeds to peel one sock off and swing it over his head as if he is giving me a perverse strip tease. A small snort escapes my body as the second sock is sent whizzing past me.

In this moment, laughing uncontrollably, completely naked with Evan, I know I am utterly in love. Because seriously, in life, how many people can you be this exposed with, this comfortable with, this 'you' with?

It's like I'm embedded in the pages of a really good romance novel. Except in my case, Evan is a real person, not a megalomaniac billionaire, rogue cowboy, love-starved vampire, British movie star, or a teacher I should know better than to pursue. *How did I get so lucky to land a real-life, honest-to-goodness man? One who loves me. One that I love. Who needs billionaires and rogues anyway? Sometimes, just sometimes, reality is better than the fantasy.*

Hmm...Evan the billionaire rogue isn't a bad fantasy though.

25 The Void Beyond the Sunset

Tossing and turning, I wake hot and sweaty. I lay awake in the darkness trying to piece together the bizarre dream that has me so frustrated and worked up. *The sunset was too bright to see beyond it. What was beyond it? I was definitely riding off towards the sunset. Evan, was there too. Why do I feel like I was chasing something? What was I after?*

I roll over and nudge Evan. "Evan. Psst, Evan." He moans and pulls the covers up to his chin. "Evan, I had a bad dream."

He moans incoherently. I watch him sleep, and stray thoughts fill my head as I try to get back to sleep. *Our third anniversary is coming up. I should plan something. We should go out. We haven't been out in ages. Seems like all we ever do is work, clean, eat, and lounge. I miss going out with friends. Maybe we should have a dinner party or something. Hell, everyone is in their own relationship bubbles right now; I wonder if they'd even come. Life is so...so blah right now.* I stare at Evan some more. *He is so cute when he's sleeping. I can't believe it has been almost three years. I always thought I would have kids by the time I was twenty-five and here I am, almost thirty and, huh...maybe we should start trying?* I roll over and drift off, thinking about little Evans running around.

"So, I was thinking..." I trail off not sure if I want to start this conversation. Evan looks at me over his pasta, but says nothing. "I um...well, I was wondering how you felt about maybe, um...well, trying for a baby." *Could I have drawn that out anymore?* I study Evan's face in hopes that he will be on board. His serious eyes indicate otherwise as he lowers his fork.

"Em, I don't think I'm ready for all that just yet. Don't get me wrong; I want kids, but I want it to be the two of us for a while, you know?"

"Oh, I get it. It's just that..." I trail off again. I guess I must have a hurt expression on my face because Evan looks at me like I'm wounded.

"Hey, don't be sad. I can give it some thought. If it's that important to you, I can start wrapping my mind around the idea. I know that I'm not ready now, but I'm sure I will warm up to the idea...eventually. I was thinking another year or two, you know?"

"A year or two," I repeat quietly so that my brain registers it. *A year I think I can do, but two years seems preposterous. Is it? Or is my brain being overwhelmed by the proverbial clock tick, tick, ticking away.*

"You okay?" Evan looks at me. He seems genuinely concerned.

"Yeah, sure." I try to brush off my fantasy that he would be so excited by the prospect of having a baby, that the dinner plates would be on the floor, and we would be baby-making on the table.

"Just so you know, I want to have your babies. So, when you're ready..." I trail off, this time shooting him the most sensual look I have.

When I look at movies and books for guidance, I am sadly left in the lurch. I find I am now the target market for stories about 'spinsters searching for love' or 'women dealing with being/getting divorced.' Don't get me wrong; I love me some *Bridget Jones* and *Sex in the City*. I'm just not dealing with the same issues.

It seems like every weekend I'm at another baby shower with random old aunts who keep nudging me. "When are you and Evan going to have a little bundle of your own?" I nod politely and wonder why women do this to one another. Why can't we leave well enough alone. Other people's family planning is none of our business anyway. But secretly, I know I'm only annoyed because I'm busy nudging myself. If I could only persuade Evan, I could be the one up there holding the tiny onesie against my baby bump.

Even my brother Jay has a little girl now. Her name is Mallory. She has the cutest little cheeks I have ever seen. She's all cheeks really. I'm so excited about being an aunt!

Charlotte, Jay's wife, is a natural at the mothering thing. I am fortunate enough to help out when 'cheeky' first comes home from the hospital. Watching Charlotte with Mallory is the sweetest thing. The gentle touches, the nurturing care she bestows, and the soothing words she coos towards her little girl make me smile. Seeing the love in Jay's eyes when he holds Mallory's tiny swaddled body in his arms makes me wonder what Evan will be like as a dad.

My happily ever after feels like it's lacking something. I think a baby will fix this nagging feeling that life is passing me by. I don't want to do this alone though. I need to get Evan on board so he'll want to be a part of this...this monumental phase in our lives.

26 Reality is a Bitch

Eleven months have gone by. Evan and I have not talked about baby-making, but as far as I am concerned, our sabbatical of sorts has almost expired. I'm ready. I told him I was good with waiting a year and now's the time to inspire him. *What can I do? Should I surround him with adorable bundles of joy to bring him on side? No, that has the potential to backfire. Last time I babysat Mallory she had a poop that went all the way up to her shoulder blades. I can't risk that. Maybe I should wine and dine him. Seduce him? That seems sleazy somehow. But, it can't hurt to make myself more desirable. The mature thing to do, though, is to talk to him. I hate being mature but, I am going to have to try.*

Evan walks through the front door with his briefcase. Maggie runs towards him, wagging her tail. As a puppy, she used to jump up all over him when he came through the door. She's not a puppy anymore. She's still a wiggly ball of energy, but she manages to keep her dancing paws firmly on the ground. *She's such a good dog.*

Her greeting is a hard act to follow. I simply wrap my arms around his strong shoulders. I breathe in his scent which fills me with a calm reassurance. After work, I put on a flirty skirt and a black tank top. I even reapplied all of my make-up. By the look on Evan's face, he's pleasantly surprised.

"Hey, you," I speak.

"Hi, pretty girl. You look nice. Did I forget some kind of occasion?" His comment emphasizes that maybe I've been lacking in the effort department lately.

"Can't a girl dress up for her husband?"

"She certainly can. I like surprises, remember?"

I decide to let him get settled in before I lay my big surprise on him. We chat about his day and I flutter around the kitchen making a primavera sauce for dinner. As I cut a red pepper, he cuddles in behind, wrapping his arms around me tightly. He whispers, "I like this skirt on you." I can feel his excitement pressed up against me. I was hoping to have the conversation before this but...

I drop the red pepper knife, turn around, and kiss him. He scoops me up and carries me to the bedroom. As he gently places me on the bed, I frantically try to search for the words to say what I want to say, but I'm afraid I will ruin the moment. He undresses as I watch. I begin to take off my shirt and Evan says, "Leave that to me. I would like to open my surprise myself."

I giggle. He climbs over me and commences my undressing. First my shirt and skirt then my bra and panties. I'm naked under his watchful eye. He reaches for a condom. We had started using them again after the birth control pill made me weepy all the time. I think he also likes being in control of the birth control. Not that he doesn't trust me; it was reassuring to us both that we were making the choice together.

That's when it hits me. I need to ask him now, in this moment, to make the choice. He's opening the package when I say, "Don't." He looks confused, as if I was shutting him down. "Let's leave it up to fate this time," I hear the words come out of me.

My eyes look intently into his, desperate for his reaction. I see a flicker of fear. He pauses momentarily then tosses the condom on the floor and possesses me in one fell swoop. There is something so intimate about it. His slow, building rhythm is intense and thrilling. We have had sex millions of times at this point in our relationship but with this new purpose it feels different, like we are doing something forbidden. My emotional senses are at an apex. He's giving himself to me in a way I've never experienced before. I'm not sure if he's ready, or just willing to do this for me, with me. I close my eyes so my body can absorb every sensation. His head is buried in my neck and I can hear every breath, moan, groan. I'm on the brink. I'm one with my body, all consumed by the building pleasure. My fingers dig into the sheets.

Without a word, he flips me over. I'm on top, dizzy and driving, taking my pleasure, desperately filling my void. I lean forward so that my sweet spot is electrified. We are nose to nose. "That's it, right there, don't move," I pant. I look at his gorgeous face as I climax around him. He follows, calling my name and pulling me tight against his chest.

We lay there, not talking, not moving, just laying there. Time seems to stand still as my waves of pleasure morph into the realization that we have taken a huge step in our relationship. Though I'm aware this is probably not going to be the day I become pregnant, this is the day we have decided to try, and that in itself is a life-altering choice. I lay comforted by the way Evan's chest rises and falls. I'm afraid to talk first, scared he may be regretting his spur of the moment decision. Nervously, I break the silence.

"You good?" I ask not knowing what else to say.

There is a long pause which frightens me more than anything he could say. "I'm a bit freaked out, but I'll be okay."

I lift up to rest on my arms and look him in the eye. "I'm scared too, but it certainly was fun trying."

Evan shoots me a soft sexy smile. "I think we're going to have to practice daily until we get this thing done."

"Daily, huh?" I giggle.

"Yep." He pulls me up to kiss his lips and I'm lost in my husband once more.

Six months go by and my period is still flowing regularly. Everywhere I look, pregnant women are parading their triumphant bellies around.

As for babies, somehow they manage to be the most endearing creatures on the planet as my longing grows within. I hold Joyce's baby girl, Anna. She coos and smiles in my arms.

Joyce moved into the neighbourhood a month before Anna was born. I met her while walking Maggie in the park. I saw a crazy springer spaniel dragging a very pregnant Joyce through the park. I volunteered to help her out and we became fast friends. Now, I find I'm at her house a couple of nights a week; rocking, snuggling, smelling her beautiful baby, Anna. Yes, smelling. She smells incredible. Comforting and warm. My desire grows.

Poor Evan never gets a rest. At the beginning of our efforts, I really tried to inspire him. Now, I am taking my temperature every morning and planning ambushes on days when I think I'm ovulating. It can't be romantic or sexy to see your wife holding her legs in the air for ten minutes after sex because some co-worker told her that helps the sperm along. Evan's a good sport. Although, sometimes I feel him losing interest in the baby-making plan. *I think he wants to scrap the ulterior baby-making motive.* Unfortunately, thoughts like that just make me more driven. *What if he changes his mind? I have to get this done.* This has become a box on my to-do list.

It's Friday morning and I'm in a rush to get ready for work. I am helping put together a school assembly at work. I want to get in early to put up the posters. I jump in the shower and do the regular breast exam thing I do. It's kind of a habit. As I soap up my breast I notice that my boobs are slightly swollen. I'm a bit uncomfortable as I put pressure on them. At first I think the worst. Then, it dawns on me. *This is a good thing.* I yell for Evan.

"Ev, come here!"

I feel the cold air enter the bathroom as he opens the door. "What is it?"

A smile is plastered across my face. I peek my head out of the shower curtain and say, "Get in."

"Oh, babe it's not that I..." he begins to deny me. I don't blame him. I've been jumping him a lot lately.

I turn off the water, open the shower curtain, and flash him.

"If you insist," he says as he reaches for his fly.

"No, no! Not that. Look at me. Do you notice anything different?" I say sure that he will perceive the new fullness of my breasts.

"You're beautiful," he says, probably trying to cover for that fact that he sees no change in me.

"No, really look at my boobs. Feel them."

"No argument here." He eagerly reaches out. I see his face change from flirty to quizzical. "They're bigger...fuller," he says.

Nodding in agreement I beam at him.

"No, really?" he whispers as he realizes the implication of what I am trying to impart.

"I'm not sure, but we can check tonight," I continue to beam.

"Holy shit!" He smiles and hands me a towel. I can see the excited shock in his eyes. I try to commit it to memory. In this moment, we are just us, us and the joy of possibility.

The rest of the day goes by in a haze. The school assembly goes off without a hitch, even though the teacher can't keep her mind off the tiny speck potentially growing inside her.

I hit the pharmacy on the way home. For some reason, I make small talk with the lady behind the counter as she rings in my dip stick. Eagerly, I mention that my husband and I are hoping for good news. It's way too personal a conversation to be having with the middle-aged cashier, but since I can't share my excitement with friends or family, it feels great to communicate it in this anonymous way.

I rush home only to realize that Evan won't be home for at least an hour. The white paper bag sits on the counter, taunting me. I sauté mushrooms and boil potatoes to occupy me. Five fifty-seven, *Evan will be leaving the bank any minute.* Twenty-three agonizing minutes later, Evan appears at the door. I throw my arms around him. He pulls away to look me in the eye. "Do you know?" He asks pointedly.

"No, I waited for you," I smile. "We're in this together."

He hugs me again, lifting my feet off the ground and twirling me around. As he lowers me back down he says, "I'm here now. Let's do this thing."

I grab the white bag and head to the bathroom. Evan waits outside the door. I read the instructions carefully, not wanting to screw anything up. "Okay, so we want a cross."

After three tediously long minutes, I anxiously bring the stick up to the light. The blue lines clearly form a cross in the little plastic window. Tears well up in my eyes. Evan's arms squeeze tight around my waist and his hands hold my stomach. "You're gonna be a daddy." The delightful words escape my lips.

"And you're gonna be a mommy," he replies.

I turn around and hug him so tight. Adrenaline somehow courses through my veins. I'm so incredibly happy!

The next few weeks are a blissful haze. I am exhausted all the time, but I don't care. The prenatal vitamins make me extremely nauseous every day, but it's all worth it. I'm consumed by reading about my little embryo's development. A pregnancy website I've found gives me weekly insights into the growth and changes that my wee one and I are embarking upon. At six weeks, it is as big as a small bean. Evan and I begin to call our little one Bean. By nine weeks, it has grown to the size of a pea pod. We lovingly change its name to Little Pea. We are super excited about going to our first ultrasound at twelve weeks. Little Pea is growing fast and we'll have to give it a new name by then but, Half-A- Banana doesn't have a very good ring to it, so we may have to be a bit more creative.

Evan takes the day off work to come with me to the clinic. The ultrasound technician hands me a paper dress that opens at the back and then leaves the room. I quickly undress and don the uncomfortable garment. Unsure what to do next, I ease myself onto the paper-covered examination table. My bladder is extremely full and my discomfort is increasing by the minute.

The technician re-enters the room. She is a petite lady, probably in her late forties. She has ashy brown hair and a nice smile. I'm nervous about the whole exposed nature of this appointment so I make goofy small talk. She's polite but to the point. She begins by smearing clear gel on my stomach and pushing the wand over my lower abdomen. My bladder cries out in pain. I muster all my concentration to keep from peeing myself. She pushes and prods. Then she asks me to hold my breath. I think it's a bit weird, but what do I know? She quickly wipes off the gel and tells me she is going to have to give me an internal exam. She asks me to go to the bathroom and pee a little to relieve some of the pressure. I'm supposed to come back because she would like the radiologist to examine me.

I walk down the hall to the restroom. I feel cold and naked in my stupid paper dress. The panic begins to set in as I wash my hands. *What is this lady not telling me?* I put my hands on stomach to get strength from Little Pea. Then, I take a deep breath before walking back down the hall.

The rest of the appointment is a blur. The next thing I know, I am sitting in my family doctor's office with Evan attentively holding my hand. I'm numb as I hear her say, "I'm afraid your baby stopped growing at nine-weeks. Your body is still exhibiting signs of pregnancy but we need to look at your options now."

I hear Evan say, "What does this mean?" He's in shock too.

"I'm afraid your baby is not alive. You can opt to have a natural miscarriage, which will happen anytime in the next month, or you can make an appointment to have a D and C."

I feel all the blood drain from my face.

Over the next few days it is as though I am looming somewhere over myself, watching the horrors that transpire. Evan and my mom fawn over me – doting on me, comforting me. I know Evan is hurting too. My own pain makes it impossible to connect with anyone though, even Evan.

"Em you have to eat," my mom pleads. I push the soup around my bowl, unable to stomach it. "I know this is hard, but I know how you feel." In my head I scoff, only thinking of my pain. She continues, "After I had Jay, I had a miscarriage. I don't think I was as far along as you were. I was admitted to the hospital for heavy bleeding. I didn't even know I was pregnant until the nurse told me I had lost the baby."

I look at my mom in disbelief. *I thought I knew everything about her.* It's weird seeing her as a woman, not as my mom. I say nothing, I just hug her. While she's holding me, my head nuzzled on her shoulder, she adds to her story. "I know it's not quite the same thing but I still felt the loss, even though, I didn't know I was carrying the baby. Eventually, I came to accept that things happen for a reason, and that nature has a way of sorting things out. If that pregnancy had worked out, I would have never had my bright, beautiful, strong baby girl. And, I wouldn't trade you for anything, Emilia Jane." I sob on her shoulder.

It takes time, but when I'm ready, I move on. Bean/Little Pea is no more. Life has kicked me in the ass. I can give up or drive on. I choose to drive.

Evan and I never really talk about our loss. It's too hard; we both know it. I can't bear to see the pain in his eyes. He wants to fix me, to make me happy. So, we fake it. We pretend to be okay for one another until time mends the hurt a bit. Then, we begin to actually be okay.

The weird thing I discover from this ordeal is that I have unwillingly joined a massive secret society of women that have all experienced one depressing phenomenon or another. There is a bizarre cultural reality where females only tell each other about the wonders of pregnancy and child-rearing until you experience a horrible rite of passage. Then, the existence of the subculture is revealed to you. I wish I could rewind and go back into the world of smoke and mirrors. I was much happier there. *I don't want to commiserate about miscarriage, stillbirth, episiotomies, tubal ligations, botched epidurals. Fuck, men have it easy!*

My sad reality has left me waiting. Evan and I have been advised to wait three months before trying again. I'm full of questions. *Why did I lose the baby? Did I do something wrong? Did I lift something that was too heavy or eat something I shouldn't have?* The scariest question by far is: *Can I carry a baby full-term?* I agonize.

When the three months are up, Evan is all over me like white on rice. His drive for a baby is different. Before, I think he was acquiescing for me. Now he's determined. When I become pregnant again the next month we are excited but rational. We decide not to name the little being. We both try not to get too attached. That being said, I talk to my belly whenever no one is listening. I hum songs to it before bed and occasionally wake to Evan kissing it. We desperately want to bond, but the recent hurt looms over us.

At three months I go back to the clinic. The same clinic. Sitting in the paper dress this time is unbearable. The ashy haired technician enters. I know she doesn't recognize me, but it was at her hands that I learned of Little Pea's fate. She does this day in and day out. I am sure she sees many sad cases. I hope to God I am not one of them today.

I breathe in deeply and try to calm my racing heart. I wish Evan could be in here with me. *Damn hospital policies.* She starts her small talk and I quickly realize that her banter is the same as last time. She squeezes the cold lube on my stomach and I feel the familiar pressure on my bladder. I close my eyes. The monitor is turned away from me anyway. *All I can do is hope.* She flicks a switch on the monitor and a swishy, rhythmical, staticy sound fills the room.

"That's your baby's heartbeat." Her words take a second to register. "Sounds strong."

Tears run down my cheeks. *My baby. I can hear it.* She swings the monitor so that I can see the screen. Then she begins decoding the fuzzy grey dots.

"That's the heart there."

I can see the movement. The grey goes from light to dark and my heart pumps with renewed vigor. *I'm going to be a mom. That's my baby, there on the screen, here in my body. I've never felt so grateful to be a woman.*

"Can my husband come in and see? Just for a minute?"

"Everything looks in order. I don't think that'll be a problem. What does he look like?"

"He'll be the pale, worried looking man pacing the waiting room. His name is Evan," I say.

Several minutes go by. I'm staring at my baby's beating heart on the monitor. Words cannot describe my relief. The sound fills my own heart with such pure delight. My trembling hand covers my mouth as a warm tear rolls down my cheek and drips onto my paper gown. A smile spreads beneath my fingers. I drop my hand to my belly and gently rub my baby bump. *What a fucking miracle!*

The door opens slowly and Evan's face is void of colour. I realize in an instant that the technician hasn't said anything to him. He is still fearing the worst. His eyes meet mine and the grin on my face restores his natural skin tone. Still in shock, haunted by fear, he grabs my hand for reassurance.

"It's okay, babe," I whisper.

A wary smile appears on his face.

"Mr. Roseblade, would you like to see your baby?"

He nods, but says nothing. I feel a calm relaxed smile stretch across my face for the first time in months. I watch him intently as he sees our baby for the first time.

"There's the heart there. Would you like to hear the heartbeat?" Ashy-hair asks.

"Yes," he says in a hushed, broken voice.

The swishy sound resumes and he closes his eyes. He looks as though he's trying to savour the sound, memorize it even. I squeeze his hand and he instantly consumes me in a hug. *We have become three.*

My pregnancy goes by quickly, I guess. It is full of unbelievable sensations. I adore the kicks and stretches of our growing baby. I try to cherish every hiccup because I never want to forget the feeling of each light blip. It's so surreal. I can't wait to meet our little angel. As we get closer, Evan and I nest away and dream of the days when we will finally get to snuggle our wee one in our arms. It's a restless, leg-cramping, queasy, sleepless, dream come true.

27 Not According to Plan

Four-thirty in the morning. I wake with a sharp pain in my abdomen. *Ow. It's probably those false Braxton Hicks contractions.* I've been having them on and off for days now. I close my eyes.

Four fifty-six. *OWW! That is definitely something.* I get out of bed. "Oh shit. Sorry Maggie," I say, realizing that I just stepped on her tail. I make my way to the bathroom and the pressure in my back makes me grab hold of the sink to prevent myself from falling. "Fuck!"

"Evan!" I yell towards the bedroom. I hear nothing. "Evan, it's happening!" Still nothing. "EV.....AN!" The pain shoots through me as I scream his name.

"Shit, Em. I'm up. I'm here. What? How? Um..." He's in a state of panic between sleep and awake. He grabs me around my waist and helps me into the living room. I sit on the couch. "No!...Ow..." It is too uncomfortable. I lower myself to the floor, putting my knees on the floor while resting my arms and head on the couch.

I can't see Evan, but I feel the fear in his voice. "Em, what should I do?"

"Call my mom." I blurt out.

I hear him on the phone as I breathe the stupid rhythm that that yoga-bitch told me would help. It's not helping. *Fuck yoga*, I think, and resort to crazy "hee-hee-who-who" breathing that I saw on *The Cosby Show* once. It doesn't help either.

"Get me a hot water bottle!" I yell out frantically.

I hear Evan emptying the linen closet. It feels like an eternity passes.

"Where do you want it?"

"My back." I gesture with my hands urgently and Evan holds the heat against me. It feels a bit better. "Oh, thank you. Evan, it fuckin' hurts. I'm so scared."

"Em, you are the strongest person I know. You're going to do great, babe. We're going to meet our little girl today. You can do this, lovely."

I feel anything but lovely right now but his words are so genuine. I try to focus on the positive. It's more difficult than I ever imagined. I'm in labour for eighteen hours. I do the first fourteen without drugs.

"You are between seven and eight inches dilated, Mrs. Roseblade. You're doing very well."

I hear the words, but the pain is so intensely relentless. Contractions are coming every two minutes now and lasting almost that long. I can barely catch my breath. *I think I might actually be dying. Can't anyone see that I'm dying here?*

"Mrs. Roseblade, we have a slight complication. Your baby has decided to turn around. So instead of facing forward like she was when you arrived, she is now facing backward."

I'm in too much pain to contemplate the dangers that this poses for me or the baby. My mom and Evan are discussing various options with the doctor but I just want this over.

Evan is holding my hand on one side, and my mom is on the other. The serious looks etched across their faces send me into a panic.

"What? Tell me? What's happening?"

"The doctors need to give you an epidural so that they can try to turn the baby around."

"Is she okay?"

"She's fine. They think she is going to be just fine," My mom says in her most reassuring voice. The way she qualifies her answer freaks me out even more though. "The anesthetist should be here in a minute. I know this isn't how you planned it, Emilia. The important thing is that we leave here with a healthy baby. That's why they're doing this."

The next thing I know, I'm lying on the bed with warm blankets covering me. It's as though I blacked out. The reality is that the pain was so intense that I have blocked all memory of it. The blankets have a comforting weight to them. Evan is holding my hand. My mom is watching the 'contraction machine.'

"I think you're having another contraction," she says.

I smile a relaxed grin. "I love drugs. Why did I ever consider doing this naturally? I'm so cozy, so mmmmm." I close my eyes and drift off briefly. I know I should be worried. I sense that the world as I know it is changing with each passing contraction, but here, in this bed, I am comfortably numb.

I start to feel pressure and the nurse tells me I'm ready to push. Grabbing my limp knees I bear-down. The doctor coaches me as she attempts to turn the baby. An hour goes by. I have pushed my last push and they are wheeling me to the operating room. My baby girl is not coming out, so they are prepping me to take her out. I'm no longer comfortably numb; I'm a nervous wreck!

The anesthetist is attentively watching me, rubbing ice on my belly until he is satisfied that I can't feel anything. 'Doctor Evan' enters the room. He is wearing green scrubs, a hair thingy, and a mask. Even his feet are covered. He sits on the stool beside me and takes my hand. I can see in his beautiful eyes that he is utterly terrified. His fear calms me in a bizarre way. It's as though he needs me to be strong; so I push my own fear aside to reassure him.

"Everything is going to be okay babe. You're going to be a daddy any minute now, Ev. We can do this."

He squeezes my hand and gently tucks my hair behind my ear. *I love him so much.* I focus on him as they push, prod, and yank my baby girl out of me. I can see her tiny red bum as they carry her over to the scale/warmer. They are suctioning and examining her. I hear the unmistakable cry of a brand new baby. It sounds like a mixture between a cat's meow and frantic bird. It is the sound of Evan and I, jointly breathing a sigh of relief.

The exhaustion of the day combined with the amount of drugs pumping through my body take over, and I am but a spectator in the wonder that whirls around me. Evan brings our beautiful Avery over to me and, struggling to rein in my emotions, I giggle and blubber my way through my first words to our daughter as I welcome her to the world. I'm still on the operating table and almost completely paralyzed. He holds her right in front of me. "Happy birthday, lovely." She calms at the sound of my voice. "I'm your mommy. I have been waiting a long time to meet you. You are so perfect." I run my finger down her cute little nose and she blinks, trying to see through the guck they have put on her eyes. "It's okay baby." Evan pulls her close and I can see the love.

28 Stretched in Every Direction

As we navigating our new reality, parenthood, we definitely have our share of challenges. It's nothing like I imagined. It's all consuming. It's a form of joy like no other, but it is exhausting too. Avery is the centre of my universe. My body is hers, day and night as she feeds. My mind is constantly thinking of how to sooth, stimulate, and nurture her.

As I stroke her fuzzy, little blond hair, she sleeps on my chest. I realize that my heart and hers have an inexplicable connection. It's the same connection I have with my mom. A tear forms in my eye as I become aware that, somehow, my hands now look exactly how I remember my mother's hands looking when I was a little girl. I'm Avery's mother. I'm the hands she'll look to – to walk her safely across the street, to teach her to tie her shoes, to print her name, to braid her hair, and to wipe her tears. I continue to stroke her hair and watch her sleep long into the night.

How can such a small person demand so much attention and consume so much of my time and energy? It seems unfathomable. *I love her so much!*

It's Avery's witching hour. Well, I guess technically it's her witching *hours*. She has colic and I'm bouncing on a yoga ball, singing every melodic song I can think of to distract her from her discomfort. This seems to be the only thing that works and I'm willing to do whatever it takes to stop her pained cry. I hear Evan at the door. *Thank God, I think my thighs are going to give out.*

"Where are my favourite girls?" He sounds happy.

"In Avery's room," I call back sounding exhausted.

"Oh, how long has she been like this?" He takes off his jacket and begins undoing his dress shirt to prepare for my inevitable hand-off.

"An hour or so. She should be ready to feed again in twenty minutes. I'm going to grab a shower if that's cool." I pass Avery over and he resumes bouncing on the ball.

Standing in the shower, the warm water cascades over my body. I breathe in deeply, relishing the quiet. I love every bit of my precious girl but I need this escape for a few minutes to restore my sanity.

It used to be that showers were part of my work day routine. I would get up, start the kettle, let the dog out, shower, and get dressed. Staying home with a baby doesn't have a routine. Sure, I would like to say Avery naps at such and such a time, and feeds every three hours, but reality is a very different thing. Twenty-four hours a day, I'm at her beck and call. Some days I'm not dressed until noon and that's not for lack of trying on my part. It's rare that I can squeeze a shower in before Evan leaves for work. For an organized, routine-oriented woman such as myself, my world has been turned on its head. The reality is that, for Avery, I'm just going to have to learn to live upside down.

My reprieve is cut short by a knock on the bathroom door. "Em, I think she's hungry."

Life continues this way for a year. I'm trying my best to juggle being a mom, a wife, and well, me. Something's still nagging in the back of my brain that I need more. Just as Avery begins to toddle we find out we're going to have more. She is barely one when I find out I am pregnant again.

Sure, I've always dreamed of children plural not singular, I guess I just always thought we'd have a bit more time in between them. Truth be told, I couldn't be happier about our oops. Nine months and one scheduled c-section later, Avery's beautiful baby sister, Parker, arrives.

From the moment Evan first hands her to me, I know that she completes our family. Her rosy cheeks and quizzical look seem to mesh perfectly with Avery's energetic spirit. I'm smitten with my girls. Busy, exhausted, multitasking to the hilt, but smitten.

29 Classic Lines

Steph is living about twenty minutes away in a trendy little neighbourhood that has all kinds of specialty shops and parks. I'm dying to catch up with her, so I throw the double stroller in my new-to-me mini-van, and we head over to visit with Aunt Steph.

Apparently she broke up with her boyfriend, Ben. I can't say I'm a fan of his. I don't know him very well, but from what Steph tells me, he lets her do all the work. She's kind of a commitment-phob magnet. Men like Ben are always all over her in the beginning, and then they run for the hills. It's so frustrating, as her best friend, to see the creeps, who don't appreciate the amazing woman Steph is, mosey in and out of her life. She plays tough, but I know it bugs her more than she lets on.

With Avery asleep in the stroller and Parker strapped to my chest in the carrier-thingy, we head to the Café around the corner from her townhouse.

"So what happened with Ben?" I ask, taking advantage of the fact the kids are both quiet for the moment.

"We had a little fight about the fact I'm always the one who plans everything. I set up all our dates, I tell him where and when we are getting together, I pick the movies, I chose the restaurants, or make dinner for him. He simply shows up all the time, and I'm supposed to get excited about that? So, after our fight, he stopped calling all together. We've been dating for about four months, and he stopped answering my texts over a little fight. After a week of nothing, I finally stopped by his place. He said he's just been busy, but come on; he cut off all contact for a week! There has to be more to it?!"

"What did you say?"

"Nothing, really. I didn't really know what to stay."

"What do you mean? You didn't chew him out? Really?" She looks at me funny so I add, "It's just that you're usually so straightforward. It's not like you to shy-away from confrontation."

"I know. What can I say? I think I've been through this too many times. I'm so tired of being the one who tries to make it work. If he doesn't even have the balls to call or text me because of a stupid fight, why should I waste my energy on him?" Her words sound empowered, but the way that she says them makes my usually strong Steph seem deflated.

"I think you did the right thing Steph. He doesn't deserve you. I can tell this whole thing's bugging you though. Were you really into him?"

"It's not even that, Em. Sure, I liked Ben, but I'm not really upset about that. It's that every guy seems to be so...I don't know...it's like they don't see me in any long-term way."

"Steph, don't let Ben get you down. You're an amazing woman with so much to offer. If he can't see that, then you're better off without him." It's the classic speech that women for centuries have been telling one another. I mean it to my core, but it doesn't change the rejection that Steph is feeling.

"I'm not getting any younger, Em. I'm turning thirty-three this year. I want to do things, and starting a family is one of them. I'm frustrated, you know?"

And, there's the problem with the 'classic speech'. Sure, Steph is better off without that bum, but she wants a relationship; she wants to build a life with someone. *So what can I say? What can I do to support her?*

Avery wakes up, so we head towards the park. I'm feeding Parker on the park bench while Steph pushes Avery on the swing. I can't help but feel like I'm rubbing her nose in the whole family-thing by having the girls with us.

"Steph, you're totally going to find someone that makes you happy – someone who will be thrilled about starting a family with such an extraordinary woman. Just wait; you'll see." The classic lines continue. As I hear this one come out of my mouth, I realize I'm perpetuating the myth.

I watch Steph pretend to grab Avery's toes as the swing draws her close to her. Avery let's out the most adorable laugh. I continue nursing Parker and get a bit introspective.

Sure, Steph may meet the man of her dreams, but the reality is that it doesn't happen for everyone. I hope it does. I want to be positive, reassuring, and supportive. But, maybe perpetuating the fairytale isn't helping her? I love happy endings; don't get me wrong. I want more than anything for her to have everything she desires. What happens if it doesn't happen for her, though? She seems to be losing some hope? Her self-esteem is taking a hit. There's nothing wrong with being a strong single woman. The problem is that she has a different vision.

Perhaps the vision itself is the issue? I've been living my fairytale lately and even I'm starting to wonder about the plausibility of the 'happily ever after' part. I mean, the 'ever after' feels real, it's the 'happily' part that could use some work. My busy life as a mother of two, while infinitely rewarding in many ways, is also starting to wear on me and on my relationship with Evan. Maybe the fairytale isn't all it's cracked up to be? I wish I could help Steph achieve her vision. Maybe there's a way we could both could get our hands on the illusive happiness that is so rampant in the pages of my favourite novels and on the silver screen? But, how?

Part Three: Smoke and Mirrors

30 Destiny or Lust

"There are three bottles in the fridge. Avery sleeps with the blue blanket. Parker sleeps with the musical bear. They'll both need a bath after the spaghetti that is on the stove." I babble last minute instructions to my mom.

"The girls will be fine. Enjoy your night out," my mom says with Parker on her hip.

Evan pulls me out the door, and I can see Avery and my dad waving goodbye at the window.

I get in the car. We are heading to Britta's for dinner. *When was the last time I had a grown up evening?* I take a deep breath. I'm so tired. Life is so complicated right now. I'm back at work, juggling teaching, daycare, playing dress up, grocery shopping, making dinners on the fly, laundry, and mending boo-boos. Something's gotta give. *I'm so glad we're going out tonight. I feel like I never spend any time with Evan anymore. It's like something's missing.*

Evan and I are in the elevator on the way up to Britta's swanky downtown condo. Everything is high-end in this place. It has a doorman. In the lobby, I saw signs indicating that there's a spa, squash courts, a gym, and a salt water pool all on the mezzanine level. I've never even heard of a mezzanine, so it sounds very opulent to me.

The elevator doors open. Evan and I meander down a stylishly monochromic hallway and locate Britta's door. It has a sleek sliver shoe as a knocker. I bang the heel down lightly. Britta swings open the door and her exquisite-self envelops me in a hug.

"Em, it's so good to see you," she beams.

Evan shakes hands with Henry, her stockbroker boyfriend. We've met him a couple times before and he's recently moved in with Britta, so we'll have to get used to him. He's a good guy according to Britta, but he is standoffish and so it's hard to get to know him. I don't mind because it's Britta I'm here to see anyway. I feel a little bad for Evan though. I fully intend to stick him with Henry. He knows it too. *I'm sure he'll be fine.*

We're sitting in a gorgeous white great-room. It's a combination living room, dining room, open-concept kitchen, and solarium. It is strikingly beautiful. The thing that throws me is that it's all white. Walls, floors, shag rug, sofa, fireplace... I make a mental note never to bring my children here. It's lavish, like something out of a magazine. Everything is modern, fresh, brand new. I can't help but feel a twinge of jealousy. The only white in my house is the kids' Penaten diaper cream and the mashed up Smartfood crumbs under my couch cushions. Not quite the same stylish appeal.

"Your new place is unbelievable, Britta," I say. I overhear Evan and Henry discussing market trends. My mommy brain prevents me from entering that conversation for now. I feel somewhat out of touch.

"Yes, well, we lucked out with this place. Right place, right time. The last owners were at a gala we attended for my market re-launch for Apple. They were pregnant and were looking for a more family-friendly address. I was ecstatic because I have been wanting to get into this condo for years now."

"That's great," I reply. I contemplate the luxurious lifestyle Britta leads; the high-powered career, the fact that her life involves galas and that she has chosen a non-kid friendly home. *We are so different now.*

Evan and Henry head out to the balcony to see something or other. I remind myself to thank Evan for occupying him.

"So things are good with Henry?"

"Yeah. I think he's good for me. He keeps me centered, you know?"

"What do you mean?"

"He is so solid and sure of what he wants. It helps me gain perspective."

"How so?" I ask, still not sure what she is getting at.

"Well, you know, everyone is settling down and having families, like you."

"Yeah..."

"I don't know whether that's for me, and Henry is the first guy I have met that sees that as a positive."

"Oh..."

"It's not that I never want kids...but maybe I don't. I really like my personal time, my career, and my freedom to come and go as I please."

I'm a little shocked. I can't picture my life without kids so I guess I envisioned that for Britta too. But, looking around, she certainly is designing her life in a way that excludes rug-rats.

"I would be lying if I didn't say that I'm a little surprised you don't want kiddies, but as long as you're happy, I'm happy for you."

"I think I am," she asserts, but it doesn't sound convincing.

I want to ask her more, to find out what's really up with her. As I open my mouth, the shoe knocker bangs and Britta rushes to the door. I stay on the sofa and admire the surroundings. The aesthetically placed glassware on the mantel of the fireplace shimmers in a way that catches my eye.

"You look fantastic Britta." Tom's voice booms as he picks her up and spins her around. His long-time girlfriend, Marilyn, looks on unamused. She's kind of a non-entity. In all the time Tom and Marilyn have been together, she and I have never really had a substantial conversation. She's a placeholder of sorts, neither adding to or taking away from our evenings together. I'm not really sure what Tom sees in her.

Britta and Tom, on the other hand, have been over for years, but the connection between them is undeniable when they're together. I can feel the sexual chemistry as I approach to greet them.

"Tom, Marilyn, it's so good to see you," I say as I give them each a quick hug.

"Long time, Em. I didn't think those babies of yours were ever gonna let you out again," he quips.

"Yeah, well, grandparents are wonderful things," I add knowing that Tom's right. *Our girls are all consuming.* I try not to let my mind wander to our girls because I know the mom in me will want to call and check-up on them.

We enter the great-room. Evan and Henry join us from outside. They seem to be getting along very well. I'm pleased. Tom and Henry shake hands but I can sense the tension. I begin asking Marilyn about her new job to distract from the pissing contest that is developing in the form of a handshake. My distraction works and everyone takes a seat. We drink wine and swap stories. I'm thoroughly enjoying our time together. *It's nice to get out.*

I'm in the kitchen with Britta, talking about something funny that Parker did the other day, when Tom comes in for a drink. I immediately feel like three's a crowd. Not knowing what to do, I busy myself by washing the appetizer platter.

"It's so good to see you Britta," Tom says, standing entirely too close to Britta.

"You too," Britta distinctly blushes. Now I really want to bolt, but I realize that everyone in the other room has a clear view of us in the kitchen, and my mere presence legitimizes their interaction as innocent. If I leave, they won't be able to continue talking. Opening a drawer, I grab some Saran Wrap. I begin covering the dips and spreads. I wash the tiny cheese knives. I'm quickly running out of things to wash so I fill the sink and begin rewashing everything. Britta and Tom are oblivious to my actions.

"I really like your new condo. I would love a tour," Tom asks in a suggestive way.

"I'd love to show you around," Britta purrs back.

Normally, I hate cheating. After my early difficulties with Evan, I hate the idea that someone would do that to another person. In the case of Britta and Tom though, I find myself in a grey area. I genuinely think that they're meant to be together but they're currently with other people so...I don't know what to think.

While I agonize in my head, they vanish into the bedroom part of the condo. *Shit. They wouldn't. No. Maybe? Should I do something?* I continue rewashing clean dishes and Evan approaches from behind.

"What are you doing, pretty girl?"

"Washing...thinking."

"You don't have to do this you know. Come join us."

"I can't," I whisper.

"Why?" He whispers with a weird smile on his lips like he thinks I'm being funny.

"Because, they're in there." I gesture to the bedroom.

"Who? What? Oh..." He answers his own question before I have to. We have talked about Britta and Tom many times and we both agree that they're right for one another. Something, maybe timing, has always been off for them. When she was ready, he wasn't and vise versa.

"So are we, like, standing guard? Are they, you know?" he asks.

"No, I mean, I hope not."

Marilyn approaches and I panic. I grab Evan and kiss him passionately in hopes that she will be embarrassed about interrupting us long enough to buy some time.

"Get a room," she quips as she places her wine glass in the sink. I should have known that she wouldn't be embarrassed. She is, after all, Tom's girlfriend. "Where's Tom," she looks around and then adds, "and Britta?"

My mind goes blank. "I think they went to check out the mezzanine," is all I can come up with. *Maybe she knows what a mezzanine is?*

"Would you like to see the view?" Evan chirps up. "Henry," he yells into the great-room, "come show Marilyn the downtown cityscape. I want to hear about the plans for the waterfront renovation again." They head out. Evan looks back at me and rolls his eyes. *I owe him big.*

I rush through the corridor to the bedrooms. The first door I open is empty. The next door...I hold my breath. This must be Britta's room. I knock and turn the handle. The bedside light is on but the room is empty too. *Phew.* Then I hear whispers. *Fuck. They must be in the ensuite bathroom.* The door is open. Something metal falls on the floor in there and I hear someone whisper, "Shit."

"It's just me," I announce as I get close to the door.

"Em?" Britta says, sounding relieved.

I turn to look at the two of them. They're huddled in the corner of the marble bathroom against the wall by the sink. They're disheveled; clothed but disheveled. It reminds me of when they were in the bathroom at the 'drag bar' many years ago. *What is it with them and bathrooms?*

"What are you guys thinking?" I scold.

The smile on Britta's face is a delight. All I ever want is for her to be happy but not at Henry's expense. Tom looks guilty but alive – more alive than I have seen him in years. Neither of them respond to my very pointed question. They look at me and then each other.

"You two, honestly," I blurt out in an exasperated tone. "I'm all for you two getting together, but not like this; not while you are both in relationships with other people – who are here by the way! That's just not cool." Now I feel like their mom.

"Em, it was nothing," Britta says. I see the hurt hit Tom's eyes as she lies.

"Yeah," Tom chimes in, in an effort to protect his psyche.

"If you guys think this is nothing, you are seriously screwed up. Britta you were feeding me all that crap about being happy before. The truth is, the only time I've ever really seen you truly happy was when you were with Tom." Britta's face turns pale. "And you, Mr. Fear of Commitment, you chose the only girl in the whole world that will put up with your shit and not challenge you to be a better person. Let me introduce you to what you are afraid of. Tom this is Britta; a girl who will be more successful than you; a girl who will call you on your shit and not let you hide behind your pranks and bullshit humour." He's pale too. "I love you both. I think you are fantastic people, but I am not going to stand here while you fuck over your partners and deny your feelings for one another."

Okay, possibly took that a little far. Possibly ruined our friendships. Hell, maybe I'm jealous of the intensity of their spark? Evan and I are not very flammable lately. I wait as a strange adrenaline pumps through me. I wait as they both stare silently at me. "Fuck, say something!"

"I think you've said quite enough for all of us," Britta affirms ready to take me on.

Tom rubs his hands over his eyes. Then he speaks. "She's right," he quietly admits to us, but more importantly, admitting it to himself.

Britta turns to him. Her look is one of concern. He's looking at the floor as if he is afraid to see her reaction. Britta takes her hands and places them on the sides of his face. She lifts his gaze to meet hers.

"What do you want?" she asks, willing him to want her.

"It scares the shit out of me, Britta." He shakes his head in her hands. Not the most romantic thing I have ever heard. He follows it up with, "Britta, it has always been you. I have always wanted you." My romance meter is in the red again. They kiss until I am forced to break them up.

The rest of the evening is awkward to say the least. Britta and Tom agree to dissolve their relationships with Henry and Marilyn over the next week and start dating thereafter. I know this; they know this; but the rest of the group is oblivious as the night drags on. Tom and Britta make googly-eyes at each other while the rest of us make polite conversation over drinks and cards.

31 Slipping Away

On the way home, I fill Evan in on the evening's events.

"So, they were going at it in the bathroom?" he asks.

"Well, they definitely didn't look innocent when I entered."

"That's crazy. What were they thinking? What if Henry or Marilyn had walked in on the two of them?"

"I don't think rational thought was driving their actions, babe. Don't you remember what we were like when we first started up?"

"We were never that brazen," Evan exclaims.

"Screwing around in the park behind Allan's parent's house was pretty brazen."

"Oh yeah. I liked brazen Emilia." He puts his hand on my thigh. I squeeze his hand and flash him a knowing smile.

He continues with, "We're really lucky we found each other when we were so young. It can't be easy still searching for love at our age."

"Yeah," I say quietly, looking out the passenger side, lost in my own thoughts.

Evan's right we are really lucky to have each other. So what's with this nagging, unhappy, unfulfilled feeling still following me around?

I don't have long to contemplate it because Evan's flirtatious tone breaks my concentration. "Your parents are staying over, right?"

"Yes. Why?" I raise my eyebrow, knowing all too well that he's suggesting a brazen adventure of our own. He turns the car onto a residential street. "Babe, we can't." I look around at house after house, as we weave our way deeper into the picturesque neighbourhood.

"There has to be a park around here somewhere," he utters.

I giggle, but my rational side is in a full-fledged panic mood. "Evan, it's not that I don't want too..."

He pulls over at the curb, clicks his seatbelt, turns to me and kisses me. Not the kind of kiss I have become accustomed to. Not the usual, hurried, and almost scripted kiss we have been planting on one another to fain romance in our hectic lives. No, this is a long, drawn out, all-consuming kiss. I should be feeling the earth shatter. I should be melting under his lust-filled osculation. I'm not.

All I'm feeling is lips. The passion of the kiss is completely lost on me. The electricity's lacking. It's dismal. His hands are rubbing and massaging my breasts over my shirt. He is seriously making out with me in the front seat of my mini-van like a frenzied teenager in the middle of suburbia. And, I feel nothing. Nothing.

What is wrong with me? Why can't I get into this?
Evan used to make my body hum with his mere presence.
Now, his overzealous smooch/grope-fest is boring me. I'd
actually prefer to go home and curl up in bed with a good
book.

He begins to remove my shirt. When the headlights
of a mid-size sedan driving towards us break his
concentration briefly, I take the opportunity to push him
away. *Evan probably thinks I'm embarrassed by the passing
car.* We both sit back in our seats without a word. There's a
long silence. *Maybe he's waiting for me to continue the
make-out session?* He says nothing. He lets out a loud
annoyed sigh, turns the ignition, signals, and re-enters the
road. The moment has passed.

Fifteen minutes later I'm standing in the kitchen with
my mom and dad. They're regaling us with cute stories
about dinner and bath time with our girls. My dad has his
arm around my mom the whole time. I watch as my mom
takes my dad's hand and leads him to the guest room. It's
sweet to see them together, but the irritating thing is that I'm
envious of their connection.

I clean off the kitchen counter and prepare a few
things for tomorrow morning as Evan gets cozy on the
couch. I hear Jimmy Fallon chuckling away on the
television. *When did we become this? Is he mad about the
car thing?* I go to the bedroom and put on my track pants

and T-shirt. I sigh when I see my reflection in the mirror. *When did this become my bedtime uniform?* I brush my teeth and pop by the living room to give Evan a kiss. He is not there and neither is Maggie. I guess he took her out for a walk. I head to bed alone. This is, unfortunately, a very common occurrence. I close my eyes, wondering if I even care and I try to drift off.

I toss and turn for awhile. Finally, I open the drawer on my nightstand and pull out my latest romantic escape. So what if Britta and Tom have the fresh sparks of new lust/love. I have trashy literature. My fantasy love-life is very rich. This one involves an up and coming rockstar. I try to push the pangs of jealousy out of my head and let the story take over, but the nagging feeling that Evan and I are sparkless persists as I finally succumb to my exhaustion.

32 Red Sauce Day

I'm lying in bed. It is 5:47am. The kids will be up in an hour. I toss and turn trying to will myself back to sleep. Evan's entirely too warm body is snoring away next to me. I roll farther away from him and put a pillow over my head. My chest has an unsettled, tightness in it. I shift again and feel utterly overwhelmed by life. Thoughts invade my consciousness...

Today Parker has that thing at daycare that I should have baked for. Instead, I bought the most homemade looking peanut-free thing I could find at the grocery store and put it in some Tupperware to fake that I made it. *I can't forget to drop them off.* When I was a kid, my mom and I would have baked treats for my school together. She would have let me pour, measure and stir. I would have helped her wash the dishes, and then play in the sink for hours in the process. A sad feeling invades my heart at the realization that I missed that bonding opportunity. Truth is, I'm just too bloody busy. Juggling a full-time job, kinder-gymnastics, swimming lessons, grocery shopping, cooking, cleaning, laundry, board games, play-dates, dog walks, and bedtime routines is harder than I'd ever imagined.

Lately, I feel so fucking used, depressed, lonely, and exhausted all the time! To see me, no one would ever know. They'd think I have it made. And, in some respects, I do. I mean, I have what I have always wanted. I have the husband, the kids, the job, the house, and even the dog I always dreamed of, right?

So, why do I feel so secretly sad all the time? I've already been to the doctor twice, hoping for an answer. Confiding in her, I have shared that I'm sad or indifferent even at the best of times. She's done blood work and confirmed that there's 'nothing wrong' with me. I should be relieved, but instead it leaves me feeling like I am to blame for my sadness. *Ugh.*

With that, I hear Parker's feet hit the floor and my 'mom' day begins. I'm up warming milk, toasting toast, dressing and doing their hair, all before I get myself ready for work.

"Okay girls. Put your coats and boots on. It's time to go." I look down the hall expectantly, hoping they will come rushing to me ready and be willing to don their outdoor gear. Instead, I face the reality that they're not coming. I can hear the screams of sibling rivalry shriek out from the back bedroom.

I put down the coats and boots and head towards the loud, ear-piercing sound that only a trained two-year-old can make. I make my way into the room where I'm surprised to see my two lovely children naked, except for their underwear. They're in a tug of war over a Cinderella princess dress. Moments earlier, I had dressed them, complete with socks, pants, sparkly belts, matching pink shirts, and two barrettes each. Now, clothes are strewn everywhere and the children are bare. I calmly assess the situation while they both loudly plead their cases. I very precisely remove the source of the argument, hanging the blue ball gown on the curtain rod high above their heads. The crying grows infinitely louder as they quickly realize I'm not going to bestow the dress upon either one of them.

I hear the bathroom door close down the hall. Evan is up and getting ready for work in the solitude that the locked bathroom provides. The shower turns on and pangs of annoyance and jealousy course through my being. *Why is it that he only has himself to think about in the morning?* I know he has a very rational reason for needing some time to himself in the morning – to be more productive at work – but for the life of me, in this moment, the only thing I can think is *bull-fucking-shit!*

The girls' incessant noise continues to melt my brain. I take a deep breath so I don't freak out on them. I lean down and say in the most polite voice I can muster, "Mommy's got to get to work. Avery, Parker, I need you to get back into your school clothes." Parker goes to daycare but we call it school so she feels big and important like her older sister Avery. I hold onto a glimmer of hope that they might do as I ask. I'm quickly given another reality check. *I am going to have to do this the hard way.*

The crying persists as I redress each one. The two-year-old kicks and slashes at me as I try to stuff her into her shirt. The four-year-old pouts and stomps around, mumbling that 'it isn't fair' and that she 'had it first.'

Not taking any chances, I take them by the hand to the pile of coats and boots in the hall. Glancing at the clock, I see I have lost twelve valuable minutes and I mentally prepare to work double-time when prepping for my classes at work.

After 'lovingly' zipping zippers and stuffing boots, we head to the car. I secure their seat-belts and tenderly kiss their noses. I do up my seat-belt and put the key in the ignition and overhear Avery say, "Mommy's so mean." I take a deep breath and ignore the shot to my heart. *Fuck, I'm trying my best!*

After work, I pick the girls up from daycare and school. I make a chicken dinner with vegetables and rice. Evan is playing with the girls as I set the table. Well, I guess technically, he is watching sports highlights in the room where the girls are sticking stickers all over the wall. He is not really playing with them. It would barely count as supervising. I look in and Avery has managed to colour Parker's entire arm purple.

"Evan could you please take care of that?" *I hope those are washable markers.* I'm annoyed that I have to direct his attention to the drama that is unfolding right in front of his face.

I guess I should be glad I have a second to plate dinner in peace. Everyone sits at the table, purple arms and all. Turns out the markers were washable but not completely as the residue now makes Parker look like she should be quarantined. As for the bathroom sink, I haven't checked, but I'm fairly certain that it looks like Barney has been massacred in it.

It doesn't take long for the dinner show to begin. Only a few seconds go by before Avery announces that she doesn't like chicken. Then Parker follows suit, declaring that she doesn't like greens. They begin arguing and pushing their food around their plates. *I just want a nice quiet meal.* The noise escalates. Evan can see the frustration on my face, so he pipes up, scolding the girls for their silly behaviour. He's attempting to come to my rescue, but in the end it sets the kids off, and now everyone is yelling and crying at each other. I start welling up. I calmly get up and remove the offending chicken and greens from the table. Peace is restored momentarily.

After dinner, I clear the table. The dishes are piled high in the kitchen. They will have to wait, much like the laundry lying in the hallway. I had started sorting it when I was waiting for the oven to preheat. Then, I forgot about it when the rice water began sputtering out of the pot onto the stovetop. *I really have to measure the water better. Shit, I forgot to scrub the rice scum off the element.*

Exasperated, I pass the mound of laundry and make my way into the bathroom to start running the bath. I hear a groan behind me, "I don't want a bath." I ignore the comment and head into Avery's room. I elicit some help from her to tidy up her toys. To my surprise, she helps with minimal persuasion on my part. I still end up cleaning most of the mess myself somehow. We finish. I grab a handful of naked Barbies in hopes of luring the kids into the tub. It works, and I breathe a sigh of relief, knowing full well that I have avoided yet another epic tantrum. Seconds later, they are splashing and kicking at each other in the tub. By the time the girls are done, the bathmat and floor are soaked. I reach down, take out the plug, and use the bathmat to sop up the rest of the water. I think about the futility of laundry as I pitch it into the pile in the hallway.

Dried and dressed in their pajamas, they look so cute and lovable. I can't help but regret my stray negative thoughts towards motherhood as I snuggle up and read stories.

Now I'm filled with guilt. They're just being kids. They are awesome creatures. Smart, loving, friendly, happy, energetic, caring, innocent, sweet... I feel inadequate and insecure as a parent. The perfectionist in me dwells on an ideal that I dreamt up long ago. I regularly fall short of my own expectations.

I think back again to my own fantastic mother. My memories of her from my childhood are all amazing. They are filled with love and an unparalleled sense of security. I can't help but feel that I am missing the mark where my girls are concerned.

Movies don't help either. The moms always know exactly what to do and say. They work through problems with their kids by having 'heart-to-heart' conversations with them. They have a quiet, unassuming wisdom that I thoroughly lack. I often feel the opposite actually, I'm loud and frenzied. I have to be if I want to stay on top of everything that the day throws me. While I am aware that movies are scripted and acted, I can't help it. I wish I could have the zen-like astuteness that movie moms possess.

I hear Evan yelling at the T.V. as I tuck Parker into bed. I kiss her on the forehead and quietly exit the room. I kiss Avery and then, as I do every night, I stand in the hallway between their rooms and sing softly to them.

I start with Avery's favourite Alison Krauss' version of "You Say It Best Went You Say Nothing At All". I used to sing it to her when she was a little baby and she had no words. The lyrics meant so much to me as her baby blues would fixate on my mouth while I sang. Then I sing Parker's pick next. She loves anything Disney. Tonight she chooses

"A Whole New World" from *Aladdin.* I struggle to do both parts as I read the lyrics off my iPad. I follow that up with three short *Beatles* tunes: "Yesterday", "In My Life", and "Golden Slumbers". They usually do the trick.

Five songs in and a sense of relief comes over me. *They're asleep. Finally, I can think about me for a split second.* I take two and a half steps down the hallway and there is a loud cry from Parker's room. I'm forced to go back in and comfort her again, despite my exhaustion.

Leaving her room some ten minutes later I remember that the dishes and laundry are waiting for me. My husband is channel surfing on the couch as I pass by the living room. I try to convince myself that Evan's probably just as tired as I am. *Who am I kidding? It's just easier not to bother him for help. I don't have the energy to argue for support.* I kind of crave the peace and quiet anyway as I dip my hands into the soft sudsy water.

I open the cupboard to put the pile of dried dinner plates away and SMASH!!! A jar of tomato sauce falls out of the cupboard, smashes on edge of the granite countertop, and continues to splatter onto the kitchen floor.

"Jesus!" I hear Evan's startled voice from the living room.

I gawk at the horrendous red mess in front of me: my clothes, the counter, my formerly clean dishes, the floor, the wall. *It's everywhere!* Evan appears at the door and laughs at the sight of me. I find it difficult to see the humour in this as I reach for the roll of paper towels that is running pathetically low.

"You want a hand, babe?" He chuckles.

"No. Don't walk in here!" I say because the last thing I need is him covered in this shit too. Besides, I'm kind of pissed at his reaction.

I begin scooping and smearing the red sauce around the kitchen. It seems to grow and spread. Pulling my shirt over my head I wipe the floor with it. *It's ruined anyway.*

At some point during my clean up, Evan went back to the couch. I re-wash the plates, scrub the cupboard door, and then contemplate the circumstance. *I have opened that cupboard like three thousand times. Why, today, did that jar fall? It occurs to me that the other two thousand nine hundred and ninety-nine times I did not appreciate the fact that the sauce didn't fall. Today however, today was a 'red sauce day', and I have the tomato soaked shirt to prove it.* I toss the shirt in the pile of laundry and carry it downstairs to the machine. I mindlessly switch over the old load into the dryer and add clothes to the washer. *When did this become my life?*

Half an hour later, I'm glued to the television watching some mindless drivel. As the night wears on, I realize that I haven't even really acknowledged Evan's presence all day. I give him a peck and say, "I'm tired. I'm off to bed." He says goodnight and I head down the hall towards the bedroom. It doesn't even faze me that he's not joining me. Sure, there was a time when we couldn't keep our hands off one another. Right now I'm quite happy to head to bed alone. I try to drift off to sleep. I'd be happy to put my 'red sauce day' behind me, but I can't sleep. I toss and turn trying to get comfortable, all the while knowing that the kids will be up at quarter to seven tomorrow regardless of how drained I am. My last thought as I succumb is that *it's garbage day tomorrow*. That's Evan job. *Who am I kidding? I'm totally going to be dragging that crap to the curb first thing in the morning. Sigh...*

33 Comfortably Numb

Married sex. Like most married couples, our first few years of marriage were filled with romantic-exciting-toe-curling sex. We christened every room of our house. We would get caught up in the moment and be dreadfully late for events. I would only need to catch the aroused glint in Evan's eyes and I'd be hungry with passion...

"Babe, did you pick up the wine for Britta's?" I ask as I enter the bathroom. Evan is busy shaving his stubble. Freshly showered, he looks good enough to eat. The aroma of soap and Evan's natural scent invade me. Inhaling deeper I close my eyes to take it all in.

"Shit, sorry I forgot." He glances at me briefly as I begin applying some lipgloss. "You look lovely tonight," he purrs. *I know that tone.* A small smile flashes across my face. *I know what he's up to.*

"Don't even think about it. We'll be late. Besides, now we have to stop for wine."

"Oh, I'm thinking about it alright." Before he is even finished uttering the words, his hands are exploring the curves of my body. I blot my lips together. In the mirror I can see the devilish glint in his eye. His hands move up to caress my breasts, and despite my rational side shooting me a pang of guilt, I succumb.

...It was that easy. He would ignite a flame and I would explode. As the years went on, we could still be explosive together, but my rational side won out more often than not. I think my ability to put a damper on his flame made him feel somewhat rejected. Evan began saving his matches.

It's not that I don't want...no...crave the passion. Life just kind of gets in the way, somehow. Now that we have two kids, I'm so tired all the time. I am so drained from constantly giving to other human beings that I forget...I just forget.

I forget the way my body felt electrified under his touch – the way life seemed more whimsical and freeing when we were ravishing one another. How carefree we used to be. I forget the way my mind made suggestive hints to me all day when I was head-over-heels. I forget...I forget how I felt attractive and somehow more confident about myself when I saw myself through the eyes of a lascivious man. I just forget...then something happens that makes me remember...

34 Jealous Much

I'm putting my boots on at the door, getting ready for work, and it dawns on me that I need to remind Evan about Book Club.

"Hey, Ev. I'm going to Joyce's tonight for Book Club. Can you put the girls to bed solo so I can get there on time?"

"Huh?" he utters.

"Book Club. It's tonight. You have the kids."

"No, I can't. I'm off for the weekend, remember? I'm heading downtown to the lenders conference thing."

"I thought that was only on Saturday night?"

"A couple of us are heading there tonight. We wanted to go tonight so we can settle in. The conference starts so early tomorrow."

"Seriously? So I have the girls all weekend, by myself, and I don't even get Book Club this week?" I huff.

"Sorry, babe. I promised the others."

"Who's going?"

"Oh, um Steve, Manny, Cheryl, Margaret and Bob. You know, the regional management crew."

I'm instantly on edge at the mention of Cheryl's name. She's always bugged me. She radiates that 'I'm stalking your husband' vibe. *I trust Evan, but a weekend away with her?* Actually, I think I'm more pissed that he is going off to have a life. I am going to be stuck listening to "I'm Elmo and

I Know It" a hundred times while slaving around, attending to the girls' whims the whole weekend. *Jealous much?*

"Fine." Inside I wrestle with telling him to stay away from Cheryl, but I can't be bothered to. *He'll just get his back up about my insinuation.*

The day drags on. Work's okay I guess. I pick up the girls from daycare. As I stir pasta on the stove, I call Joyce to tell her that I can't come to Book Club. She commiserates and we plan a play-date after the kids' gymnastics class tomorrow. It'll be nice to have some adult conversation. Sure, we'll probably be dressing Barbies or fixing a Play-Doh ice cream machine during our conversation, but I still crave the interaction.

I climb into bed after standing outside waiting for Maggie to 'do her business' in the freezing cold. I crawl under the covers with my Book Club book. Eat Pray Love has been around for a while, but none of us have read it. Joyce always chooses life affirming stuff and it was her pick. I'm three paragraphs in when the phone rings.

"Hey, you." It's Evan. He sounds like he is enjoying himself, perhaps a little too much? *Is he drunk?*

"Hey, yourself." I hear voices in the background. They're pretty rowdy.

"I'm calling to say goodnight."

Oh, that's sweet. "That's nice, babe."

"I feel bad about your Book Club thing." His sentiment is great and all, but I'm totally distracted by a woman's giggle in the background.

"Thanks, Ev. Where are you?"

"We all came back to my room. A couple of lenders wined and dined us."

"That's great. Who's with you?" My jealousy can't help but lure me deeper.

"Kevin from accounts, Cheryl, Steve, Margaret and Bob. We're having a couple of drinks." The incessant girly giggle sends my brain into a tail spin.

"Evan," I say in a you-should-know-better, kind of tone, "watch yourself with that Cheryl. She's got a thing for you." It feels weird as it comes out. I can't help it. I know I'm just fueling his libido with a 'forbidden fruit' angle. *What am I doing?*

"Em. Seriously? What are we, in high-school? You have nothing to worry about."

I take offense to his implication that I'm being childish, even though I am.

"Ev, I know how frisky you get when you're drinking. I just don't want you to do anything stupid." I instantly regret saying it.

A door closes and the voices are now muffled. He must be in the bathroom or the hallway. *That can't be good.*

"Em, I'm not sure what's wrong with you. I can't believe you would think I would cheat on you. We have a family. We have a life together. You think I would fuck that up?"

"Evan..." I try to defend myself but he cuts me off.

"I don't know what's gotten into you lately. I miss you, Emilia. You're so...so not yourself." I'm silenced. I have no response. After a long uncomfortable pause he says, "I gotta go. I'll call tomorrow. Night." Click. He hangs up before I can even muster a lame 'I love you, goodnight.'

What a shitty conversation. It seems like all I see is Evan's annoyingness lately – his shortcomings, distance, and lack of support are bombarding my vision of him. *That Cheryl can have him.* I can't believe my own thoughts. I pull the covers over my head questioning my own resolve.

What does he mean, 'I'm not myself'? I remember back to high-school when Evan was prowling around behind my back with that Sarah girl. *It was so devastating. It seems like a lifetime ago. I'm not sure I'm the same girl anymore. Sure, it would be devastating if Evan slept with someone else, but frankly, not for the same reason it was back then. Then, it killed me because it completely ruined the emotional connection I had with him. It destroyed my trust and put my concept of intimacy into question.*

Now, I think I love Evan in a different way. Sadly, I think it's more out of convenience and a sense of loyalty than anything else. It's hard to think about, but I question whether Evan cheating would just give me the impetus to alter my existence in some way. It would be devastating because it would change the dynamic of our family and it would be a legal nightmare.

I vaguely remember Steph's mom leaving her dad when we were young. The look in her dad's eyes was like he had been totally blindsided. That sticks out in my memory so clearly for some reason.

I used to feel like her mom leaving was selfish and inconsiderate. My perception seems to be changing. *Who knows how long she felt used and alone?*

I fall asleep dizzy with depressing hypotheticals whirling through my brain. I'm pretty sure I don't want a life without Evan, but the way life feels right now, well...I don't want that either.

35 More Beige

<<BRING>> <<BRING>> The phone jolts me up. I fumble to find it on the bedside table. Three forty-two in the morning. *What the fuck is he thinking?*

"Evan, what the..."

"Em," I hear my brother Jay's voice. I freeze. My heart instantly kicks into turbo drive as I listen, "it's Dad. Mom's taken him to the hospital. I'm not sure what's going on, but it doesn't sound good. Mom wants us to come." His last line hangs in the air. Consumed by fear, I robotically prepare to make the hardest drive of my life.

I call Evan. When he doesn't answer – *let's face it he could sleep through a freight train* – I call the front desk. They send someone up to wake him. I can't wait. I call Joyce. It is now four ten in the morning. I wouldn't call her if I wasn't desperate. She's at my house in record time, still wearing her pajamas.

I'm in the car when my phone starts buzzing. I can't answer because I'm driving, but the buzz is somehow comforting. *Evan knows. Evan is trying to help.*

The hospital is on the other side of the city. Tears of panic are streaming down my face as I pull onto the highway. I try to console myself. *He's going to be just fine.* But the nagging thought that *Mom would have waited until the morning if that were true* invades my brain.

My relationship with my dad flashes through my memory. His kind heart, gentle guidance, and constant love and support. Physical pain begins to swamp my own heart. I'm on the off ramp when my thoughts drift to my mom. *My poor Mom. He's her everything. What the hell will she do if...?* I can't bear to finish the thought. *What the hell is with all the fucking red lights?* I beat the steering wheel out of frustration. I'm overly conscious of the fact the sun is beginning to rise on the scariest day of my life. *My poor Mom. Why is it taking me so long?*

I pull into the visitor parking near the emergency doors. My mind is racing as I rush past the 'Please Disinfect Your Hands' kiosk towards information. It's closed. *What the fuck!!!* I pick up a phone on the desk that has a sign saying, 'After Hours Information.' I swear I can hear my own rage as I wait for the electronic voice to list my options.

"Em," I turn and Jay is standing behind me. He is ghost white as he says, "Mom's in the Critical Care waiting room. Follow me." *Critical Care,* the phone drops from my hand and I silently follow Jay into the elevator. Oddly, it dons on me that he's not wearing his coat. *He got here before me. He's seen Mom. He knows what's going on.* My thoughts are brief, staccato. Shock has set in. I take a deep breath, afraid of what is to come.

Jay breaks the silence. "Em, it's not good. Dad was complaining of a sharp pain in his stomach for the last couple of days." A pang of guilt shoots through me. I've been so consumed by my own life that I haven't talked to my mom for about a week. "Tonight he woke up sweating and shaking. Mom called an ambulance." I don't think our family has ever had to do that. Mom must have been extremely worried for her to call an ambulance. "When they got here, Dad was examined and admitted for emergency surgery. He's in surgery now."

"What's wrong with him?" I sputter out, desperate to know, but frightened at the same time.

"It is pretty technical. The doctor told Mom he has a perforated bowel." I hear the words but they don't really hold any meaning for me. I could easily figure out what it means on a normal day. The frenzied hysteria in my brain right now is rendering me dumfounded.

"What does that mean?" I search Jay's eyes for hope. They are as vacant as mine.

"He has a massive internal infection. They're going to have to take part of his intestine out. It's not good, Em."

I hug Jay. I never hug Jay; we aren't really that close. As the elevator door opens on the top floor of the hospital, I mentally prepare to be strong for my mom.

The fluorescent lighting in the hallway hums and our footsteps are the only other sound in the long corridor. I'm glad Jay is leading the way because everything seems the same in the sterile tunnels of this hospital maze. It's an endless stretch of beige.

We turn and enter a small, cheerless room. *More Beige.* My mom rushes to me and throws her arms around me. I hold my panic-stricken mom.

"Thank you for coming," she says like Jay's late night call wasn't a forgone conclusion.

We edge over to a bank of seats and I can feel my phone buzzing again. I'll get to Evan once I have more to tell him. I hold my mom's hand and look into her ghostly face. Shock has set in for her as well. She fills me in with the same information Jay gave. I listen as though it's the first time I have heard the details. She is telling me as much for her as for me. She is trying to make sense of it. I hear her optimistic spin as she repeatedly reassures me "...your dad is strong. He'll be just fine. I am sure he'll be just fine..." She tapers off. The Critical Care sign looms over our heads. We all know it.

After an hour of hugs and hand holding, I excuse myself into the hallway to call Evan.

"Em," he answers on the first ring. "Em. I got your message. I rushed home. Are you okay?"

"I am..." I try to be strong but I've left my strength in the waiting room with my mom. "Ev, it's bad." I sound like Jay, but it's the only thing I can struggle out before the lump in my throat attacks my vocal cords. I sob into the phone and lean my forehead against the beige door frame.

"Baby, I'm so sorry. What happened? How is he?"

I explain my dad's reality. My mom's optimism sneaks in as I try to reassure him and myself that he can beat this. It helps, talking to Evan. I feel like I can let my vulnerability out and I hope that will help increase my strength for when I'm with my mom.

"What can I do? How can I help?" I hear his genuine concern. *It is nice to hear Evan so invested in something. It is sad that this is what it takes to hear it these days.*

"Just look after our girls. I've gotta get back to my mom."

"Emilia," the word catches me before I hang up, "I love you so much, babe. Be strong." It is exactly what I need.

I swallow the lump in my throat. "I love you too."

Several hours later, Jay is getting coffee when the surgeon enters the waiting room. Still in scrubs with fabric booties over his shoes, he reads 'Mrs. Somerville' from the clipboard in his hand. My mom and I stand and follow this complete stranger, who holds our fate in his hands, into a small room marked 'Private Consultation'. I search the steely eyes of the doctor for hope. The physical exhaustion that he exudes scares me. I squeeze my mom's hand.

"Well Mrs. Somerville, I have never seen anything even close to the amount of infection your husband was dealing with. It's a wonder he did not end up here months ago." I'm shocked by his frank bedside manner. I'm holding my breath because he hasn't given any indication that my dad is okay yet.

I look at my mom. I can see in her eyes her desperation for reassurance.

"How is he now?" I ask because I know my mom cannot speak.

"It's complicated. He's stable for now. But because of the amount of infection, we were unable to close him up." My brain heard 'stable'. After that it was all a jumble.

The surgeon goes on to explain that they will finish the surgery on Monday provided the infection responds to the medication they're administering. I'm confused. A saner me would have all kinds of questions. Instead, I only really hear words that are either comforting or that freak me right out. The rest is just noise. One of his sentences replays in my head as I try to register its implications.

"There was so much infection, it would be a miracle if we got it all." *Are doctors really allowed to talk like this?* When the doctor leaves the room, I see his words are ping ponging around my mom's brain as well.

Now is the hard part. We wait. We wait and we hope. To pass the time we update friends and family. It's hard to sit here with my mom and pretend we aren't both thinking the worst. I can hear her updating my aunt in her chipper way. I do the same as I talk to Avery and Parker on the phone.

"Grampa's tummy was hurting but the doctors are fixing him up. Mommy's going to stay here with Gramma today. Maybe you could make him a picture. I'm sure that would make him feel better." *If only it were that easy I would Crayola a bloody mural right now!*

The hardest part is that neither my mom nor I are willing to acknowledge aloud that there was a look of terror in the surgeon's eyes when he discussed the infection. *It is his job. He does it every day. So why the horror?* I lock the question in my brain behind my optimist facade.

Day turns into night. Jay's wife, Charlotte, has brought us clothes and snacks. She and Jay have left for the night. Mom and I are still glued to the vinyl chairs when a nurse comes in to tell us we can visit briefly with dad.

We walk into the room. He is sleeping. Machines are buzzing and flashing around him. I.V.'s and tubes seem to be attached to him everywhere. I watch as my mom gently strokes his cheek. *He looks so small.* I am so used to him being a beacon of strengthen and wisdom. He is lying there *so frail.* I wince at the thought.

Dad's eyes flutter open weakly. He reaches for mom's hand.

"Shh, it's okay," she soothes. My mom looks at ease for the first time all day. They're together. She can touch and feel and see him.

I give Dad a quick kiss on the forehead, fully aware that he has been through too much today. I prepare to take my leave. "I love you, Daddy."

His voice is weak as he says, "I love you too, kiddo." A tear escapes and trails down my cheek.

"You rest. I will be back in the morning."

I don't even ask Mom to come with me. There's not a chance she'll leave his side tonight. It takes everything in my power to drag myself from the room. I know though, that together they're fine. Together, regardless of circumstance, they are better.

On the drive home the fatigue hits me. It's amazing how sitting and staring at four walls can be so draining. I flip through the radio stations trying to find something to perk me up. I fail as I catch the tail end of Death Cab For Cutie's "I Will Follow You Into The Dark". I listen to every word with new found appreciation.

I am sobbing. Seeing my parents together, so completely connected makes me wonder about Evan and I. It hurts too much to consider the agony that might ensue if I give it any more consideration.

I pull into the driveway. I can see the bluish flicker of the television bouncing off the walls inside the house. A slight worry about seeing Evan creeps into my consciousness. Before all this stuff with Dad, our last conversation was so awful. I don't know if I have the energy to discuss it. Fumbling with the lock at the front door, Evan rushes over to let me in. I've texted him the details of the day. Until now I have not seen the concern in his eyes. *He does care. I mean of course he cares, but lately we have both been too busy to give each other any real emotion.* I see real emotion in his eyes and I cling to it. I toss my coat on the floor, kick off my shoes, and wrap my arms around him.

He lifts me up and carries me to bed. Without a word, he pulls back the covers and gently places me down. He climbs in and holds me close. I can feel his breath on my neck as we spoon. He whispers, "Today was hard. Tomorrow will be better." Emotionally drained, his warmth fills me up. I fall asleep with my spark of hope ignited. *I hope I'm not dreaming this feeling.*

36 Insight and Resolve

I have breakfast with Evan and the girls before heading back to the hospital. It's Sunday and traffic is light. The sky is dull as I case the parking lot rows in search of a space. The sad thought that *the hospital is really busy today* crosses my mind. It's depressing that so many people are here this early on a Sunday morning.

I text Mom to find out where they are. My dad has been transferred to the I.C.U. I quickly make my way to that part of the hospital. The large 'Intensive Care Unit' sign freaks me out. My mom is sitting in the waiting room with her back to me.

This waiting room is very different. It has an air of importance. It has large comfortable chairs in it. I see a couple sleeping in two chairs in the corner. Another sad thought occurs to me: *this place is different because it's meant to comfort the people unfortunate enough to be in this area of the hospital. The waiters in this room are often waiting for the end.* I shudder, take a deep breath, and make my way over to my mom.

My mom fills me in. Dad has had some complications during the night and they have brought him here to stabilize his heart rate. He even has a nurse assigned solely to him. *That can't be good.*

With my brave face firmly in place, I insist that my mom go home and rest. I explain to her that I will sit vigil all day and she can come back in the evening. She looks ruined. She's no good to him in this state anyway. She has been by his side all night and is only in the waiting room because there was an issue with a nearby patient. The nurses asked her to give them a few minutes to sort it out.

A nurse buzzes me into the I.C.U. It is the craziest place I have ever been. I walk past bed after bed of seriously injured or gravely ill people. One person after another, on the brink, in limbo between life and death. The beds are divided only by a curtain. At the end of each bed is a nurse recording in great detail every blip, beep, fluid intake, or output. It is a scene right out of a science fiction movie. Most of these people are only alive because of the electronic contraptions they're attached to. They can't eat, move, and in some cases, breathe without assistance. The fact that my father is in bed 32 in this room is more than a little disturbing.

I try not to look as I hear someone weeping behind one of the curtains. I do look though. I can't help it. The image of a mother sobbing at her daughter's bedside burns its way into my brain. The girl is young, maybe twenty. Her head is bandaged and she has lots of bruising. Tubes are running in and out of her body. She is there, but one look and the painful sound of her mother's cry tells me she's not really there. I only glanced at the heart wrenching vignette in passing, but I know instantly that it will be an image that haunts me forever. I'm not sure why, but it has been tattooed in my memory. *It makes me want to live...really live. That poor girl. Her poor mom. What horrible misfortune has brought them here?*

Time has always seemed very linear for me. I have always been driving forward. What if my time is cut short? You just never know? It is hard not to think about your own mortality when you can taste death in the air.

27, 28, 29, 30, 31. Dad's next. The nurse at Dad's feet stands up as I approach.

"Hello. You must be Emilia. Your dad and mom have told me about you. I'm Beth. I will be your dad's nurse for the next three hours or so. I've been here all night with him and he seems to be perking up." She grabs a tray from Dad's bedside and leaves the curtained area.

Thanking her as she walks away, I turn to face my dad. *He's still frail and small.* His skin is grey and sweaty. I'm relieved when he quips, "It's about time. I thought your mom would never sleep again."

I smile and quip back, "Yeah well, you haven't got the best timing you know. Next time, give a girl some notice before you pull a stunt like this."

He laughs and then winces grabbing his stomach in pain. I remember my fear of laughter after my c-sections. I apologize for the joke and try hard not to be funny. Unfortunately, humour is my defense mechanism for stressful situations. *This is going to be hard.*

Hours go by. I pass the time by reading the sports section aloud to him. I watch him sleep. I pat his brow with a moist towel. It's nice being here for my dad, supporting him and, in a small way, giving him what he always gave me: comfort and love.

Jay comes by midday and I slip out for a bite in the bleak cafeteria. It is a relief to be among the living even, if they are random lunch counter workers.

When I get back into Dad's room, he is asleep. On the other side of Dad's curtain, I can hear a nurse talking to her patient. He is in a vegetative state, but she talks to him gently anyway. *It's sweet.* I look at my dad. Now that he's sleeping, I can really appraise his situation. The blanket that used to cover his stomach has rolled down slightly. I can see a large tube sticking out of the bandages covering his still open wound. It creeps me out, but I stare anyway. The rawness of his sudden brush with death is so disconcerting. It makes me contemplate my own life again.

It's around dinner time and Dad's up. His mood has changed. He knows I'll be leaving when Mom gets here. Only one visitor can be in here at a time.

"Emilia, there's something I need to say." His tone and the way he is holding my hand tells me that I'm not going to like this conversation. He pulls me close so I'm looking him right in the eye. "Em. If anything happens to me, I need to know that you will be there for your mom. She's gonna want her independence, but Em, I want you to promise me that you will bring her to live with you."

"Dad, don't..."

"Em, I need you to promise me. I mean, I may not have been the best husband, but the least I can do is make sure she's taken care of after..." He tapers off.

"Dad, stop. You were and will continue to be the perfect husband. You can't talk like this. You need to be positive." *The irony of my statement is not lost on me. I'm queen pessimist these days.*

"Em, I was far from perfect. Your mother will attest to that." He laughs slightly and quickly holds his stomach. I can see by his expression that a thought has flashed into his consciousness. *It is strange seeing my dad as a man.* "You know when you kids were young I was so distant. Your mom used to say if we had any more kids I would have been a doctor. I started night school right after your brother was born. I continued until your mother almost left me."

What is he talking about? They were so great together. I remember them always being so in love. I must have a quizzical look on my face because he goes on.

"Your mom was...is my best friend, Em. I took her for granted during those early years. As I'm sure you're finding out, there are no rule books for how to be married and have kids. I did what I thought I should and left your mom to do everything else. She was so good with you kids that I didn't realize she had taken on so much. Her life became consumed with the care of everyone else. She had lost herself. I'm so thankful she had the sense to shake things up before it was too late." I'm not sure why he is telling me all this. *Maybe he knows. Maybe he can see through me.*

"She's the love of my life, Em. It's things like this," he points to his open wound, "that help me realize how lucky I really am." He pauses, lost in his thoughts. "Your mother has always cared for us wholeheartedly. That's why I need you to promise to care for her if..." He closes his eyes, unable to complete the plea.

"Dad, I promise. But I know that you're gonna be fine so don't..." I can't finish my statement either. I sit holding his hand in silence for a while until the nurse tells me that my mom is in the waiting room.

I kiss him on the forehead before an orderly escorts me out.

My mom gives me a big hug filled with genuine gratitude. She looks worried but much more put together then the sleep deprived basket-case I saw when I arrived.

Driving home, everything starts to make sense to me. *The marriage I have been striving for was romanticized by my memory. I still think my parents are great role models, but I have to consider that I was seeing what they wanted me to see, and what I wanted to see. It's a strangely liberating insight.*

It's all so clear now. I have been so busy deflecting my sadness onto my surroundings that I didn't realize Evan and the kids aren't actually sad. Have I somehow martyred myself in support of their happiness? Evan's right. I haven't been myself lately. I have forgotten who that is. It's my relationship with me that's the problem! My family is oblivious to my sadness. It's not Evan. Well, maybe Evan's complicit in it too, but it's me. I'm the one who's withholding. I'm the one who's withdrawn. I'm too busy doing life to live it. It sounds so cheesy, but it's true! And, the scary thing is, I have no clue how to live any other way.

Just like Dad described, it's my fault that I'm being taken for granted. When did I stop asking for support? When did silence become easier than honesty? When did it become easier to do everything myself? Is it really easier if it builds up to this dissatisfied feeling?

I need to be honest with me. I need to be honest with Evan. I need to connect again, to feel again. But how?

37 Book Club

I'm in the bathroom desperately trying to read the last thirty pages of *Eat, Pray, Love.* The irony of Joyce's choice this week is not lost on me. *Maybe it has added to my internal struggle lately? I might not be lying on the bathroom floor, but the inner turmoil of the lead character, Liz, resonates with me. Maybe I need to step out of my comfort zone a little more. Italy, India, and Bali may not be the answer for me, but, something's gotta give!*

Evan's calling me for dinner. Since I've been busy with work and the hospital, Evan has started stepping up at home. Tonight, he has been slaving away in the kitchen for an hour.

I know that if I don't finish my book now I will be the only one tonight who hasn't. I dog-ear my page, add a little bit of blush and lipstick, so I look alive, and head to the kitchen for dinner. Evan and our girls are already seated. It's the first dinner I have had with them all week. Between work and the hospital I've barely been home. We eat Avery's favorite pasta. I make quick work of the dishes and then play 'Snakes and Ladders' before bathing the girls and tucking them into bed. I've missed these little things so much. It is 8:30 as I walk the block and a half over to Joyce's house. I'm armed with my book and a bottle of wine.

It has been a week since my dad went into the hospital. Dad has been moved to a regular room and the doctors seem optimistic. *Fingers crossed, he is going to be okay.*

"Come on in," Joyce says as I step over her kids' backpacks at the door. "Will is putting the kids down, so make yourself at home."

Deb, Joyce's friend, and Steph are already here, drinks in hand.

I make my way to the kitchen for a glass and pop the cork on my bottle of 'Girls Night Out' wine. I take a sip and savour a quiet moment in the kitchen. I grab the bottle and make my way to the living room.

"Hey you, how's your dad doing?" Steph smiles at me.

"Better today. They think he might start fluids tomorrow." I sit beside her on Joyce's overstuffed brown sectional. I put my feet up on the ottoman and relax for the first time all day.

"Everything else okay?" She senses my stress. Maybe it was the loud sigh I omitted when I sat down.

"Yeah, same old shit, you?" I don't really feel like going over my week so I ask, "How are things with Ben?" Her on again off again relationship with him drives me nuts! I know she really likes him, so I try my best to be supportive, but it makes me crazy that she still seems to make all the effort in their relationship.

"We're good. I haven't seen him that often over the past couple weeks, but we're good." I'm not sure if she is reassuring me or herself.

Deb places a tray of veggies and dip on the table and starts ranting, "Steph, you don't know how good you have it. I mean, I love Barry and the kids, but the freedom you have. What I could do with even an hour to myself." Deb has twin four-year-old boys.

"It's like the book," Joyce chimes in. "Steph, you are the only one of us who could really make a journey like that – who could pack up and leave everything to find what makes you happy."

"Steph, if I were you I would be packing my bags," Deb adds.

"I don't think the book is saying you have to leave your life to find yourself. She says something about seeking truth internally or externally," Steph says.

"I think she means through meditation," I pipe up.

"Yeah, like I have time to meditate. I don't think my postnatal yoga video or the hour of guided meditation in the church basement with that crazy-hippy lady is going to bring me the same kind of enlightenment Liz traveled the world to find." Deb is always so pessimistic. I think it's sad that I agree with her.

I take a swig of wine and then ask, "Do you think you can find yourself when you're in a relationship...when you have kids that depend on you?"

Silence befalls the room. I think we're all introspectively considering the question.

"I don't know but I want to feel inspired," Joyce chimes in with flare. She is always full of spunk. It is part of her charm. Her comment saves us from the awkward silence I single handedly created with my question.

I think out aloud, "Family is a huge part of what makes me, me. I mean, shit, I'm not sure I could find myself without them." I feel satisfied and reassured by my answer.

"You say that because your family's perfect," Deb says with a hint of disdain.

"We're far from perfect," I defend. Or wait. Maybe I'm throwing us under the bus. I'm not sure.

"You guys are pretty perfect," Steph chimes in as Joyce nods in agreement.

"I'm glad you ladies think we have our shit together." I register that I'm swearing way too much this evening. "But I'm just as exhausted, frustrated, and fed up as you are with the constant demands on my time. I need inspiration just as much as you do." *It's true.*

"I gotta tell you; I'm relieved to hear you say that. It's nice to know you're human too." Joyce seems to commiserate. *It's funny that they think things are so perfect*

with us. I'm not sure if I like that. It's probably a testament
to the fact that I go out of my way to project a perfect image.
Why do I even care what others think?

There is a noticeable silence. Twice in one night, it's
very unlike us, especially on evenings where wine is
involved.

Deb breaks the silence with, "What is it about us
women? Why do we feel like we have to do it all – and with
a smile on our faces to boot?" She proceeds to finish her
merlot.

"I think you're all fantastic. Marriage, kids, work...I
have trouble keeping track of things sometimes, and I only
have work and the odd boyfriend to deal with." Steph
attempts to boost our egos.

"You know, this is the only time I get off all week?"
Deb quietly admits.

"I'm glad we've decided to do this. Regardless of the
books, it is refreshing to get together with you ladies, to relax
and be ourselves with no one needing us," I affirm.

"It is nice, but in keeping with the theme of the book:
how can we make things better for ourselves?" Joyce
always brings us back to the book on nights like this. She
was a literature major in university.

"Well, we've already established that we can't make
for Italy. So, I don't know," Deb scoffs.

I reluctantly open up. "I think my issue is with me. I need to figure out what inspires me. It sounds a bit odd, but maybe I need to date me for a while." I'm not sure where the date idea comes from, but ever since the talk I had with my dad in the hospital, I've been contemplating taking some 'me time'.

"Date yourself?" Deb inquires.

"Actually, that's an interesting idea, Em," Steph says. "At the beginning of my relationships, I always feel really stoked. Maybe treating myself to things that make me happy would have the same effect."

"So, what are we talking about? I take myself out for dinner?" Deb says as she rolls her eyes at the idea.

"No, I get it," Joyce chirps up. "We need to remember the simple pleasures that we neglect because our lives are so hectic. We need to allow ourselves to be consumed by the things that make us giddy."

"I guess," I say. "I need to think more about it. Maybe we could make a list of things we could do for ourselves; a self-dating guide of sorts." The idea sounds promising, albeit weird, as it comes out.

"If it gets me out of madly trying to read three chapters of a new book by next week, I'm in," Deb jokes. Joyce gives her a sour look.

"I'm in too," Steph affirms. "I think it could be fun."

"Okay," Joyce chimes in, "but we have to choose a book for the following week," she adds pouring herself another glass of red.

38 Yes Instead of No, Sex Instead of Sleep

My dad is scheduled to go home from the hospital next week. The doctor is still monitoring him closely, but it seems miracles do exist. The infection that was threatening his life is responding to the medication, and he is recovering well from the surgery. I call my mom to check in. Dad is resting comfortably. A sense of relief washes over me. Life is slowly returning to normal.

I turn my attention to my Book Club homework. I have always been the studious type, so making a list of date ideas is at the forefront of my brain all week. I have a blue pad of sticky notes that I have placed on the counter to scribble stray thoughts on. At first I start writing answers I think the other women will agree with. Each time I do, my ideas seem so boring and forced. I need to see the beauty in my everyday life. This is easier said than done, of course. This list isn't for the girls anyway. Sure, we'll discuss it, but I don't really have to share anything I don't want to. I need to be honest with myself.

I start with a list of things that make me happy. *Scratch that; it needs a cooler name than that. My Self-Dating-Guide? No, I don't like that either. My Pleasure Inventory. Yes, yes I like that.*

I write My Pleasure Inventory:

        -my family

        -reading relationship novels

        -watching uplifting romantic movies

        -the perfect cup of tea

        -long baths

        -belly laughs

        -music, any kind really

        -dressing up

        -sex

I read it over. *Of course my family is first on the list. Watching the girls grow, learn, and play together is so incredible. I love seeing Evan's pride and sheer joy as he tickles them mercilessly. Fixing boo boos, good night cuddles, reading stories together, playing play-dough, doing puzzles, and listening to their crazy insights about the world makes me truly happy. Sure, I've been less than enthusiastic about family life lately, but the fact remains, that deep down they provide me with unfathomable joy...*

"Mommy, I made you a picture." I look down, and on the page is Avery's endearing rendering of our family. Evan's very tall, with a huge smile plastered on his face from ear to ear. Avery is holding his hand. She's wearing a little shirt with a rainbow etched on it. Parker is smaller, her curly hair encircling her head. Maggie is drawn with fuzzy pencil strokes jutting out to make her appear furry. Then there's me. I'm large, like Evan. I have long curly hair like Parker and a rainbow on my shirt like Avery. I'm smiling larger than everyone and right beside my head is a large heart. The picture is beautiful. It is how I always hoped my children would see our family. Tears form in my eyes as I bend down and hug Avery. *Maybe I'm not missing the mark.*

"Your picture is lovely. Tell me about what you have drawn." As a Grade One teacher, I have learned to 'ask the question' instead of assuming anything about a child's drawing.

"It's us mommy. This is Daddy, Me, and Parker. That's Maggie and you."

"We look very happy," I say.

"We are, 'cause we're all together."

I don't think she could be more adorable.

...This is kind of happiness I need to hold on to. It is the feeling that I need to channel when I'm frustrated and feeling pulled in every direction.

Next on the list is reading, movies, bath, and tea. *I find it hard to imagine when I will possibly find more time for these things, but if I'm serious about dating me, these aren't bad options. I can do all of these things after the girls go to bed. Perhaps I can combine some of them. Maybe I will try to have a bath with my book and a tea, once or twice a week. Sure, I think I can squeeze that in.*

As for movies, I will make a solid effort to watch one movie each week. Evan plays hockey on Tuesday nights, so that could be my movie night. I should see if Steph wants to come. We didn't say anything about double dating. I like the idea. I grab the blue sticky note and write 'Steph time' on it.

Since belly laughs can't be scheduled, I guess I will have to remember to enjoy every last chuckle when it come along. Enough said.

Music...huh. I can't deny that music has always elevated my mood. It's not like I'm going to take myself dancing or anything. How can I actively increase music in my life? I need to finally tackle, iTunes, upload my CDs, and immerse myself in it. It will take time...ugh. Maybe I can resolve to add one or two albums a week? That sounds do-able. Maybe I can play songs when I cook dinner and have the girls dance around my feet. Sounds quite fun actually. Done and done.

Dressing up. Well, that takes effort too. On weekends, I'm in my mom gear: track pants and a fitted tee.

Through the week, I'm in cheap cotton-blend slacks and a sweater or blouse – nothing I would be too upset about spilling orange paint on, since it is in my job description. It's no wonder dressing up makes me feel happy. I seldom do it and when I do I'm usually headed to a wedding or an anniversary dinner. I would make an effort to look good if were going on a date with anyone else, so why shouldn't I look good for me?

*Secretly, I sometimes wish I had a high-powered job like Britta. Being in marketing, she always looks pristine, tailored, sharp, and sexy. Three inch heels are simply not practical in my life. My footwear choices typically revolve around the requisit that my shoes need to let in as little sand as possible. This is imperative when you stand in a playground multiple times a day. If they're waterproof, even better. Not quite the sexy appeal of a stiletto. If dressing up gives me pleasure, then I'm going to put in more of an effort. Perhaps I'll even purchase some sexy shoes of my own. I should enlist Britta. She would love to help sexify my footwear, w*hich brings me to the last thing on my inventory, Sex.

It's beginning to feel like everything on my list requires more effort, more engagement on my part. I'm already drained just thinking about all the changes I have to put in place. It's starting to feel overwhelming.

So, Sex. How am I going to fix that department? Even though I'm supposed to be dating me, I think it goes without saying that I can cheat on myself with Evan. I can't imagine a one woman show being nearly as rewarding. So for now, I think I will resolve to take Evan up on his overtures. I will simply say yes instead of no, sex instead of sleep. I will be present, and look for that familiar glint in his eye. 'Familiar'. Hmm...perhaps that's a problem too?

39 Creating a Sorority

I listen to Deb as she rants about the things on her list. It sounds a bit more like a requisition for a maid or a nanny. It's more like a list of things she doesn't want to do than a real stab at making things better. Then, Joyce reads her list. It sounds like it could be satisfied quite nicely by a general contractor. Her list even includes saving up for new windows, for Pete's sake. She must think changing her surroundings will change her outlook on life.

Steph begins her list. "Well, um...here goes. Ways to date myself. Get up earlier so I have time to enjoy my morning coffee. Read the newspaper on the train on my way to work. Take a long lunch, now and then. Dance nude." She pauses while we chuckle and nod. Steph is not embarrassed at all. She seems to enjoy sharing this with us. "Hang out with the girls more often. Drink expensive red wine. Have Sex."

"Well, I certainly envy you in that department," Deb chimes in.

"You ladies get more sex than me," Steph replies.

"Maybe but yours is so new and fresh," Joyce adds and then blushes with embarrassment.

"You know what I just realized?" I say, because the revelation just occurred to me "We don't talk about sex unless we're talking about you, Steph."

"Yeah...so, that's because no one wants to hear about my bedroom," Deb laughs.

"Maybe not, but it is kind of funny, don't you think? Why doesn't it ever come up? It's like we're ashamed of it or something. We're all adults. I put sex on my date list," I admit.

"Okay, so why don't you tell us about your sex life then?" Joyce challenges me and blushes again.

I pick up the gauntlet without shame. "Evan and I have been together since we were teenagers. We still have a good sex life," I say, even though we have been off lately.

"So, like, how often?" Deb asks, staring at me intently.

"I don't know. I guess once, sometimes twice a week."

"And, you're saying you guys are still hot and heavy after all these years?" Steph inquires.

"Well...it's not the same as it used to be, but it's still good." I totally feel on the spot so I deflect, "What about you ladies?"

"Since we had the kids, we're lucky if we have sex once a month," Deb scoffs.

"We're a bit better than that, I think, but, I miss the random, hot, mid-afternoon, early morning stuff." Joyce blushes more than ever and puts her hands over her face.

"So, how can we fix it? It's not like we have a ton of free time and Greek gods waiting for us in our beds?" Deb says.

"I think I'm partly to blame for our slow decline." There is a pause as we all become a bit introspective. I continue, "I rarely initiate and sometimes I'm just so tired..." my voice peters out. It's a far cry from my earlier assertion that our sex life is good. I feel somewhat exposed.

"I know what you mean," Joyce agrees but seems sad at the thought.

"I'm just not motivated," Deb pipes up.

"Ladies, you're not selling me on the whole marriage with kids thing," Steph interjects, trying to lighten the mood.

"Okay, so what should we do?" I ask as if we are now a sorority.

"Have more sex...hot sex!" Deb spits out.

"Just like that?" Joyce says. "I'm not saying Will won't be on board, but how do we make it 'hot sex'?" She asks as if she is a fourteen-year-old girl talking about sex for the first time with her friends at a sleepover.

"You add the things that made it hot when you first started out," Steph answers.

"We're gonna have to put some effort in ladies. Primp and flatter our bodies. Maybe wear some lingerie. I don't know...try and seduce our husbands," Deb proclaims. I smile at the thought of lighting a fire under Deb. She's so often negative. It's refreshing to hear optimism in her voice.

"Sex at least three times this week girls," Steph rallies. "Make me want to live vicariously through your sex lives for a change."

"Operation Seduction," I say in a whisper, and then snicker to myself.

"Next week we report back. Deal?" Deb declares.

"Deal!" We say collectively.

40 Operation Seduction

Parker has an ear infection, Evan has hockey on Tuesday night, and I have a parent council meeting on Thursday night. As I lay in the bath, listening to Adele's majestic sound, I try to mentally schedule in three sex nights. I take a sip of my tea, mostly sugar and milk really, and then do a thorough job shaving. I decide that, next month, I will treat myself to a spa day and get some much needed waxing, massaging and maybe even a facial. *It's a date.* I giggle to myself. *It's still a strange concept.* I pluck, primp, and examine every line and blemish on my face way too closely. When I am sufficiently satisfied that there is nothing more I can do to improve my appearance, I prepare to commence *Operation Seduction.*

The girls are in bed. I suspect Parker will be up again when the Advil runs out so I'm on borrowed time. Wearing a towel, I head into the bedroom for inspiration. I pull open my underwear drawer. I wade through the granny panties and nude coloured bras. *Man, I didn't realize it was this bad.* It takes me ten minutes to find a fuchsia bra and matching panties. They were part of my pre-kid collection. Putting the bra on, I realize that my boobs have changed so much. *Feeding two babies will do that to you, I guess.* They're not bad; they're just different. They have lost their youthful charm, but the bra squeezes them tightly, creating an appealing bust line.

I slide the panties on and, like magic, my c-section scar is masked in pink lace. I glance at myself in the mirror, trying to muster some confidence. I'm pleased with my disguise. I slink over to the bed and lie across it. I try a couple of different poses, finally settling on my side. My bent elbow holds my head up and I cross my legs at the ankles. I grab my iPad off the nightstand and send a quick text down the hall: Hey babe, could you help me with something. I am in the bedroom.

I figure this sounds slightly suggestive, without being overt. I resume my pose as I hear the ping of the message being received. My anticipation builds. I here a frustrated sigh as if I'm bothering him and then footsteps.

The bedroom door opens and his shocked expression quickly fades into a devious smile.

"What do we have here?"

"I have an itch that needs scratching," I say trying my best to be coy.

"You do, do you?" His eyebrow raises. "I think I can help with that. Why don't you lay back and I'll see what I can do."

"I haven't told you where it is yet," I tease.

"Oh, perhaps I can find it myself."

"Alright...I'll let you know when you're getting warmer."

"I'm plenty warm already," he whispers as he looms over me.

He starts by kissing me. Slowly. His mouth takes command of me. His tongue expertly navigates its way. Flirting. Teasing my senses. One hand is holding him up and the other is lightly caressing the back of my neck. He pulls back and looks me in the eye. I see his lust. *I want it all.*

"Cold" I whisper, barely audibly. I feel anything but cold. The comment throws him for a second. Then, I see my game register and my worthy opponent smirks. He gently kisses my shoulder and looks to me for a response. "Cold," I repeat with a slight giggle. He moves steadily down towards my breasts. He kisses the bust-line of my bra. The light tingling, feeling sends a warm rush below. He pulls at my bra exposing my nipple and takes it in his mouth. I arch and squirm. My nipples perk up under his expertise. I breathe in the sensation. It's so tender, so...tantalizing. Relishing the feeling, I crave more. "Warmer," I moan. A hum of pleasure emits from deep in his throat. It sends my senses into overdrive. His wicked intention is so welcomed. He trails kisses down my side and over my navel. I can feel his heated breath on my skin. "Oh, Evan," I moan. He smirks up at me briefly between kisses. "Warmer, Warmer," I plead. He travels lower. His fingers stroke the delicate lacy panties in a slow deliberate motion, starting at my sides and working their way to my apex. I feel a moist rush as two fingers exert pressure, rubbing my most sensitive parts over my underwear. I'm primal as I beg, "Hot, hot, more, more..."

"Shh!" He looks up at me as he pulls at my panties, dragging them down my legs, over my thighs, my calves, my ankles. He kisses my ankle. I say, "Colder." He laughs and moves up to my knee. "Warmer," I purr. He runs his hand up my thigh and quickly thrusts two fingers inside me. The action is so warranted after his slow seduction. I cry out "Evan!" He uses his other hand to stimulate my sex. Abruptly, he pulls out and proceeds to use his tongue to magically massage me to the brink. I am in a state of total consumption, utter bliss. I explode, completely satisfied. Pure pleasure.

Evan moves up my body, planting kisses as he goes. His hard erection is pressing against me. Before I can collect myself it is inside me.

"How's that?" He grunts between thrusts.

"Hot, so hot, burning hot...FIRE!" I scream out at his smooth but punishing pace. It's indescribable ecstasy. He lifts my legs up to his shoulders and continues to drive into me. The intensity is mind blowing. My body is his. I'm building around him. I cry out again and his smooth motion becomes faster, ragged. It pushes me over the edge. As I quiver, he releases himself. We are one. We collapse, a mess of legs and shoulders. My knee is firmly pinned beneath him but I couldn't care less.

I lay there excited by my revelation that *we still have it!* *What made this time so, so hot?* *How can I bottle it?*

41 Why Purple

The next morning, I'm standing at the sink scraping the leftover cereal off the girls' breakfast bowls and Evan comes up behind me. He kisses my hair and wraps his arms around my middle. I feel so cared for. It is such a simple action, but it feels new. I consciously feel loved. It lasts only a minute, but it's all I need. The rest of the day, I can't get him out of my head. My husband, the man I have known for sixteen years, is making me giddy like a school girl. *What's happening to me?*

At lunch I text Evan: Hey, babe. Last night was fun. Thanks for scratching my itch.

Within seconds there is a reply: My Pleasure. I like you itchy.

That flirt. I reply: Warmer...

Instantly he responds: Warmer indeed.

Yes, I think the "..." spoke for itself. I smirk to myself as I tuck my phone back into my purse, imagining its possible connotations.

After our sexcapades yesterday, I decide to pick up some lingerie on the way home from work. I know it's a Monday, and usually sex is the last thing on my mind during my drive home, but today I feel different. I can't stop thinking about Evan and Operation Seduction.

If I'm going to pick up the kids from daycare on time, I will have to go to that adult store by the dry cleaners. I don't have time to hit a boutique or go to a mall. *They should have something there, right?* I park in front of the dry cleaners. I quickly scan the vicinity to make sure I don't run into anyone I know. The XXX sign over the door doesn't exactly scream, 'Welcome mother of two/Grade One teacher'. I walk briskly to the entrance of 'Sexification'. As I heave open the heavy door, I try to avert my eyes from all the naked postcard sized pictures pinned to a cork-board on the wall. My best guess, without reading them, is that they are escort or rub and tug advertisements. As the door closes behind me, I hear the quiet hum of the flashing OPEN sign shaped like a pair of lips. I instantly think I have made a bad decision.

I'm about to cut and run when the girl behind the counter chimes in.

"First-timer?" she says. She is everything I'm not. She is short with long blond hair that's loosely gathered in a spiky ponytail. Her black eyeliner and bright red lips draw my attention. She steps out from behind the counter and is wearing a black corset with a red miniskirt tutu thing. It's her twelve-hole, cherry Doc Martins and fish net stockings that shock me the most.

Here I am, dressed in my muted blue blouse and grey dress pants with flats. I have lip gloss on and Parker's shiny barrette holding my hair just so. I look like I should be in a library not a sex shop.

Feeling completely out of place I shyly say, "Yeah."

"I love virgins," she says and I'm confused.

She can't possibly think? "No, um, I meant it was my first time here," I clarify.

She laughs, "So did I. I think I'm gonna like you."

A nervous laugh escapes me. She is obviously more comfortable about sexuality than I am. Hell, her whole body screams sex-fiend. "Don't be shy," she continues. "I'm the only one here. I won't bite, unless you want me to?" She toys with me and then adds, "What are you looking for?"

"Oh, um, do you have any lingerie?"

"Sure. Follow me." Sex-fiend sashays off in front of me.

We head to the back of the store past a ton of lotions and potions and an incredibly distracting wall of dildos. *Why purple?* I think to myself glancing up and fixating on the largest schlong. When we hit the lingerie, I realize that most of this stuff is for S and M. *Not really my scene. I'm not even sure how I would put half of this stuff on.*

"Do you have anything a little less...I don't know. Maybe more simple?"

"Boring, you mean?"

"Not boring," I assert. "Just not so...overt. Something without metal studs or...what is this?" I hold up a strange item with a band across the top and two lacy strips that hang down.

"Crotchless panties," she smiles.

"Seriously?" I drop them back into their display basket. I'm a grown woman. I thoroughly enjoy sex. *Why do I feel so wrong about being here?* "Listen, I'm sorry. I don't really think this is...I mean...I think I'm gonna go."

"Aw, come on. I'm just messing with you. I know this isn't your thing. I mean, look at you. We have more run of the mill stuff over here."

Run of the mill? Well, she's definitely not their star sales person. Am I a prude? The idea is disconcerting. I reluctantly follow the sex-fiend to a small rack of lingerie I recognize. I find a violet satin négligée with a matching thong. I want to get out of here, as quickly as possible, so I head straight to the register.

Sex-fiend says as she begins ringing my purchase in, "You know. This is alright, but if you really want to liven things up for you and your man, you might want to think about one of these." She holds up a purple rubber thingy and pushes a button on the bottom. I have never seen one in real life before, but I know instantly that it is a vibrator. She continues pressing the button and the buzz changes speeds and pulses rhythmically. I'm mesmerized. She hands it to me and I can't help but take it from her. It wiggles and buzzes frantically in my hand. *Why purple?* I think to myself for the second time since entering this place.

"I think I'm okay, but thanks." I hand it back, intrigued but not sold.

"Your loss. I'm telling you, this baby doesn't disappoint."

I find myself seriously considering this bizarre impulse buy. *Perhaps Sex-fiend's sales skills aren't as bad as I thought.* She places it back on the shelf behind her and hands me the debit console. I start to enter my pin number and a strange thought enters my head. *Why not? Why shouldn't I try something new with Evan? He might like it. If he doesn't, well that's cool too. It would certainly spice up the girl talk at Joyce's this week.* I blush and push cancel on the console.

"I'll take four of those." *If I am gonna try this thing, I may as well share the wealth. I can't wait to see the look on Joyce's face when I whip these things out.* I giggle nervously to myself.

"Really? Why four?" the fiend asks.

It's my turn to mess with her so I say, "They should spice up our key parties. And they are probably useful for orgies too. Don't you think?"

Sex-fiend gawks at me openly. Satisfied with her lack of response, I carry the lovely lingerie and four vibrators to my mini-van. *What am I doing? Seriously, what are the girls going to think? I guess there is only one way to find out.*

That evening, as I walk the block and a half to Book Club, I mean our Seduction Sorority, my mood is very different from last week. I've actively implemented almost all of the items on my Pleasure Inventory. I downloaded Maroon 5 this week and really enjoyed having Avery and Parker "Move Like Jagger" at my feet as I make dinner each night. I read three quarters of a romance novel in the tub with my milky, sugary tea. Evan and I managed three sex nights and one early morning quickie. *I'm really digging this plan!* Best of all, I'm carrying a bottle of wine and four vibrators in a bag to Book Club. I haven't told Evan about my purchase yet. I thought I would run it by the girls first. They are, after all, responsible for my new outlook.

I enter Joyce's, unable to rein in my beaming grin. If you had told me last week I was going to be here with a bag full of sex toys, there's no way I would have believed you. Yet, here I am.

I open the door and my new heels, courtesy of Britta, click loudly on Joyce's hardwood floor. They're open-toed, black, sling-back wedge heels. I love them. I head to the living room where the girls are in mid-conversation. *I guess I'm a bit late.* I see Deb first. When she lays her eyes on me she breaks out into spontaneous laugher. It's probably because of the stupid grin I have on my face or because of the fact that I'm actually dressed up and not in my mom gear. I'm not sure why, but I'm laughing too. My chuckle stems from the fact at I have never seen Deb so alive. It's a delight to behold. We're both giddy. Steph and Joyce say almost simultaneously, "What?" And, like a yawn, the contagious giggling spreads to them too.

Our collective laughter continues for some time…no one saying anything, just chuckling. Finally, without any explanation, I open my bag and toss a vibrator at each of the ladies. My laughter intensifies when Joyce's face grimaces openly as she realizes what I have given her. Tears are now streaming down my face.

After some time, we regain our composure and begin talking about our week. It seems that everyone is reaping the benefits of Operation Seduction.

First, Deb regales us with Barry's table-top sex venture:

"I feel stupid telling you this," Deb begins.

"Oh, no! We had a deal! You were gonna make me jealous, remember?" Steph urges her on.

"Okay, okay. Well, Barry was typing away on his laptop at the kitchen table. The boys were asleep. So…" she fades out, fully embarrassed by whatever vision is dancing around in her head.

In unison Joyce, Steph, and I say, "So what?" We're riveted.

"So I ... I came up behind him and began massaging his back and shoulders. When he turned his head to look at me, I couldn't resist. I started kissing him like mad."

"Aw," Joyce utters.

"And, then?" Steph asks, eyes wide.

"Then, I...we...had sex right there on the kitchen table!" Deb blurts out.

The cheering and laugher that follows is only natural.

Collecting ourselves, we focus our attention on an already blushing Joyce as she begins to describe her first ever strip tease for Will:

"I can't believe I'm talking about this."

"Oh come on; it's only fair." Deb is now the pusher.

"Well, on Wednesday Anna had a sleepover at my mom's, so Will and I were on our own." We all nod mischievously at one another. "I had been trying to figure out how to spice things up for days and decided that I was going to need some inspiration."

"You're killing me. What kind of inspiration?" I chime in.

"I scrolled through my iPod and found a song that I thought was kind of...you know...sexy." At this point Joyce is beat red and giggling.

"Go on," Deb nudges.

"What song?" I giggle too.

"It's an old Portishead song, I think it's called something like "Glory Box", but I know it as 'Give Me a Reason to Love You'."

"I know that song. I love that song. You're right. That is a sexy song," I say.

"So what did this sexy song inspire you to do?" Steph asks.

"I can't...no, it's too embarrassing." Joyce's hands are covering her face now.

"Spit it out!" Deb demands.

"Or, would you prefer we use our imagination and fill in the blanks?" I joke.

"No, no. Don't do that. Lord knows what Deb would have me doing." Joyce laughs and she continues, "I danced for Will."

"You mean you danced, or you danced-danced...like stripped?" Steph asks with her eyes wide in shock.

Joyce nods her head with her face covered by her hands.

We all laugh profusely. *I honestly didn't think Joyce had it in her.*

"What did Will think?" Steph asks.

"Are you kidding? He probably couldn't think because no blood was going to his brain!" Deb snort-laughs.

"He was...um...surprised and 'excited' I guess." Joyce giggles as she put air quotes around the word excited.

The focus turns to Steph as she wows us with her surprise ambush of Ben at his office:

"I walked into his office, locked the door, closed the blinds, and dropped my dress. I thought Ben was going to faint from his sudden blood loss." Steph chuckles and elbows Deb.

My mouth hung open in shock as I gawked at Steph's sheer ballsiness.

"I've always heard of stuff like that happening. I just never thought..." Deb sounds impressed.

"I know, right?" Steph shakes her head, almost as surprised as the rest of us. "That was my thought. I wanted to do something crazy. Something...uninhibited. Let me tell you, it was a lot of fun! But I'm not sure Ben's rolling office chair survived." Astonishment quickly turns into belly laughter with her last comment. Her hands quickly cover her mouth as if she can't believe what she blurted out. Her hands do little to conceal the smile in her eyes. They are filled with new-found vigor and delight.

My turn:

"I never thought the girl who brought you a bag full of vibrators would end up being the prude tonight. After hearing your stories, I'm going to have to step up my game," I joke.

"Have you used it yet?" Steph asks at the same time as Deb spits out, "What did Evan think of it?"

"No, I haven't. Ever the teacher, I figure it could be involved in next week's Book Club homework." I wink at them and chug the last of my cabernet. Nervous laugher ensues.

"Evan and I had lots of great sex this week though. It was nice. Fun again, you know?" The girls all nodded in agreement. A memory from the early morning romp I had with Evan today runs through my mind. *Who knew trying to be quiet could be so awesome?* My goofy grin is starting to hurt my cheeks. "The weird thing is that it wasn't just the sex that was better. I don't know...Evan and I were just different with one another."

"How so?" Steph pipes up.

"I don't know. It was like he saw me again. He started paying attention to the stuff I do and has even started helping out more." *I still can't believe that he picked up the girls from school/daycare on Wednesday so I could meet up with Britta and go shoe shopping. Having a whole night off in the middle of the week was so amazing! He also made the kids' lunch all week and remembered to take out the garbage. It's the little things, the everyday things that matter. This week, his support mattered and it went a long way towards fueling my desire for Operation Seduction. And I don't think he's complaining about that. I wonder what he would think if he knew I'd hatched this plan with my Book Club girls.*

"Now that you mention it, Barry was more involved this week too."

"Yeah, even Ben, mister lack of initiative, called me like ten times after I jumped him at his office. He's sent me flowers at work and has already arranged a date for this weekend." It's hard to miss the twinkle in Steph's eye. *I love seeing her this way. She deserves a man who really sees her, who truly appreciates all the phenomenal qualities she possesses – a man who gets to know and love the 'Stephness' that I adore so much.*

"I guess he isn't holding a grudge about his chair then?" I smirk at her and she throws a pillow at me.

"Will's been following me around like a lovesick puppy. It's kind of funny, actually." Joyce smiles knowingly.

"Who knew, right? I'm not saying that a little sex has put Evan into some kind of a trance. But I'm not gonna deny that I like the way he's looking at me and pitching in."

"Seriously, though, why are men so driven by their penis' that their behaviour changes so dramatically when they get some?" Deb interjects.

"Maybe, it isn't just the sex. Maybe *we* were different this week too. We were probably in a better mood because of our self-dating thing, and we were also making an effort to really see our men, to give them attention. Maybe it was just easier to be nice to us?" I pontificate.

Steph picks up where I left off, "In the past, dating the way I have, I've noticed that when one part of my relationship starts to go downhill, it isn't long before the whole thing goes to shit. I guess I just never thought that the opposite could be true; that improving something like my sex-life could change the whole couple dynamic thing."

We all become slightly introspective for a moment. *It seems funny to think sexifying your relationship can change things so much, but I think Steph's on to something. I hope Evan and I can continue to keep this up.* Before the momentum of the evening is doused into a haze of seriousness I raise my glass and make a toast, "Long live Operation Seduction." <<Clink>>

After topping up everyone's wine glasses, I recount a slightly exaggerated and shocking version of my trip to Sexification for the girls. Then I proceed to enlighten them about the multiple settings of our new purple friends.

<<BUZZZZZZ>> "I imagine that this light humming setting is for those quiet times, to start you off slow. The pulsing one <<BUZZ>> <<BUZZ>>

<<BUZZ>> is to get things going, if you know what I mean." I crack-up a little. "And this, <<!!!!!!!!!!!!!BUZZZZzzzzzzz!!!!!!!!!!!!!!>> this must be the money setting!" I place the frantically buzzing purple bad-

boy on the coffee table and watch it shake, throb, pulsate, rattle, and rock against the glass. I think Joyce might faint as it falls off the table onto the carpet.

Hysterical laughter erupts once more.

Towards the end of the evening, Deb announces our new book club selection:

"The girls at work have been talking about it and it sounds...well it sounds pretty intense. It just came out. We might have to buy it online because I'm not sure it's in bookstores yet," Deb says. "I wasn't sure it was your thing Joyce, but after hearing about your pole dance..."

"It wasn't a pole dance," Joyce chirps up.

"Oh, in my head it was," Deb laughs.

"What is the book called again?" I ask Deb.

"*Fifty Shades of Grey.*"

42 Beginning Anew

I'm in the laundry room. I take a scoop of laundry detergent and add it to the mass of clothing piled in the washer. I see a tiny T-shirt float to the top of the machine. It's Parker's favourite. I see a smear of orange paint on it and smile as I think of her most recent picture. *It's the cutest painting. It's her under a rainbow. She even managed to put all the colours in the right order.* That's something Avery has been trying to teach her. *They really are growing up fast.* Avery is off to Grade One in the fall and Parker will be starting 'big girl school': Kindergarten.

I hear the stomping of little feet above my head and it breaks my concentration. I know that somewhere on the main floor, my girls are dancing around, probably in princess dresses. They are always fantasizing about their own Prince Charmings. *I should read The Paper Bag Princess again. I'd really like them to know that there are worse things in life then heading off into the sunset alone.* But for now, *maybe when I get upstairs, I will help them build a castle out of couch cushions.* The thought makes me smile.

As I spin the dial on the dryer to perma-press, I contemplate how much happier I've been lately. When I think about why, I realize that somewhere along the way I chose to be completely selfless, putting my husband, my kids, my job, and my own unrealistic expectations ahead of myself. The result was depressing. I existed in this sad space between reality and the ideal.

Now, for the first time in my life, I feel that a degree of selfishness is as critical to my relationships with others as it is to my own well-being. *Huh. It seems funny, but dating myself has put me in touch with the things that make me happy. When I'm happy, I'm simply a better person to be around.*

I stare at the basket of clean clothes on the floor and spot my violet négligée on top. I blush, as I remember waltzing around the dining room with Evan to Norah Jones' rich voice. I slowly reach down, pick up the basket, and twirl around with it. I want to revel in the memory a moment longer.

I hear Evan's husky voice calling my name. "Emilia." It's not an urgent call, more of a 'where are you honey' kind of call. It sounds like he's coming down the stairs in search of me.

"There you are, pretty girl. I was looking for you." He takes the laundry from me and gives me a gentle kiss.

"The girls and I are starting a movie. They want to watch *The Princess Bride*. I know how you love that one."

"Totally. Thanks, babe."

Once upstairs, I step over a wagon and an old slipper in the hallway. I flick the switch on the kettle for a tea. As I stand in the kitchen, I can see Avery and Parker snuggled up on the couch together sharing a sleeping bag, and I can hear Fred Savage scoffing at Columbo. Evan comes up behind me and envelops me in his arms. He whispers, "Come on, we don't want to miss it."

"As you wish," I mumble back. He grabs my hand and leads me to the couch. We spoon together beside our girls. Maggie is wagging her tail at our feet.

This is the man I love. The man I have grown up with. In the back of my brain I am fully aware that I have everything I have ever wanted. In this moment, I can't help but think, *I'm so thankful that this is what I signed up for.*

Acknowledgments:

I would like to thank my amazing husband, Denham, for his support and encouragement. I find it difficult to put into words the depth of my appreciation, so I will simply say, thank you for all that you do and all that you are. I love you eleven.

To my girls, Rae-Rae and Bean: Your energy gives me inspiration. I love seeing the world through your eyes. Thank you for giving mommy the chance to play in the grown-up world sometimes too. I love you to the farthest star and back.

To my mom and Rachel: Thank you for your friendship and generosity. I was nervous the first time I sent this novel to you. Your kind words and reassurance made me feel like this writing thing could actually happen. You were both a part of this book every step of the way, and I cannot express my gratitude enough; not just for your involvement in this project, but also for the integral roles you have played in my life.

To Jennifer Pooley: Thank you for enhancing my story and supporting my evolution as a writer. Your insights into my character development and the flow of my plot were spot on. I appreciated your positive support and gently critiques. I look forward to working with you again in the future.

To Lorraine Chiarotto: You have a gift. Thank you for putting up with my lack of commas, my inability to use quotations appropriately, and my general love of typos. I must love them to have so many, right? You may think of yourself as 'just a grammar geek' if you like but, I think of you as a 'grammar goddess'.

To Megan Pike: Thank you for your expertise on the cover design. You have been a great support since I first approached you when the novel was in its infancy. You

have provided me feedback, options, and skilled assistance with the world of social media. You have raised my level of digital professionalism and I have thoroughly enjoyed working with you.
http://society6.com/megpike

To Lindsay, Kate, Leigh-Anne, Alison, Rebecca, Karen, Vanessa, and especially Julie: Thank you all for taking the time to read the novel, for listening to me flesh it out, and for giving me feedback along the way. Your insights went a long way to making this book what it is.

To my readers: Thank you for reading Em's story. I hope you enjoyed her evolution as much as I did. I look forward to hearing from you:
www.facebook.com/thesexificationofem
@LauraKatAuthor

www.ingramcontent.com/pod-product-compliance
Lightning Source LLC
Chambersburg PA
CBHW061924170626
46813CB00006B/2295